T0063991

Flying Saucers

Emil Venere

authorHOUSE®

AuthorHouse™
1663 Liberty Drive
Bloomington, IN 47403
www.authorhouse.com
Phone: 833-262-8899

Published by AuthorHouse 03/27/2024

ISBN: 978-1-4918-3899-0 (sc)
ISBN: 978-1-4918-3898-3 (e)

Library of Congress Control Number: 2013921583

Print information available on the last page.

CHAPTER 1

The newsroom was mostly deserted.

It was one of those perfect late-summer days. A day perhaps more fitting for Southern California than Midtown Manhattan, and the writers had taken to the streets; the family-friendly, well-policed streets of Rudy Giuliani's New York.

Jane Hale had just returned from lunch when she noticed the manila envelope on her desk. Her name was handwritten on one side of the envelope with a bold, black marker.

"Jane Hale" was all it said. No stamp, no return address. She flipped over the envelope and saw the word "PERSONAL," underlined three times to emphasize the upper case script. It had obviously been hand-delivered to the newsroom at Thompson's Defense Weekly, an international publication reporting on the multi-billion-dollar business of war.

Inside the envelope she found a collection of papers, including what appeared to be old magazine articles, various memoranda and a series of letters penned by high-level aviation and aerospace executives from top American companies back in the 1950s. Jane recognized the names right away. These were the heaviest hitters, key players in the nascent military-industrial complex. Some of the documents were signed by the authors and printed under official company letterhead.

She studied the memos. One, dated May 31, 1954, was from a senior engineer by the name of Thomas England and was addressed to Glenn L. Moore, founder and CEO of the Moore Aircraft Company, a major military contractor. A blocky CONFIDENTIAL was stamped across the top of the communication. The nut graph of this communiqué contained the following incredible statement:

> *As you know, we achieved proof of concept with the anti-gravity flying disc platform several years ago and are now proceeding toward commercialization. The 12.5-meter disc has been shown to accelerate to mach 3, and we've taken her up to a ceiling of about 40000 feet. The next step is a full-scale 20-meter prototype. We are on schedule to meet the objectives of the timetable, and should have the airframe constructed by January. We will report back soon the results of further work on the propulsion system, and we should have an update ready for you in time for the next mid-month briefing.*

England advised Moore in another memo dated September 13, 1954:

> *We are ahead of schedule on the full-scale project and should have it ready for military review by December. The power and propulsion hardware for the disc have been completed, and we are in the process of completing the airframe. All in all, integration should be finished*

in November and a first flight scheduled for early December.

Then, in a memo dated December 1955 and addressed to U.S. Air Force General Nathan Twining, Moore dropped this seemingly earth-shattering bit of news:

The Moore Aircraft Company has completed test flights of its 20-meter disc. This follows high-level demonstrations of earlier prototypes (e.g. Presidential Directive, 1952, Washington). Designs for the propulsion system, electrical controls, airframe and additional hardware are ready for production. As you know, flight tests over the past year have shown the overall platform capable of outperforming all U.S. and Soviet fighter interceptors. The current contract proposal calls for production of 2000 units, delivery date 1961."

How had this envelope suddenly materialized on her desk, and who had delivered it? She glanced around the newsroom furtively, but no one seemed to be the least bit interested in what was going on at her workstation. The managing editor was transfixed on his computer screen, laboring to make someone's mediocre prose more readable. A few copy editors chatted casually while clacking away on their keyboards. The executive editor was out of the office, his door closed and shuttered, and his secretary was talking on the phone. CNN played on a wall-mounted television.

She continued leafing through the sheaf of papers. The package contained a series of blueprints and schematics for what appeared to be electronic components. Not being an engineer, she had no idea whether these were technically correct. She unfolded one of the documents, which covered the top of her desk when completely unfurled. It contained a diagram of something that looked exactly like a flying saucer. The plans showed various views depicting portions of the craft, with detailed breakout cross-sections of specific features. One cutaway was entitled "gas-turbine power plant," and another, "zero-point gravitator," and one other view dealt with hydraulic controls for the landing gear.

Jane left the document sprawled over her desk and went on to the next item in the stack of papers. Included were three pulp-magazine articles from the same period as the memos. One, dated March 1955, featured an artist's concept of the classic flying saucer. It was silvery and had *U.S. Air Force* inscribed on its upper surface. The article quoted Moore and other aviation insiders who said an antigravity propulsion system was within reach and that jet-engine technology would soon be obsolete.

Illustrations accompanying the articles reflected the angst of the era, a time when people were increasingly jittery about the emerging "super science" of nuclear physics, microelectronics, modern astronomy and cosmology. Strange hovering discs and rocket ships limned against backdrops of ghastly greens, eerie mist, star fields and the planet Saturn, that obligatory symbol of cosmic mystery.

She continued perusing the material and came across an item she had written herself a few years ago. It was just a three-paragraph tidbit in the "News Briefly" section of Thompson's. If not for the impeccable credentials of the source, Thompson's wouldn't have considered publishing such a dubious story. It read:

From The X-Files or a U.S. Black Project?

> *Robert Marsden has seen every type of military aircraft that ever took to the skies during his nearly 50 years with Britain's now-defunct Royal Observer Corps, but he spied an apparent U.S. plane he couldn't identify one day last month. Marsden was on a cruise ship in the North Sea when he spotted a huge triangular craft being escorted by three F 111 bombers. He watched the planes traverse the sky in an easterly direction for nearly 10 minutes, using a pair of binoculars to get a good look at the craft.*
>
> *"They were flying no higher than 10,000 feet," Marsden said. "I have been observing aircraft for many years, and I can tell you without a doubt that this was unlike any plane I'd ever seen before. I would describe it as an equilateral triangle with very sharp edges, much larger than the B-2 stealth bomber and without the distinctive flying-wing profile of the stealth plane."*

Marsden was a bona fide expert, a living encyclopedia of modern military aircraft. The Royal Observer Corps had been the twentieth century's preeminent organization dedicated to identifying enemy airborne threats and played a huge role in helping the Allies intercept Luftwaffe planes during World War II. For his part, Marsden had identified everything from early German jet aircraft in the final days of the war to the latest Soviet MIG fighters flown during the waning years of the Cold War.

In his "retirement," the aged Marsden had become somewhat of an aviation historian, penning two books on military aircraft, one exclusively focusing on World War II and the second concentrating on postwar innovations in the United States and the Soviet Union. Jane first met him during a conference of the American Institute of Aeronautics and Astronautics. It was one of those two-day affairs of technical, jargon-filled sessions dealing with such matters as "novel designs for liquid-fuel rocket nozzles" and "clean-burning hydrogen-peroxide fuels" and "oxidizer-rich stage-combustion cycle engines."

After it was all over, she was able to eke out several short pieces based on these highly technical talks. Far more entertaining was Marsden's plenary lecture about the history of military aircraft in the Western world. His presentation included an overview of likely future advances in aviation, and then diverged into some highly speculative ideas about possible top-secret designs.

"These concepts are based on certain things that have been observed by people hanging out in places like the Mojave Desert," he said at one point during his presentation. "They are seeing things that are definitely not stealth fighters, I'll tell you that. So, unless you are prepared to accept the very unlikely possibility that we're being visited by ET on a regular basis, there is only one logical conclusion: Uncle Sam's flying some pretty nifty prototypes these days."

His talk drew some polite applause, but mostly cynical whisperings. Afterward, Jane had exchanged business cards with Marsden, and she mentioned his talk in a feature article about the conference. He appreciated the favor. The article gave him some good exposure, which resulted in a few clients.

After his unusual encounter about a year later, he gave her a call to see whether she had ever heard of the triangular plane he had observed. Marsden was pretty sure the United States had its hands on some sophisticated new hardware that was years ahead of anything else. He was drawn to this conclusion, he said, after reviewing estimates for the American military's "black budget" over the past few decades. Any way you sliced it, Marsden figured, the budget for ultra-secret research and development was thriving, probably a figure that outstripped the gross domestic products of many sovereign nations and surpassed annual combined spending for NASA and the departments of Justice, Energy, Interior and Housing and Urban Development. And, if history was any indication, he argued, there was no telling what sorts of secrets were being maintained in the name of national security.

Witness the SR-71 Blackbird. It was developed in complete secrecy during the 50s and 60s by the Lockheed Aircraft Corporation, and it remained largely unknown despite its incredible performance record. The plane was capable of exceeding Mach 3, a speed unmatched by any other spy planes of the time. And the same atmosphere of hyper secrecy surrounded the stealth fighter. Its development involved hundreds of people, yet it remained entirely shrouded from the public until it was unveiled in 1988. No one had written about the stealth fighter in large-circulation newspapers like *USA Today*, the *New York Times* or the *Washington Post*. Sure, there were rumors in some small niche publications, but no photos had been published.

No insiders had leaked any detailed information. It was the journalistic equivalent of a black hole.

Marsden had always thought that the stealth fighter and bomber programs were, in fact, very successful conspiracies. He preferred Webster's secondary definition of the verb to conspire: "to act, or work together toward the same result or goal." A conspiracy wasn't necessarily evil. As far as Marsden was concerned, the stealth programs were the perfect argument against the naïve but commonly held assumption that there were no longer any secrets in America, that everything was an open book.

The SR-71 was the world's best high-speed, high-altitude reconnaissance aircraft. Therefore, since it had been decommissioned in 1989, Marsden thought it only reasonable that the United States had replaced it with some other extremely fast airplane. He simply could not believe that the last remaining superpower would leave a gaping hole like that in its military repertoire. There just had to be something new, something capable of flying at least as fast as the Blackbird, something that could be launched into the heavens at a moment's notice and reach its far-flung destinations anywhere in the world within a matter of hours. Satellites were not nearly as versatile. It wouldn't make sense for America to retire the nation's most capable reconnaissance aircraft without first fielding its successor. Such inaction just didn't mesh with past behavior.

The Pentagon, after all, always had a new secret weapon.

Marsden's observation that afternoon in the North Sea should have served as evidence that there was, indeed, something dark and mysterious roaming the skies, something unique and fearsome. Yes, it all made perfect sense, but exactly what kind of technology was this? What sort of "plane" could fly without wings? How could anything shaped like an overgrown kite keep up with F-111 bombers?

These and other questions led Marsden to pick up the phone and consult with Jane. Alas, she had nothing for him, as none of her sources had ever suggested that a replacement existed for the SR-71. As far as she knew, the aircraft had simply become too expensive to operate and expendable after the Soviet Union's disintegration. Anyway, robotic drones were all the rage. Although they were not capable of supersonic flight, officials insisted the "unmanned aerial vehicles," or UAVs, when combined with satellites and the aging U-2 spy plane, satisfied all of the military's reconnaissance needs.

Jane dwelled on Marsden's sighting as she kept looking through the envelope's contents. She came across several articles from British tabloids regarding something she had never heard of before called "the silent Vulcans." The tabloids had apparently had endless fun with a series of UFO sightings dealing with triangular objects that resembled the 1950s-era, V-shaped Avro Vulcan bombers. The enormous triangular UFOs had "invaded British airspace," according to one article. Another piece retold how pilots landing a British Airways 737 at England's busy Manchester Airport were startled by the sudden appearance of the huge craft flying directly at their plane. The object came so close to the commercial airliner that one of the pilots instinctively ducked.

A lengthy investigation by Britain's Civil Aviation Authority eventually concluded the pilots had, in fact, seen a real aircraft, but it never was identified. The silent Vulcan articles segued nicely into some news clips detailing similar sightings in New York's Hudson Valley. Hundreds of citizens and local police had seen the large ship cruising overhead at very low altitude.

Jane had scanned most of the items by the time coworkers began trickling back into the newsroom after lunch. She hastily returned the documents to the manila envelope.

Later, though, she pondered flying saucers, prompting a spontaneous shiver of the spine.

CHAPTER 2

Tommy Swift was raised in rural Indiana, where kids sprouted up tall and Teutonic and loyal to god and country.

He began flying as a teenager, working as a line boy at the local airport, pumping gas, washing and waxing and towing airplanes, supervising the office cash register while saving his pennies for flight training.

Tommy received his pilot's license at sixteen. He had inherited his passion for airplanes from his maternal grandmother, Bessie Shoemaker, she herself a pilot who learned to fly with her husband back in 1955. Waiting until the harvest was in, they took their first lesson in a Piper Cub over Labor Day weekend and became lifelong members of the Flying Farmers of Indiana.

The barnstorming breed of general-aviation devotees frequently took wing over the nation's heartland, following air charts that showed the precise meanderings of roads, rivers and railroad tracks below.

Many a night old Bessie would sit her grandchildren on her knee and recall various flying adventures, albeit slightly dramatized for the benefit of her audience. There was the time grandpa Shoemaker suffered a gallstone attack in

Edmonton, Canada, and Bessie had to save the day, flying home for emergency surgery. In the northwest corner of Illinois she hit a hazy wall of fog, a perilous predicament for pilots like Bessie who flew strictly under visual flight rules.

"We was flying blind for ten minutes or more but got home just in time to operate on your grandpaw," she recited. "Doctor said his gallbladder was dang-near ready to burst with gangrene."

Bessie told and retold a seemingly endless assortment of riveting bedtime stories. A favorite involved the time gramps made an emergency landing in a pasture, threading a narrow passage defined by rocky terrain, trees and hedges. They rolled right up to a farmhouse, and the people, complete strangers, put them up for the night.

Even mundane experiences she embellished with tantalizing tidbits to make the stories entertaining.

Tommy's parents weren't sure what to make of grandma's influence, but they encouraged their son's obsession with flying, even if they hadn't shared his passion for airplanes. His father was a utility company lineman. His mother was a stay-at-home mom who spent her days administering her own sort of wholesome brainwashing. She was no rocket scientist, but she did understand some things about child rearing that many failed to grasp before it was too late.

There would be no latchkey kids in her home. She dutifully attended all of their academic and sporting competitions, providing emotional support and bolstering their nascent competitive drives. Her fundamental formula was to raise her kids from the very beginning to have confidence and self-esteem, and everything else would follow. Encourage them and provide positive reinforcement, but don't dole out gratuitous praise. Challenge them, but don't push them too hard.

Try to go easy on the corporal punishment, but by no means spare the rod entirely, especially for the boys.

"I'm not raising any sissies," she'd say.

Deal an impromptu swat to the butt, a smack to the cheek, a show of force when warranted. Not so much out of anger but of purpose. This measured use of violence would hard-wire a latent aggression into their malleable nervous systems. Make sure they have some compassion, but not too much. The necessary quantum of empathy, but that's all.

Impressionable neural connections in the brain formed indelible associations between love and pain, authority and consequence. Laying the foundation, installing the basic software for a restrained rage, waiting to be unleashed. This would serve him well as an alpha male.

The old man also fulfilled his fatherly duties, performing the requisite male-bonding exercises: the sports; the Boy Scouts; the fishing; the stupid fucking bowling.

These parental efforts weren't lost on Tommy. The eldest of four children, he emerged as one of those kids who just seemed to have his bearings right from the start. A model high school student, he excelled academically and in sports and became the first member of his extended family to earn a college degree.

He'd been memorizing mathematical theorems since the seventh grade and solving quadratic equations for at least that long, so he tested out of the first year of calculus while studying freshman engineering at a Midwestern university famous for its technical programs. The curriculum was difficult for most of the students, but not for Tommy, who felt right at home with his Texas Instruments scientific calculator and head full of nonlinear algebra. It was obvious that he could run with the best and brightest, even those computational whiz kids from abroad, who made up a full quarter of the engineering student body. The university had the largest number of international students of any school in the United States, and nearly all of them were pursuing careers in the sciences. These were the cream of the crop, the best foreign minds, people who came to America for diplomas in electrical engineering, computer science, physics and mathematics.

The university was a wellspring of talent for NASA: Numerous alumni would go on to become pilots and astronauts. Some would walk on the moon. Some would fly the space shuttle.

It seemed that Tommy, too, was destined for a similar fate.

His professors had never seen a student quite like him. He raced through the difficult curriculum enthusiastically, cradling his books like a football as he hurried from class to class, taking scarcely three years to earn a B.S. in aeronautics and astronautics. Then the young engineer plowed through a doctoral program in physics in record time: two years. Just two years for a guy who had only taken freshman physics, competing against a bunch of topnotch physics grads who looked down their noses at everything engineering.

The way they saw it, there was only one hard science: physics.

Yet even those geeks had to marvel at the kid who earned a Ph.D. in their chosen field faster than anyone in the school's history. His advisor had been teaching physics for thirty years, and he knew how rare it was to find a student with such a combination of technical know-how, ambition and raw intelligence.

Tommy seemed to spend every waking hour studying textbooks and working in the lab and also found time to keep up his flying. The university had its own full-service airport and offered a certified pilot-training program.

He wrote seven research papers, each of which was published in well-respected physics journals. His four hundred-page thesis was roughly twice the usual length and based on two experiments, either of which would have been sufficient to earn him a doctoral degree. One of his experiments yielded findings considered important enough to merit publication in *Physical Review Letters*, a prestigious science journal.

His jealous peers started calling him Tom Terrific, but he silenced their sarcastic whisperings as a parting shot when he won the Karl Minsk-Horowitz Prize, the physics department's highest honor for graduating doctoral students.

And as if all of these accomplishments weren't enough, he quickly landed a place in an elite U.S. military jet-pilot training program. The boy genius was one of a hundred people chosen for the program, out of a thousand applicants. Those numbers, however, didn't begin to adequately describe the rigmarole involved in qualifying for the school.

In addition to the usual academic requirements, he had to pass muster in rather severe physical endurance and coordination exams, including a centrifuge-like test at Wright-Patterson Air Force Base and a nausea-inducing trip over Alaska in the back of a supersonic jet. The plane's pilot flew in numerous loops and banking maneuvers to probe an applicant's susceptibility to airsickness.

Tommy was one of the few who didn't puke.

So it was that he had easily bounded over yet another hurdle. Soon he would be flying T-37 and T-38 training aircraft, the latter being a supersonic high-altitude jet. And not long after that, he'd be at the controls of an F-16.

Imagine that! A fighter jock with a Ph.D. in physics.

Everyone could clearly read the handwriting on the wall. It was not a matter of if, but when, Tommy Swift's name would be added to the list of astronaut-alumni.

Some people, however, had him in mind for an even higher calling than the astronaut corps. Something so compelling, something so monumental in the history of science and technology that it really had no precedent.

Something truly unique.

CHAPTER 3

It was primarily a bad marriage that had landed Jane Hale at Thompson's Defense Weekly.

Her resume was full of newspaper credentials, most notably her nearly ten years in the field, the Thompson's stint being the only exception. An exploration born out of necessity. She'd had a fairly cushy technology beat working at Boston's best newspaper, but her ex-hubby was the city editor and the divorce had been ugly.

What it all boiled down to was this: He'd left her for a model. A fucking swimsuit model.

And she hated him for it. In this case, 'hate' was not a metaphor for despair or fear or loneliness or the other emotions people experience in life-changing episodes of rejection. Seeing him every day. Mr. Confidence. Perfectly coifed. Smelling like a ladies' man. And, meanwhile, everyone knowing her humiliating story.

No. This was actual hate.

There were times when Jane thought she might kill the man. Literally. Right there in the newsroom. It was a real possibility. She had grown terrified of the prospects of losing control. Ending up in society's destitute fringe. Then, there was the depression. She'd tried big pharma, but in the end she emptied her Prozac capsules and filled them with marijuana. That seemed to help.

Jane could have sent her resume to the other bigs; the newspapers in the five-hundred-thousand-plus circulation category. However, finding a job among the elite papers could take months. She didn't have the luxury of time: Something had to be done, and soon.

Owing to her particular beat as a business reporter focusing on aviation and aerospace, she'd made contacts among the specialty trade publications - contacts like the managing editor at Thompson's.

There was an opening, effective immediately.

ଓଓଓଓ

As a journalist, Jane had enjoyed her share of small triumphs, the various awards and honors, the exclusive tell-all interviews and exposés. But her career had been primarily marked by consistency: She had staying power. She was resourceful, if nothing. A resourcefulness that was based on a need to survive and an instinct, spawned sometime before adolescence and nurtured over the years, owing to a strange childhood and a single-parent home.

Jane grew up in a blue-collar family forty miles from New York City, a metropolis that scared the be-jeesus out of her construction-worker old man. Her mother had fled the household as soon as she could figure out a workable exit strategy, an event that only served to enhance her father's dark descent. A man who incessantly worried about everything, aloud, so that Jane, an only child, could absorb and cultivate his angst. He administered discipline with the back of his hand and words of discouragement and was wont to watch baseball games in his boxer shorts, beer gut protruding under a stained sleeveless undershirt. Occasionally he'd fart and exclaim, "I'd like to bottle 'at and send it to Kroos-Jeff."

When she was quite young he'd often mock her chubby nature and had constructed a touching little bedtime lullaby for her. It went something like this: plain-ee Jane-ee, that's ma name-ee, plain-ee Jane-ee, that's ma name-ee, what a shame-ee, plain-ee Jane-ee.

In the end, the child had learned little from the parent that could be deemed good. She did, however, acquire some useful traits: a tireless work ethic motivated by an inexhaustible sense of fear and longing; and a deep-seated cynicism of human beings, their institutions and traditions, including those devoted to the divine.

Jane thought of herself as a "devout agnostic."

"My lack of faith sustains me," she once told a horrified Jesus freak who was trying to get into her pants. Morality was entirely a manmade construct, and if a god existed at all it was some totally objective entity whose nature was completely beyond man's comprehension. Humankind was no more important to this god than were any of the world's other species, just as the Earth is only one of countless other bodies and not the center of the universe.

Such a philosophy, being inherently dark and pragmatic, didn't jibe well with the conventional trappings of young womanhood, normally a time of bright optimism and grand vision. The college years brought a drug-addled Nihilism period marked by youthful anomie, but not in a good way. And then came marriage, and with it stability, for a time. Now the marriage was over, but hopefully not the stability.

Her apartment building was one of those faded-grandeur affairs with hardwood floors and concrete gargoyles in Tudor City, a pricey Manhattan neighborhood. She'd lucked into a cheap efficiency.

In her mind it was temporary housing. Though, after the divorce, changing jobs and cities, everything seemed temporary now.

The desk clerk was an officious relic named Benny, a very proper seventy-something African American man who held quaint traditional values and always seemed just a little too rigid for Jane's liking. She noticed him raising an eyebrow when she came in awfully late once, sometime around midnight, hand-in-hand with a guy younger than she.

"Anything wrong, Miss Hale?" he asked.

The corridors smelled of mothballs and the apartment was small and a little depressing, but if she looked out of the window, staring her right in the face was the United Nations building, a proud, mirrored monolith that partially blocked her view of the East River. Speedboats churned up white foam, and Jane felt there was something oddly contrasting about those two images. The UN building and speedboats, high-stakes geopolitical intrigue and pointless, exhilarating abandon. The historic neighborhood, draped in cold granite and festooned with copper building decorations, versus thundering engines and gas-guzzling decadence. Virility versus verdigris. Confinement versus escape.

The view made her feel ever so slightly confident about the future. Perhaps, eventually, things would be all right again, but this perhaps came with a big maybe. Jane was not usually positive these days. She would come home from work, exhausted and drained, and crash in her tiny shoebox of an apartment. Get up the next day, walk down to Grand Central Station only a few blocks away, hop on a subway and do it all over again.

That was the cycle she'd grown used to lately.

CHAPTER 4

Tommy Swift flourished in the Air Force, reaching captain in no time.

But his true fantasy was spaceflight, and he diligently pursued a coveted slot in NASA's astronaut training program. He underwent an excessive variety of tests, quantifying and correlating numerous physiological and psychological parameters, personality traits, even social attitudes and moral bearing.

In the end, there was virtually nothing mysterious about him, and this engendered a smugness in Tommy. Surely, his right-stuffness being defined, he'd be at the top of the competition. He was, after all, nearly flawless. Yet, Tommy's aspirations foundered. The space agency told him his application was on hold, officially because of a surplus of astronauts and "few new opportunities for human spaceflight."

This rejection he'd come to accept with humility. He had moved on to more realistic pursuits, when, one day, his commanding officer handed him orders in a sealed envelope. He was to report to a training facility someplace in Utah.

And thus began a most surreal turn in Captain Swift's military career.

He would learn that NASA had a far superior sibling, a shadow space program that had quietly explored the full breadth of the solar system and was now poised for interstellar travel. The space shuttle, International Space Station, planetary probes and other NASA milestones were child's play compared to the military's clandestine achievements. It was a program based on a technology that had been hatched by the Nazi war machine and perfected by America in the decades that followed the war. A program based not on rocketry but on a radical new kind of locomotion: electric field propulsion.

Officials were very particular about the kinds of people they chose to skipper America's secret fleet of antigravity vehicles. These "non-terrestrial" commanders must meet the same requirements needed to run a nuclear submarine. That meant having an advanced degree in the hard sciences, preferably physics or some branch of engineering.

Tommy, of course, met the academic qualifications.

Psychiatric specifications and various other criteria also indicated he was ideally suited, as did the particulars of his social life: unmarried and otherwise unattached -- vital data points considering the extreme security measures surrounding the assignment -- perhaps the most intrusive of any job in military service.

All contact with the outside world would be carefully recorded. His actions, both professional and personal, would be monitored meticulously. And he would be thoroughly schooled in the art of deception, the lies he'd have to tell his nearest relatives, dearest friends and colleagues, when they happened to ask him what he did in the military. These deceptions must be entirely consistent, with absolutely no deviation from the script. Certain people would always be watching, and they'd know.

All of this was just fine with Tommy.

Soon he'd be flying ships like something out of Star Trek, and there was no other place he'd rather be.

CHAPTER 5

The phone rang at 3:30 in the morning. A man's voice on the other end of the line said: "Have you ever asked yourself how police officers in five different jurisdictions could independently see the same gigantic unidentified object hovering a thousand feet in the air and then describe exactly the same thing, to a T?"

Jane didn't know how to respond. Contrary to romantic portrayals of journalists, she'd never received odd calls in the early, early morning from would-be deep-throat sources. Of course, she'd always had an unlisted number to protect herself from such assholes.

"Ah, what?," she said, looking at her alarm clock in perturbed disbelief. "How the fuck did you get this number?"

"Let's just say I have a friend who owes me a favor," said the man.

"Well, I'm not impressed. Give me one good reason why I shouldn't hang up right now."

"If you do, you'll be missing the biggest story of your career. Actually, the biggest story in history, unless you count things like the parting of the Red Sea and Jesus walking on water."

"Oh, really, and what story might that be, flying saucers? You didn't include a self-addressed stamped envelope, so I pitched your stuff right into the circular file."

The man uttered a smug sort of chuckle. "You know, as a journalist, I would think you'd be interested in uncovering the greatest conspiracy of all time."

He broke into a paroxysm of coughing and hacking.

"Excuse me. I have a condition," he said, wheezing. "Paradoxically, I have found, between the medicine and mental anguish, a sick man sleeps less than a healthy man. Hence, here I am, wide awake in the middle of the night."

It was the voice of an old man, but it conveyed a sense of great depth and surety. He expelled a tired sigh.

"You've probably read somewhere that, oh, probably before you were born, people were seeing a lot of strange things in the sky. I mean a lot of people were seeing a lot of strange things. And good, solid people. Pilots, cops, military guys, people from all walks of life. And this weird flying saucer craze just sprang up out of nowhere. Suddenly people were seeing flying saucers. Why flying saucers? There certainly was no real precedent for disc-shaped vehicles."

Jane slipped easily back to sleep, the phone's handset wedged between the pillow and her head. She had popped a Valium at the start of Letterman's opening monologue, and now all she could manage were fleeting spells of wakefulness. She drooled into the phone as the man's droning discourse turned increasingly soporific.

"So, anyway," he continued, "all of a sudden, forty years later, everyone's seeing all these triangular things. Why? What the heck is going on here? Were people also just imagining these vehicles also? And good people. Are you still listening? Are you there? From 1989 to 1990, something like two thousand people in Belgium reported seeing the damned thing. Belgian Air Force F-16s, the best technology, the best training in the world, chased it all over the place, but it executed a series of maneuvers that would have generated g-forces great enough to kill any human being, or so it seemed. What do you make of that? G-forces too great for humans to endure, and yet there it was, in full view of witnesses, tracked by radar. I said, what do you make of that?" the old man said, raising his voice enough to nudge Jane temporarily from her slumber.

"Yes, but, people see a lot of things," she said in the lazy, inchoate speech of someone half asleep.

"Ok, fine. Let me just spell it out for you, alright?" he said. "Let me just do your job for you, here. The United States military has developed, let me rephrase that, has been developing a fantastic new aviation technology for the past fifty years and nobody, I mean nobody in the media, seems to have a clue about what is going on. And the whole thing stinks to high heaven. The ramifications are just astounding. It's the sort of thing that should really make you mad, should make every red-blooded American citizen piping pissed off. And you know why? First of all, people are dying needlessly in unsafe vehicles like commercial airliners, space shuttles, sport utility vehicles.

"Meanwhile, guess what? We're sitting on a truly revolutionary transportation technology that could catapult humanity into the twenty-first century. Not just that, but we've been sitting on this thing for five decades. You want to talk about political scandal. Well, this is big-time political scandal. This is orders of magnitude beyond Watergate.

This is, quite simply, the most profound dirty little secret ever kept from the world."

The man's ranting reached a fever pitch, jarring Jane fully awake. Was he going to go postal on her? He had her phone number, knew where she worked, probably had her home address, as well. You definitely did not want to hang up on a guy like this. No telling what the hell he might do. The best approach would be to reassure him that you were listening, that you were taking him seriously, buy some time for the problem to resolve itself.

"Do you have any idea what an innovation like this would mean for the auto industry alone? Think about it. You eliminate the need for a drive train in your car. No transmission. No drive shaft and a million little gears and metal doohickeys. Practically no suspension. Think about wear and tear on the interstate highway system. You've got a bunch of hover cars that never touch the road. We're talking about major ramifications for the entire transportation infrastructure.

"Then think about the airline industry. Jet engines are completely obsolete. Runways are unnecessary. They just take off vertically. Pilot training is a snap. Hell, if you can drive a car you can drive one of these things. It takes no real skill at all. Jesus, you can't crash, for crissakes, the thing just hangs in the air.

"And, in aviation research, no need for wind tunnels and all sorts of fancy, shmancy aerodynamic design anymore because these things don't have wings. They don't really fly like a regular plane at all. If we really wanted to, heck, we could practically eliminate airports entirely. Just create a whole new generation of personal vehicles that could take you anywhere you wanted to go. Am I getting through to you? Do you have some sense of what I am trying to communicate? You park the damn thing in your driveway. It's no larger than your basic sedan. You want to fly from your house in Chicago to the in-laws in Florida. No problem. You punch in your destination, and off you go. The damn thing flies itself.

"And the technology is cheap. I mean much less expensive than today's cars. After all, you eliminate all kinds of complicated engineering. Have you ever seen the insides of an automatic transmission? Jesus! With these things, all you have is a gravitator for vertical takeoff and then some gravitators for thrust and steering. You have a joystick, and that's how you drive. We are talking about a vehicle with hardly any moving parts, except for the electrical generator, which could be powered with natural gas. Just a standard gas-turbine generator. And some day even that will be replaced with some kind of fuel cell. Then you'll have no moving parts at all.

"Of course, the one application I haven't even really mentioned is that of space travel. We could be rapidly colonizing the moon and Mars and traveling to nearby solar systems. You know how expensive it is to haul cargo in the space shuttle: ten thousand dollars a pound. Rockets are less pricey but limited as all hell and still way too dangerous and complicated."

Jane again succumbed to Valium's seductive allure.

"Excuse me, sir, this is all very interesting, but ..." Her mind slipped into sleep mode in mid-sentence.

"What would you say if I told you I had proof? Actual documentation. Original films of flight tests from the 1950s and 1960s, and still photographs, archival-quality pictures, even blueprints."

She snoozed as the old man described how he'd previously approached the New York Times and the Washington Post, the weekly news magazines and aviation publications. How they'd all snubbed him. Nobody understood. Nobody cared. Not even Seymour Hersh. Now, his health failing, she was his last hope.

Hearing nothing from Jane, his voice rose higher, but she'd dropped the handset to the floor by then, her grasp relaxed in a dreamy torpor.

ଓଓଓଓ

Three days later Jane came home from work to find a note from the apartment manager's office taped to her door: "Miss Hale, there is a package for you at the front desk."

A package? She was not expecting any packages. And that note: "Miss Hale." When were these people going to get with the times? Jane went downstairs to see if the front desk clerk could provide an explanation.

Two old men sat in lobby chairs listening to a Mets game on the radio, and Benny was reading a paperback book.

"Why, hello Miss Hale," he managed amiably.

"Hi Benny. There was a note on my door saying I had a package."

"Why, yes. I do think I have something here for you. I just came in a short while ago, but I do seem to remember seeing something here."

Benny began looking over some large pieces of mail and FedEx envelopes that were arranged on top of the front desk.

"Let's see now, hmmmm," ruminated the clerk, a tall rail of a man. His bony fingers played over the various envelopes and small boxes. "Well, Jane, I coulda sworn there was something for you – oh, wait, now I remember."

He turned around and stooped down, and she saw him struggling with a rather large box on the floor behind the front desk.

"This is heavier than I thought," he said. "Maybe I should get the hand truck."

"No, that's Ok, Benny," Jane said. "I think I can manage it."

She went behind the desk and helped the aged clerk wrestle the box off the floor.

"Who's it from?" she asked, not really directing her question at anyone in particular.

"Well, don't you know?" Benny said annoyingly. "A lady shouldn't be accepting packages out of the blue."

"That's OK, I can manage," she said, and yanked the box away from the man.

Jane was a little surprised by the heft of the package, which must have weighed forty pounds. She could barely get her arms around it, and she swayed slightly backward and then forward before gaining her balance and trudging off toward the elevator. Once inside her apartment, she checked the return address. It read "1217 Broad Street, Albany, New York."

Visions of the Unabomber flashed through her mind while she retrieved a steak knife. She sliced through the packing tape and unfolded the top of the box. It was stuffed with newspapers and Styrofoam peanuts. Under the packing material she found a letter-size manila envelope inscribed with a handwritten label, "instructions."

She set aside the envelope and continued rooting through the box. Next she found two round metal canisters, separated by a piece of cardboard. She removed the canisters and set them aside on the floor next to the box. Then there was a smaller box, sealed again with plastic tape. Jane removed that box and immediately cut it open, revealing several videotapes, and placed the box next to the stack of canisters. The remainder of the box's contents consisted of some graph-paper notebooks. She removed one of the pads and opened it, glimpsing pages of neatly written laboratory notes.

The mysterious package yielded new artifacts the deeper she dug. Jane got a wine cooler from a miniature refrigerator that also served as an end table and surveyed the contents of the box, now spread out on the hardwood floor of her apartment. She drank slowly, contemplating the strange set of circumstances and the old man on the phone. It had been several hours since she last ate, and she was already catching a cheap buzz by the time she finished the bottle. Suddenly remembering the "instructions" that came with the shipment, she found the envelope and removed a single-page letter.

Dear Ms. Hale:

I offer this brief instructional memo to help you comb through the cache of material before you. The videotapes contain footage originally shot on 16 mm film by corporate. That is, before their work was deemed "above top secret," as it were.

I had already come to possess several reels of film documenting this work following the war. These were produced by the company, and most were destroyed by government decree. At any rate, I converted some of the footage to video. I have the original reels in a safe place and have taken great pains to keep them properly preserved! Two reels are included in this package so that you might verify the veracity of the video footage. A careful scrutiny of these films will demonstrate their authenticity, and comparing the tapes and films will clearly show that the footage matches the scenes in the video.

In addition to the films, I also have stored laboratory notes from engineers, scientists and technicians during the earliest days of this research. Any trained researcher should be able to verify to you the authenticity of these records.

Well, that's about it, for now, anyway. I will be in touch, and I trust you will find this material rather compelling.

The letter was not signed. Jane remained sitting on the floor, her back against the bed frame. She picked up the small videotape box, opened it and inspected the contents. There were four regular VHS cassettes, labeled simply "Film One," "Film Two" and so on.

Sipping her second wine cooler, she turned on her television and stuck the first tape into the videocassette recorder. There were some unrecognizable symbols and a numbered countdown and then black-and-white footage. The film showed men in white lab smocks working on a disc-shaped apparatus suspended in the air by a cable or rope. The disc was small, only about three feet in diameter, Jane guessed. One of the men fiddled with switches and knobs on a control panel. The disc began swinging back and forth, and the researchers took notes. The camera was evidently on a tripod, and the view was fixed.

The scene ended abruptly, and another began. The same men watched the disc as it whirled around in a circle like some sort of amusement park ride while suspended from above. They stood back as the thing accelerated to blurring speed. The faster the disc went, the farther out it moved from the center of the imaginary circle it described. Similar scenes followed, each one ending abruptly and the new scene beginning just as suddenly.

There was no audio, adding to the strange sense of historic authenticity.

Jane fast-forwarded the tape until she came across a completely new setup in which technicians worked around an object roughly the size and shape of a large church bell sitting on a wooden pallet. One of the technicians fiddled again with some knobs on a control panel. The machine began to glow. After a few seconds it started shaking and shuddering. Then it abruptly lifted off of the pallet and hovered a short distance from the floor.

It floated motionless for about thirty seconds and then slowly lowered back onto the pallet. Jane thought she noticed some sort of distortion surrounding the object, a fuzzy or blurry region just a few inches from the edges.

A new segment began almost immediately, but this time there was a brief introductory title in stark white lettering on a black background that said: "Half Scale Model of Disc

Configuration." The cut-in title lasted a few seconds and was followed by another page of white-on-black lettering: "June, 1952." The date disappeared and was replaced by the usual cast of laboratory workers, this time seen tinkering with a silvery disc about ten feet in diameter. Several thick electrical cables were attached to the saucer, and it sat on four legs. The men finished preparing the object and stepped back. Within a few seconds it lifted off of the lab floor.

Jane ejected the cassette and skipped to the fourth and final tape in the collection. She had noticed that all of the footage up to that point contained scenes of the same workers, suggesting that this was a very restricted project involving a small number of people. She cracked open her third wine cooler and popped the fourth tape into the machine. A title flashed on the tube for a few seconds: "Full-Scale Test, Mojave Desert Facility." The title vanished and then a new message popped up: "April, 1955."

Unlike the footage in the first tape, this film was in color. The craft was parked on a paved surface, possibly a runway, with craggy mountains sprawled in the background. A tall stepladder was standing next to the silvery ship, which was shaped like two soup bowls attached at the rims. It was about twenty-five feet across and sat low to the ground on four wheels. The top "bowl" was a little more dome-shaped than the bottom one. Cut into the upper dome was a hatch, and its door was propped open. As technicians busily worked around the craft, readying it for the test, a pilot dressed in a flight suit walked up to the ship and climbed the stepladder. He deftly stepped from the ladder onto the top of the craft and through the doorway, descending into the saucer. A moment later the pilot reemerged from the waist up, reached up to grasp a handle on the door, and swung it shut. The technicians moved away from the ship and stood watching. The saucer lifted effortlessly off of the ground and remained hovering.

The next scenes on the tape showed the craft flying at low altitude, perhaps five hundred feet, the same mountain range in the background. Jane thought the geological backdrop looked familiar, possibly the Black Mountains, or the Catalinas in Arizona, where she had worked as a reporter for some years, or the Papoose Mountains that framed the government's notorious Area 51 test site in Nevada.

Toward the end of the tape there was a scene that included a photo session for military brass and civilian officials. These were not the white-smocked laboratory workers from all of the other footage, but rather men in uniform and gray flannel suits. Jane was having a great deal of trouble taking this at face value: a record of military muckitymucks and corporate yahoos hamming it up for the camera in front of a big honking flying saucer on the tarmac of some aerospace proving ground in the high desert?

How could this be true? More to the point, how would she sell the story to her editor?

He would likely laugh her out of his office, and for good reason.

CHAPTER 6

They called her Big Black Delta, a moniker that applied to all of the triangular cruiser-class vessels, and she was under the command of Captain Tommy Swift.

Tommy was now an experienced and decorated fighter jock, "non-terrestrial officer" and cosmic traveler. He had run covert missions in the thick of hostile territories and close surveillance over Russian and Chinese missile bases; tripped across the solar system, surveyed the gas giants Jupiter and Saturn, the rocky swarms of planetesimals in the Kuiper belt and the outer edges of Earth's stellar neighborhood, roughly defined by a swath of comets making up the Oort cloud.

Nearly every mission offered a new set of truly seminal and mind-blowing experiences, and tonight would be no different.

The pilots and technical personnel sat in a small briefing room, some slouching in uncomfortable chairs, some taking notes. A sign mounted above the whiteboard read: "Faster Than Light Speed, Non-Terrestrial Exploration Wing – Integrated Space Command." But the routine disposition of the men and women in the room belied the unusual nature of their business. Tonight, for example, they would take a jaunt just beyond the second Lagrange point a million miles from the Earth, easily dodging past the Hubble Space Telescope and International Space Station, leaving NASA hardware in the cosmic dust.

There, with the sun at its back, the giant spacecraft would have a clear view of the universe. The galaxy beckoned, its countless star systems offering fertile ground for human expeditions. Big Black Delta was now poised to take the next leap: an investigation of the nearest solar systems within a perimeter of fifty light years from Earth.

A real starship, and the new millennium hadn't officially begun.

Meanwhile, who knew?

From the president to Congress to the most elite members of the research community and the public at large, all are distracted by the intricate details of their own lives and the consuming world events of the time: Unabomber sentenced to four life terms; NASA turns 40 and announces John Glenn may fly in space again; Pope John Paul II visits Cuba; tornadoes kill dozens in Florida; Bill Clinton impeached; Elton John is knighted.

Elton John is knighted!

Society is oblivious to the nation's secret antigravity juggernaut, a fleet that encompassed several models: the standard saucer, which existed in various dimensions from thirty to one hundred twenty feet in diameter; triangular interceptors the size of fighter jets; and cylindrical things that resembled huge flying submarines and traversed water and air with equal ease. They were all "classics" in the sense that they instantly outperformed anything that ever took to the skies. Individually crafted masterpieces.

And Big Black Delta was the crown jewel of the fleet. Its builders were ecstatic over the huge ship's boundless potential; its herculean capacity to lift and transport hundreds of times the cargo of conventional airplanes; its expansive storage bay that doubled as a hangar for little flying saucer scouts and triangular interceptors to be unleashed against enemy fighter jets.

It immediately became the linchpin of the nation's deeply cloaked military space program, an airborne aircraft carrier central to America's quest for cosmic conquest and global dominance well into the twenty-first century. The fleet was operated by an invisible entity called the Integrated Space Command, headquartered in the Intermountain West, but the ships were housed at various military facilities around the world.

Some represented the ideal stealth platform and were coated with radar-absorbing paints or composite materials. The United States sometimes used the antigravity vehicles in reconnaissance missions over the skies of Europe and the Middle East, particularly to probe the defensive systems of potential adversaries. Small saucers hovered amid the clouds, their round, gray fuselages blending nicely into overcast skies. They collected heaps of data about foreign systems and eavesdropped on short-range radio traffic, the FM stuff that stops at the horizon. These communications usually weren't encrypted because they were so localized, providing intelligence for military and CIA programs. It was amazing how candid people could be when they didn't think anybody was listening.

Most of the ships in the fleet employed conventional turbine engines to drive megawatt dynamos that powered the field-propulsion systems. Then there was a new, elite class of nuclear-powered vessels, equipped with reactors like those on submarines. The atomic-powered vessels carried enough fuel to last at least five years and plied the vast reaches of space. Always out there, patrolling the solar system while the people of Earth went about their business.

The antigravity vehicles were not to be used in actual combat because the possibility of losing one of them to the enemy was too grave. They did, however, participate in mock military strikes, playing cat and mouse with unsuspecting air force pilots in venues as geographically diverse as the Arab world to the United Kingdom, South America to the U.S. homeland. These exercises were conducted only against countries friendly to the United States. That way, just in case one of the vehicles went down the Americans would be able to retrieve it. Hence, Western Europe was fertile ground for these "living lab" assignments. The missions yielded volumes of data vital to assessing and fine-tuning the fleet's performance and capabilities in a real-world environment.

Tonight's was primarily a reconnaissance exercise over rural Indiana: a technology test to see how well the ship could evade the nation's defensive systems, a dress rehearsal for the practical machinations of war.

Big Black Delta would swoop down over American soil in the early morning hours, traversing several towns and skirting a U.S. Air Force base. Such nighttime endeavors focused on three overall goals: first, study the ship's facility and readiness for low-altitude warfare and surveillance over populated regions of technologically sophisticated nations; second, probe BBD's ability to overwhelm the military and other authorities; and last, a psychological-operations component. Specifically, how would people react to the sight of something so potentially menacing? Would they be awed, or demoralized? Would they fear for their lives? Would they question their gods or flock to churches, get drunk, smoke dope?

Many of these results should be easy to learn simply by monitoring media coverage and perusing official reports from police and military agencies. From these data, strategists might assess the psychological-warfare value and the impact on civilian populations. To learn, in effect, whether a people might happily yield to a shockingly superior and ominous presence: Big Black Delta as a razor-sharp instrument of emotional terror, inflicting existential anguish instead of physical injury.

The huge craft was moored in its underground hangar at a restricted section of a military base in Utah, one of a small number of sites housing facilities related to the advanced propulsion technology. The captain and his crew boarded the ship shortly after dusk and began the rather extensive readiness checklist required for each operation; a rundown of the nuclear reactor's fuel rods, cooling system, steam-pressure vessel, electricity-generating turbines and the field-propulsion drives.

Inside the stainless-steel viscera of the General Electric model 26G reactor, things kicked into high gear in a hurry. Neutrons bombarded the nuclei of highly enriched uranium-235 atoms, causing them to split and releasing two neutrons in the process. Those neutrons then went on to bombard other U-235 atoms, ramping up exponentially. Control rods kept the fission reaction from going "supercritical." They absorbed neutrons to maintain the process at a nice, steady pace -- a pace that would allow the fuel to last years rather than exploding in a violent chain reaction.

The ships were more like oceangoing vessels than aircraft, and the ranking scheme of the crew was a mixture of Air Force and Navy.

The flight engineer, Senior Chief Petty Officer Carl Hand, monitored the reactor control panel. He ordered personnel to retract the fuel rods, throttling up the nuclear reactions and generating enough heat to produce steam for the turbine generators. Senior, as he was called, prosaically recited a string of crucial data.

"Temperature readings, normal. Radiation readings, negative. Pressure level, normal. Turbines running at optimal RPM. Powering up central gravitator. Powering up steering and thrust gravitators. Activating hyperdrive assembly."

The leviathan came to life, lifting silently out of its grave-like berth as the crew went about its tasks, checking various instruments and reviewing mission plans.

"Ok Senior, stand by to assume high-altitude orientation at selected parameters," Captain Swift commanded.

The engineer responded on cue: "Central gravitator configured. Hyperdrive configured."

Commander Swift immediately countered: "High-altitude orientation in ten seconds."

The ship suddenly shot out of sight, instantly arriving at its programmed destination sixty thousand feet above the ground. There were no G forces, no sense of acceleration, even though they were zipping through the airspace a zillion times faster than sound.

Officers in the ship's control room studied their computer monitors.

"Stand by to assume low-Earth orbit," Commander Swift said.

A few seconds later, the colossal craft emerged two hundred and twenty miles above the planet. The ship had just made orbital flight look as uneventful as a Sunday drive in the country. Something that normally required a perilous rocket ride on top of controlled explosions, pushing man and machine to their physical limits.

The twelve crew members in the spacious control room continued to view their computer monitors, strapped to their seats in the now-weightless environment, some of them clicking away on keyboards, others simply concentrating on mission data.

The captain addressed the crew, speaking into a headset that fed his voice to a sound system.

"Listen up. We'll begin with recon at twenty hundred hours to confirm satellites of interest to the intelligence community," he said.

Although the brightly lit control room was full of busy people, there was no sense of claustrophobia. The environment was strangely clean and fresh, owing to carbon dioxide scrubbers and other systems that continuously absorbed airborne wastes. Filters and dehumidifiers controlled air quality, keeping it suitable for people and electronics.

Two large-screen monitors, one each on the starboard and port sides of the control room, displayed real-time views of planet Earth below; wispy cirrus clouds, blue oceans, lush continents. Stacked along the portside of the control room was a bank of electronic boxes housing the ship's navigational systems, including the vital Navstar global positioning gear. Red and green lights blinked on and off on panels facing the boxes. The GPS system, which provided a three-dimensional fix with an accuracy of three meters, showed the precise latitude and longitude of the ship's position.

And computers for various and sundry purposes were crammed into another row of cabinets. All told, they represented the raw power of five Cray supercomputers. The machines hummed audibly in the background.

A mission plan came up on individual computer screens and also appeared on a large display centered in the front of the control room. The print was in a large bold font, with the title "Satellites of Interest."

Captain Swift explained how the mission was to include mock "orbital-object-sequestering" exercises. The idea was to rendezvous with foreign satellites and then simulate the operation of a robotic arm capable of plucking a spacecraft from orbit and hoisting it into the ship's cargo bay. NTOs had performed the simulated operation hundreds of times and had actually done the real thing on more than one occasion, not with foreign birds but with obsolete U.S. communications hardware in geosynchronous orbit.

BBD's crew also would practice "killing" satellites with a system that shot high velocity metal shrapnel, the equivalent of space buckshot. Because of Big Black Delta's precision maneuverability, obliterating satellites constituted little challenge. The missions yielded virtually a one hundred percent success rate -- simply too easy for thrill-seeking, highly trained combat personnel. Banality aside, however, eliminating an adversary's orbital assets could prove vital to U.S. military strategies during the earliest days of a war. Within a single hour, the NTOs could cripple the opposition's ability to coordinate crucial elements of combat.

Captain Swift reviewed the mission statement. After several screens of text, images of a half dozen satellites appeared in succession, each remaining on the screen for about five minutes. The animations rotated and magnified certain features. Rendezvous coordinates, already programmed into the ship's computers, were included in the briefing. Estimated time to complete the satellite sortie was a little over three hours, Swift said, in summing up that portion of his briefing.

"Now I want to take some time to review the heart of tonight's mission," he told the crew.

A new portion of text appeared on the monitors under the heading "domestic recon."

"Well, we've been through this many times," Captain Swift said. "I don't think I need to remind anyone that a lot of people will be watching. We're going primetime tonight."

The mission plan summarized in bulleted fashion precisely how the crew would assess its effectiveness in penetrating both military and civilian airspace, although, BBD's superlative stealth capabilities had already been demonstrated in a smattering of previous missions. Fields of text flashed on the computer monitors one after another, culminating with a special segment focusing on the most delicate task.

"We're going to run a low-altitude operation over a civilian population and within military airspace at two hundred hours," Captain Swift said. "The objectives are as follows."

A new page immediately appeared on the monitors.

GENERAL OBJECTIVES

LOW-ALTITUDE OVERFLIGHT OF POPULATED COMMUNITIES

1. *DOCUMENT ANY OFFOCIAL GOVERNMENT AND/OR MILITARY RESPONSE*
2. *PENETRATE MILITARY AIRSPACE*
3. *TEST ABILITY TO CONTROL AIR SPACE*

The captain's voice took on a more relaxed tone.

"Folks, the results of this mission will be tracked by the directorate for purposes that are outside of our need to know, but suffice it to say this is considered high-priority. It's fairly obvious why. Think of it as a kinder, gentler form of shock and awe."

Some of the NTOs got a kick out of their commander's attempt at humor.

At exactly eight o'clock that night the crew began its satellite reconnoiter, using precise rendezvous points that brought them within snatching distance of their quarry – slightly more than a dozen Chinese, Russian, French, Indian and Pakistani military spacecraft. Such a satellite flyby with conventional spacefaring technology would have taken days, requiring perfectly timed rocket burns and mathematically meticulous trajectory planning. Yet Big Black Delta just configured its field-propulsion system for the proper coordinates and instantly appeared in a parking orbit next to each satellite.

The first part of the mission was completed by ten o'clock, and the crew stood down for a few hours before the night's main attraction. Carl Hand made his way aft, down to the mess hall, pulling himself along on railings and handholds bolted to the walls to help weightless shipmates negotiate the narrow corridors. A labyrinth of cavernous passageways led to various rooms, services, facilities and systems. Some of these corridors, such as those near the nuclear reactor, were restricted to specialized personnel. Radiation warning signs marked the way. Other symbols and notices stipulated exactly which personnel were permitted in certain areas.

The control room, engine room and life-support systems were housed on the ship's first level, as was the mess hall and most of the living space for the crew of more than thirty. The dining area was a hub of activity, combining cafeteria, movie theater and game room, not unlike the arrangement on U.S. nuclear submarines. A large warehouse stored everything from peanut butter to frozen meats, freeze-dried consumables and the most vital commodity of all: coffee.

Although some portions of Big Black Delta were relatively spacious, most segments were very tight. It took some practice for crew members to learn how to avoid bumping into everything, and everyone, spelunking weightlessly through the ship's lacy network of hallways.

Shipmates floated around the control room, while others visited their quarters to kill some time.

The sleeping habitats were cramped, coffin-size bunking units stacked three high on both sides of a narrow corridor. Curtains enclosed each berth, giving a very small degree of privacy, but at least it was a familiar space where crew members could lie down, read a book or magazine, write a letter or check out a recent "familygram" from a loved one. It was a highly restrictive, unnatural way to live, both physically and psychologically, yet the NTOs embraced their world, happy in the knowledge that they were a privileged lot.

Captain Swift remained in the control room, where he sat reading various training manuals, swiveling in his captain's chair, his short hair fluffing out slightly in the absence of gravity. He unsnapped his harness, lifted buoyantly out of the chair and drifted toward the ship's navigator, Lieutenant Junior Grade Regina Klein, who was updating the inertial navigation systems with the latest GPS data. Klein was not a large person, and Swift sometimes had the feeling she might be swallowed up by all the equipment in the navigation station. Like being engulfed by a large electronic amoeba -- numerous LED eyes fixed unsympathetically on its prey.

"How's the gear looking?" he asked her, leaning close enough to be heard over the hum of cooling fans.

"Everything's checking out fine. We're mission-ready, sir," she resolutely told the commander.

All things considered, this was, more or less, a fairly routine outing so far -- nothing to get excited about. Select crew members were summoned to report for a midnight briefing in the control room. Then, shortly before two a.m., Big Black Delta was "repositioned" to new coordinates at sixty thousand feet, forty thousand feet, and then only five thousand feet over Indiana farmland.

"Ok, take her down to one thousand feet, standard field propellers," Captain Swift told the helmsman, who manipulated controls on a panel of switches and knobs.

Now the ship floated easily over the sleepy town of Lawrence.

"Take her down to five hundred."

The control room lighting was dimmed so that the crew could better view the night-vision images displayed on their monitors and large screens. Their faces were illuminated a creepy greenish cast from the monitors.

"Taking her down to five hundred," the helmsman replied in monotone.

Big Black Delta passed over the town.

"Ok, standard drive with a heading of zero six five degrees at forty-five knots," the helmsman said. "Here we go."

The ship was illumined like a football stadium and just about as large.

"Alright, surveillance crew, let's get ready to record the moment," said the captain.

The surveillance unit consisted of three officers, officially called electronic warfare operators, or EWOPS. They were cryptologic technicians and reconnaissance equipment specialists who concentrated on operating the various snooping gadgets on the ship -- several cameras, including infrared and night vision systems, radars, acoustic listening devices and radio receivers. A Chief Petty Officer in the unit oriented the cameras to capture video of a civilian as he craned his neck to watch the gargantuan craft glide overhead.

"Continue on current heading," Captain Swift said.

Navigator Klein was hunched over a computerized monitor resembling a radar screen, tracking the ship's slow, precise trajectory over the town. The sky was cloudless, the ride smooth as silk. The airspeed was a glacial seventy knots. Klein studied the ship's GPS coordinates.

"We're right on the money," she reported

Big Black Delta meandered above the sprawling farm country for roughly twenty minutes, traversing five police jurisdictions and the environs of Anderson Air Force Base, home to facilities and aircraft specializing in medical evacuation and refueling. Not a single officer on the base was aware of BBD's presence until the police dispatcher called. Then, the response was swift and imposing: Two heavily armed F-15E Strike Eagle fighters were scrambled out of Benson Air Force Base, about seventy miles to the north.

The Air Force listened in on police channels, providing updates to the pursuing jets, while BBD's surveillance unit snooped on both the military and the cops. The ensuing radio traffic had the ship's control room collectively smirking. The clear -- if somewhat staticky -- chatter was being piped over the sound system, as the tone of discussion changed from amusement to anxiety to awed disbelief.

Within twenty minutes the jets had drawn close enough to see BBD's rear running lights. The lead pilot, a Texan with the call sign "Hondo," could make out the ship's broad outline and overall size. He'd been a fighter pilot for two decades, a hard-bitten warrior who'd won dogfights against MIG-17s over North Vietnam and flown sorties in Desert Storm.

Together with his wingman "Mad Max" the pair constituted a formidable fighting force, finely honed killing machines armed with the latest and most lethal technologies.

"Bogie, ten left, slow and low, in the weeds," Hondo radioed the tower. He spoke in the laconic language of "brevity code," a system for communicating the most salient facts as tersely as possible.

The Air Force personnel manual advised pilots to record a UFO's altitude, direction of travel, speed, description of flight path and maneuvers. It was to be treated like any other hostile intruder, and a detailed report was to be prepared for NORAD, the North American Aerospace Defense Command, protector of U.S. and Canadian airspace.

The two jets approached Big Black Delta at more than four hundred miles per hour, screeching over rural Indiana in the early morning hours. Just as the fighters drew within five miles of BBD, the ship's powerful field-propulsion system started driving their instruments haywire.

"Benson tower, alpha check, gadget bent," said Hondo, sounding a little agitated.

Adding to the intrigue was the object's failure to observe the standard IFF protocol, or identification friend or foe, emitted by electronic transponders on aircraft. But this aircraft had issued no IFF data, suggesting its transponder had been turned off or its signals compromised by atmospheric interference.

The tower radioed the pilot his coordinates and a precise fix on BBD.

"Hondo, copy bogie dope, committed," the pilot replied, indicating his intention to intercept the UFO.

Captain Swift alertly ordered the ship repositioned to forty thousand feet, and BBD instantaneously disappeared. At this point, Hondo violated one of the primary tenets of brevity code: Always err on the side of reticence.

"Target has vanished," he said, voice betraying a mixture of horror and amazement. "It's just gone! How can it be gone? Tower, do you have contact with target?"

"Benson tower, checking medium and high." A pause followed as controllers searched for BBD on their screens. "Hondo, possible contact high, forty angels."

"Copy," said Hondo, offering no other reply, a conspicuous omission considering the urgency of the situation. Surely the tower didn't think the high-altitude target was the same object. Nothing moved that fast.

"Tower, are you painting that object?"

"Affirmative."

"Break, break to high," Hondo barked to his wingman. "Will try to bracket. Repeat, bracketing."

Both jets pulled into a steep climbing maneuver, shooting upward toward Big Black Delta. The intent was for the jets to reach a position on either side of the big ship, an action that would allow the pilots to assess the object's size, shape and other defining characteristics.

"Copy that, continue," came the tower response.

Tommy Swift had been anticipating just such a tactic, and he immediately dispatched five saucers to intercept the jets. The tower picked them up at about twenty thousand feet.

"Heads up, new picture," the tower air traffic controller radioed to the pilots. "Bandits at your ten left and two right positions. Repeat, bandits, angels plus twenty."

"Copy, tally and closing," said Hondo, exasperated, his breath labored.

The tower was now buzzing with officers, watching in bewilderment as the two jets and five targets merged into one indistinct smudge on the radar screen. The saucers intercepted the fighters and deftly surrounded them, training powerful spotlights on the jets and blinding the pilots, which enhanced the whole fear factor of the moment.

"Warning, red," exclaimed Hondo, sensing imminent attack, his voice rising an octave.

The fighter jocks, men for whom machismo is a core value and intimidation a foreign concept, rarely broadcast feelings of fear. But now they were experiencing something completely different: utter vulnerability, and, worse yet, subordination to another presence in the sky, heretofore their sole dominion.

Now they were shitting bricks in their form-fitting flight uniforms, lit up like a couple of bugs under a microscope. Cockpit alarms blared and various gauges were compromised by such close proximity to the field-propulsion drives. The saucers easily paced the fighters, keeping a parallel trajectory that prevented the jets from pulling away. This went on for several minutes, as the fighter pilots worked up a sweat trying in vain to out-maneuver the saucers.

"Break left!" Hondo shouted into the radio. "Hard left! Hard right!"

The jets banked every which way, climbing and nose-diving at crushing speeds. With every move, though, they found themselves in exactly the same position relative to the saucers, as though glued to the mysterious objects in perfect synchrony.

These strange events horrified air traffic controllers, a commanding officer peering anxiously over their shoulders.

"What is your status? Can you describe bandits?"

"Unconventional," came Hondo's reply. "Very unconventional. They've got us blinded with some sort of beam. Defensive, missile threat imminent."

At the same time, BBD repositioned itself to sixty thousand feet.

"New picture, mother is very high, angels sixty," the tower informed the pilots.

Tommy Swift sat back in his captain's chair, listening to the tension-filled radio traffic. By now the saucers could have easily annihilated the jets with their twenty-millimeter cannons. Satisfied, he terminated the exercise, and the flying saucers veered away at three times the speed of sound to rendezvous with Big Black Delta.

"Tower, bandits have gone!" said Hondo, expressing equal parts wonder, confusion and relief.

The fighters returned to the base, and both pilots completed extensive reports.

However, media accounts in coming days focused exclusively on the police encounters with BBD, making only passing reference to sketchy reports of the possible appearance of fighter jets and "other lights" in the sky. After all, the brief but harrowing UFO dogfight unfolded at twenty thousand feet and was over within minutes.

The mission provided a bonanza of data. BBD had recorded all radio traffic and captured extensive video. Intelligence analysts would later study these records, also monitoring the aftermath, primarily in the form of media reports, police filings, letters to the editor, documentaries and graphical reenactments.

The living laboratory was yielding a bounty of knowledge.

ଓଓଓଓ

Sergeant Steve Sullivan was two hours into the midnight shift at the Lawrence, Indiana, P.D. when the odd call came in from the dispatcher. It seemed that local businessman Eddie Earle, owner and operator of Eddie's Diner, had just filed a report at headquarters that was providing an endless source of comic relief for the weary desk sergeant and the woman working dispatch.

Earle, a fixture in the rural Indiana farming community who'd been running the greasy spoon for decades, had just experienced a close encounter of the first kind.

It was 2:30 on a frigid February morning. Earle had locked up for the night and was walking to his pickup truck with a moneybag of the day's take. He happened to look skyward and noticed an unusually bright star. But then the "star" seemed to be growing brighter, and Earle surmised it was probably a low-flying airplane.

"That's funny," he thought, "can't ever remember seeing a big plane coming in so low before."

A military base was nearby, but this plane wasn't flying in that direction. It was heading straight over town, pretty much due east and not remotely in line with the runway approach. The plane was remarkably quiet, and soon it was gliding straight toward Earle when he came to the realization that this was no ordinary aircraft. First of all, it had no wings and seemed to have an angular shape.

"Why, that's lit up like all getup," he said to himself as the object moved so slowly, almost hovering. It slipped silently beyond the treetops and out of sight.

He pulled out of the parking lot and drove aimlessly for a few minutes. Without consciously doing so, Earle soon found himself rolling up to the Lawrence Police Department. He wandered into the lobby like a zombie, uncertain what he was going to tell the desk sergeant.

The cop looked up from his paperwork and asked politely, "Can I help you, sir?"

"Well, I'm not sure what I got to report. I was hoping you might know about a situation that just happened," Earle offered vaguely.

"Sir, you'll have to be a little more specific than that," the desk sergeant said.

"Okay, ah, what I mean, is, I was wondering if anybody might have called in any reports of low-flying airplanes and such," Earle said.

"I'll check with dispatch, but I am not aware of any reports. Why, did you see an aircraft flying too low?"

"Well, not exactly. I, I mean, sort of," Earle said.

The desk sergeant folded his arms in consternation.

"Now, look, buddy, which is it?"

"Ah, well, here's the thing. I was walking out of my restaurant and I seen a really big plane or something fly right over the trees. I mean, this thing made no sound, no nothin."

"Could you describe the object?"

"Oh, sure."

"Well, go ahead, sir," the cop said with a hint of annoyance.

"Okay, it was really big, about the size of a two-story house, with a couple-three bright winnders on top, and it was kinda square."

The cop recorded the restaurateur's name, address, phone number, the time and location of the "incident" and a brief narrative. Earle had scarcely left the building by the time police were dispatching the report over the radio to sergeant Steve Sullivan, who was just finishing a property-damage call when he received the transmission.

"Ah, four-ten. We have a subject reporting lights in the sky over the area of State Road Twenty-Eight and Lincoln Drive. Can you tell me your twenty? Over."

"I'm winding things up here," he responded.

"Well, we've got a gentleman here who was very upset about something flying in the area of his business." The dispatcher broke off her communiqué at this point, and laughter could be heard in the background.

She had the raspy voice of a heavy smoker.

"Was he ten fifty-five?" asked Sullivan, code for driving while intoxicated.

"That's negative."

"Ten-four. I'll check it out."

Sergeant Sullivan turned his cruiser around to begin heading toward the location of the sighting. He topped a ridge and immediately spied what appeared to be an extra-bright spotlight from a farmhouse. He pulled over, and the light was moving slowly toward him. He could see then that there were actually three or four lights on the object.

Leaning out of the patrol car's window, he was surprised to hear no drone of engines. The policeman had grown up as a military brat, and he knew all about aircraft, from A-10 "warthogs" to big lumbering C-150 cargo planes. This plane was different: It lacked the usual green, red and white recognition lights. Instead, the lights were a uniform white and abnormally bright.

Sullivan got out of his car to get a better look at the curious object. It was probably about half a mile away and closing, following a course that would bring it over the cruiser's position. As it grew closer, he could see that the thing was much larger than a military cargo plane.

He grabbed the radio handset.

"Dispatch, this is four-ten. I have that object in sight now."

"You're kidding," the dispatcher said. For the first time she sounded serious.

"It's huge," Sullivan reaffirmed.

The sky was clear and nearly moonless, but the object was even darker and well defined against a voluminous collection of stars on display that night. He turned off the overhead strobe lights and the engine, peering straight up at the UFO. It appeared to have features on its underside resembling beams or some other kind of structural elements. The cop watched in disbelief as it drifted over a cornfield. An eerie silence hung over the spot.

The entranced officer gazed at Big Black Delta for a minute or two. He was suddenly startled by the sound of screeching brakes as a trucker pulled off to the side of the road to take a look. Then a car passed by, its brake lights flashing brightly as the vehicle skidded to a stop right in the middle of the southbound lane.

The driver stepped halfway out of the car and stared at the object.

"Ma'am, you're in the middle of the road," Sullivan shouted at the young woman. "Please move your car now!"

She turned to the officer.

"What is that?"

"I don't know," was all Sullivan could tell her.

She moved her car to the shoulder and joined the officer and the trucker, gawking skyward as BBD projected a brilliant beam of light straight down. It didn't sweep back and forth, as a helicopter's searchlight might. The ship blotted out stars as it passed closer to the three spectators, and its sheer size was frightening to behold. The police sergeant felt the sensation of something heavy pushing on him as the craft floated nearly directly over them. And everything -- the road, the car, the very air -- seemed to be charged with energy and vibrating slightly.

Sergeant Sullivan also noticed that surrounding the triangle was a hazy envelope, distorting the stars near its edges before they were occulted by the object itself. He realized at that moment that he'd been holding his breath for quite some time. The woman motorist started sobbing. She ran to her car and drove off, never saying another word to the two men.

Sullivan reached into his cruiser for his radio handset, and when he looked up the craft had inexplicably disappeared. It had darted some twenty miles away in the blink of an eye and looked to be over the town of Millberry.

"Ah, dispatch, you might want to get on the horn to Millberry P.D. I think this thing should be visible now to officers there."

BBD's surveillance unit picked up the ensuing radio traffic. Technicians busily operated a suite of snooping gadgets, recording every detail. By the time the UFO flap had ended, half a dozen cops had encountered the remarkable craft, and all of them came away with the same unsettling feeling. They had just experienced a life-changing event, something that couldn't be neatly compartmentalized or conveniently clarified with conventional explanations.

If nothing else, it would make for some good storytelling, or grist for those exceptionally vivid nightmares, the ones that woke you up in the middle of the night sweating bullets and thanking god it was all just a dream, just a bad dream.

ଓଓଓଓ

Despite the truly bizarre nature of the encounter, it was virtually ignored by the major media outside of little Lawrence, Indiana. Some local radio stations covered the story, and the Lawrence Daily News, the only real newspaper in the area, published the following article:

Cops chase 'really big' UFO

From Staff Reports

For nearly an hour early yesterday police in Lawrence and four surrounding communities chased a huge, mysterious object that floated silently over housing developments and agricultural fields before zipping away at tremendous speed.

Shortly after 2:30 a.m. on Wednesday, officers watched what they later described as an immense triangular craft, which was thought to be at least the length of a football field.

"It was really big and made no sound, except like a humming noise," said Sgt. Stephen E. Sullivan. "It moved very fast, from one place to another, like a blur."

Edward T. Earle, who owns Eddie's Diner, 1826 State Road 28, was leaving work when he spotted the object moving toward his business. He reported his sighting to the police department, insisting that an officer be dispatched to investigate the strange lights.

"It flew over my parking lot and then just kept a movin'," he said.

Sullivan followed the strange object in his squad car. Several times the UFO sped away at great speed and came to an abrupt stop, skipping around the night sky, he said.

A few minutes after it was reported to Lawrence police, officers in Millberry saw the UFO, said Millberry police spokesman Daniel E. Shea. Officer Mike Martin tried to take a picture of it with his Polaroid camera.

"But it was really cold and too dark, and the only thing that came out was the lights," Martin said.

Just as quickly as it had appeared, the UFO vanished. Air traffic controllers at Indianapolis International Airport and Chicago O'Hare International Airport said they saw nothing unusual on radar during the time of the sightings. Likewise, the Federal Aviation Administration could shed no light on the mystery.

Meanwhile, residents living near Benson Air Force Base were awakened by the deafening roar of fighter jets around 3 a.m.

"It's possible that the jets were scrambled in response to the UFO," said Joseph Braun, director of the National UFO Network office in Indianapolis

The base's public affairs office did not immediately return calls.

The story was picked up by a handful of publications in the newspaper's parent chain, engendering coverage by a Chicago television station, which produced a sarcastic feature riddled with clichés and poking fun at the police officers and poor Eddie Earle, who was depicted as a first-class hick. The TV story included an interview with a famous UFO debunker, who characterized the witness accounts as delusional and attributed the sightings to either a blimp, the planet Venus or a streaking meteor.

Then, perfectly on cue and with a smirk, the anchor suggested that perhaps the encounter was alcohol-induced or fabricated to drum up business for old Earle's restaurant.

"I don't know what those guys are drinking down there, but maybe they were celebrating the weekend a little too early," he said. "Speaking about the weekend, here's Cindy with the five-day weather forecast."

CHAPTER 7

Jane dragged herself out of bed, shaking off the residual nausea from those lousy wine coolers the night before.

Less than an hour later she was huffing it down to Grand Central Station, at Fifty-Third Street and Second Avenue, just a few blocks from her apartment building. Her office was on Ninth Street and Fourth Avenue, in Manhattan's East Village, so she always took the Six Train on the Green Line, which let her off right on Eighth Street. The cars were usually crowded, but the Four and Five express trains were even more packed.

She slid her fare card into a slot in a turnstile and ambled onto the platform along with a throng of rush-hour commuters. The Green Line trains, like the shuttle to a gentrified Times Square, were new and relatively fancy, in seeming contradiction to the stereotypical, gritty New York subway experience. Tourists frequently rode these particular trains, and Rudy Giuliani never could pass up a good marketing opportunity. Showcasing them was a way of reinforcing New York's freshly rebranded image as a more wholesome, family friendly place; a chance to circumnavigate the sordid components of a megacity; to cast a handsome veil over the various sins, the riffraff and depravity; while bolstering the mayor's presidential ambitions at a time when his Democratic adversaries reeled under Bill Clinton's moral transgressions.

Nevertheless, riding the subway was still a wholly unnatural circumstance; all those people crammed together, most of them confronting the stressful drudgery of their crummy nine-to-five existences, a mindset that brought out the worst in some. She took pains to avoid eye contact, gaze fixed to a section of the New York Times, opened before her like a paper shield. Sometimes she wasn't even reading the damn thing, but it provided some cover, a private moment where she could think about the upcoming workday. This morning, however, as the train snaked its way under the city, her thoughts led to a vague intuition, an unpleasant distraction that wouldn't go away, a formless premonition of danger.

She arrived at her office, and, as was her routine, immediately consulted her desk blotter for the day. She was one of those people who stubbornly rejected the modern, mobile world of electronic organizers, or "personal digital assistants." One look at her blotter confirmed that nagging intuition. In an instant her heart rate and body temperature kicked up a notch, and that sickly wine-cooler feeling returned. She tugged a little on her shirt collar to pull the fabric away from perspiring skin, eyes glued to the date's entry: "AR due."

Horrors! This was the day she was to hand in her annual review, including a rather lengthy evaluation form, complete with detailed performance figures, statistics supporting the contention that she had met the expectations of her managers; that she had, in effect, been effective and efficient and productive.

What a nuisance.

It was to be handed in by COB, and her editor, William Walsh, was not a very understanding sort of guy. He was a conceited, unimaginative, impatient man; an intellectual snob; a college-professor-turned-editor with a Ph.D. in journalism. To Jane, it seemed, he lived for the chance to belittle others, especially on paper. Everyone called him Bill, but whenever he ripped the hell out of your copy with red ink, his comments scrawled in the margins were always signed WW. Not Bill, or BW, or B.

He walked around with his nose in the air bellowing journalism truisms.

"If your mamma says she loves ya, ya still better check it out," he'd say at least once a week, in a tone that smacked of some literary blueblood trying to sound like Joe Sixpack.

Often she would hear his resonant pomposities from halfway across the newsroom. Frequently these were sarcastic witticisms delivered at the expense of some underling.

"Well, as the great Baltimore Sun columnist Jack Germond once said, 'Starting from seemingly incontrovertible evidence, one can come to erroneous conclusions.' Ha, ha, ha, ha!"

She especially detested that gaudy laughter, which some staffers affectionately regarded as "contagious." To Jane, Walsh's faux joviality seemed ridiculously affected at best and obnoxious at worst. But he was the managing editor, and she had to please. The paperwork for the annual review was a painstaking, tedious exercise: How many articles had she written on specific "strategic" subjects deemed most important by editorial bosses? How many new sources had she developed? How many hard news stories, feature stories, enterprise stories, etc., etc.? And the most dreaded of all data points: How many errors of fact had she committed? She was thinking about her predicament when her phone rang.

"Is this Jane Hale?" asked a man with a British accent.

She wasn't sure she recognized the man's voice at first.

"Hallo, this is Robert Marsden."

Could it be? The same Robert Marsden who sees UFOs? And why now, so concurrent with all this strange flying saucer business she'd suddenly been burdened with? True to her pragmatic nature, she never really entertained the whole metaphysical notion of synchronicity. Again, an eerie premonition: Something was up.

"Hallo." Marsden said. "Hallo?"

"Ah, yes, hello Robert, how are you?"

"Just fine," he said. "And how is everything in the world of aerospace intrigue?"

"Intrigue?" she said. "You make it sound so romantic."

"Listen, I happen to be in town this week for some meetings with my publisher and thought we could touch base on a project I'm working on. There are some, well, issues, some matters of importance."

The last thing Jane needed this morning was a complication. On the other hand, she wouldn't mind a diversion.

"Well, I do have a deadline this afternoon, but …"

She hadn't finished her sentence when Marsden interrupted.

"Brilliant! Why don't we meet for dinner? I promise not to take too much of your time. It's just that I feel very strongly that we should discuss these issues sooner than later and …"

Now it was Jane's turn to interrupt. Why the hell didn't he just tell her what was on his mind?

"I think you're the one with all the intrigue, not me."

"What's that supposed to mean?" he said with a light-hearted giggle. "You Yanks are suspicious people."

Jane laughed at Marsden's coyness.

"Well, is it animal, vegetable or mineral?" she said. "You're the one who called me."

Marsden cleared his throat.

"To be completely honest, I don't feel very comfortable discussing this over the telephone," he said.

Jane was now very interested.

"Alright, I guess I can appreciate that."

"Splendid," he said. "The publisher put me up at the Marriott. Ghastly place, full of vacationers and their annoying children. At least the pub seems civilized, though. How about meeting there for a chat? I don't mind telling you, I'm quite anxious to discuss this matter."

Jane spent the rest of the day in clerical Purgatory, preparing the annual report. Eight pages of meaningless folderol: numbers, comments, checklists.

She escaped the office in late afternoon, saying she had to see a man about a story.

CHAPTER 8

She found Robert Marsden in the hotel bar, already fairly drunk on vodka martinis. He was sitting at a table all by himself, nursing a drink and completely lost in thought. It wasn't until she had sat down opposite him that he noticed her.

"Jane, I am so glad you could make it! Please have a seat. Would you like a drink?"

He was very fit for a man in his 70s. A former marathon runner, he still jogged a few miles almost daily.

Marsden summoned the waitress and Jane ordered a screwdriver.

"I have to apologize for being so pissed," Marsden continued while Jane waited for her drink to arrive.

He explained that he hadn't been himself since Lynn, his wife of forty-three years, passed away. That was almost two years ago, November, but it all seemed so surrealistic living without her. Traveling was especially difficult because they often took these kinds of business trips together.

"At home I can just burry myself in work, but when I'm on the road, well, that's when I miss her the most," he said.

Marsden suddenly snapped out of his dark introspection.

"Sorry to be such a depressive sort. Are you married, Jane?"

"Divorced," she replied.

"Pity."

The waitress arrived with her screwdriver and Jane immediately lifted it to her lips, her hand trembling slightly.

"Ah, well, the reason I contacted you is that I've just completed a manuscript for a book. I'm afraid it's a bit on the fringe, though."

"Really?" she said.

"Look," Marsden told her with a hint of impatience, "I know you are aware of this whole bloody business."

"What business are we talking about?" she said. "I mean, throw me a bone. You're the one who's written a damn book. I'm just a weekly hack."

"I brought a whole box of bones," he said. "My manuscript, eyes only."

"What I don't understand is why you want anything from me. Your book is finished, right?"

"Well, you see, yes, my book will be published, and it might raise a few eyebrows in some circles, but it represents only the tip of the iceberg. I mean, it's really gonna require some attention from the American press to bring it out into the open. Now, I know you've been contacted by an interesting chap who was directly involved in the development of this technology. I am certain that he is telling the truth, based on numerous anecdotes, historical clues and the few real sources I could get to speak off the record. But, you see, therein lies the crux of the problem. While my book may draw some interest, it lacks broad appeal. But, mark my words, this thing is just waiting to blow wide open. All it needs is an enterprising journalist to start digging, in earnest. You could come out with an investigative package by the time my book hits the newsstands. See what I mean?"

Jane found his idea tantalizing, in a sleazy sort of way. She turned it over in her mind, running it through that built-in ethics filter that's imprinted in journalism school. She certainly had no intention of shilling Marsden's book, but she'd let him think otherwise. The waitress came by, and they ordered another round.

"You know, Robert, I like your idea, even if it is sordid. I mean, in effect, you're asking me to promote your book, aren't you?"

Marsden took a gulp from his martini, and he blushed slightly at her suggestion of unprofessionalism.

"It's not like that, Jane, I swear to you. I don't think you fully understand the magnitude of what we're talking about here."

Jane quickly drank half of her second screwdriver, critically assessing the vodka content.

"What I mean to do is speak more candidly," he said. Marsden reached down with his right hand, pulling up a brown leather valise.

"I have a copy of my manuscript here, which I am willing to give you an advance look at. It's a hell of a story, but I need help with it. I mean, to really suss it out," he said with slightly slurred speech.

"Why Robert, how generous of you," she said, extending her open hand.

"In exchange for information," he said, withholding the manuscript.

They picked up some takeout from the bar and set out for Jane's apartment.

ଓଓଓଓ

She let Marsden pay the cab fare.

"Well, it's a bit austere, but it's home," she said, flicking on the light switch.

Marsden surveyed the tiny apartment and was surprised by its Spartan furnishings. It didn't look like the domicile of a thirty-something journalist doing reasonably well in her career, all things considered. There was a small desk, one of those cheap particle-board affairs with a plastic veneer that was supposed to resemble wood grain. An ergonomically incorrect, straight-back chair accompanied the desk.

He sat on the chair, and it immediately started rolling on the smooth floorboards. He smiled awkwardly, steadied the chair and began fumbling with his valise to retrieve the manuscript. Jane settled on the edge of her bed, which afforded the only other place to sit down other than the hardwood floor. He pulled out a box and tossed it on the bed next to her. The heavy manuscript bounced on the springy mattress.

"Well, here it is," he said.

Jane found her box of UFO matter, reached in and pulled out one of the videotapes, turned on the TV and stuck it in the VCR.

"I'm hoping some of this will make sense to you."

She pushed the play button on the VCR and removed her sandwich from the bag of takeout food, sitting on the floor while unwrapping it.

"Please don't mind if I eat," Jane said nonchalantly. She scooted across the floor with the restaurant bag to where Marsden was sitting, handed him his takeout sandwich, and then scooted back to the television set. The video appeared on the screen: "Full-Scale Test, Mojave Desert Facility." Color footage showed the lab workers readying a classic flying saucer on the tarmac of a runway. Then the pilot climbed aboard and took off, majestic mountains in the background.

Marsden watched in disbelief, his sandwich untouched.

"My God, Jane! Do you know what you've got here?"

Jane could see that Marsden was coming unglued. She had half expected him to declare the video an elaborate fake.

"Do you think it's authentic?" she asked him.

"Absolutely authentic!" he replied.

The tape ended with the photo session.

"Robert, do you think you could identify any of these men?"

"Not offhand, but I think that we might, given some time," he said.

Marsden rubbed his chin as though pondering a weighty problem. He got up and started pacing around the small apartment.

"It's bloody brilliant!" he said. "A breakthrough that seems so much more advanced than anything on the planet couldn't possibly be from the U.S. military. A program more secret than the Manhattan Project. A decades-long government disinformation scheme to convince everyone that flying saucers are alien spacecraft. There's never been any real media investigation, you know."

She didn't understand most of Marsden's excited rambling. Yet, if ever there was a Eureka moment in Jane's career, this was it. She suddenly understood that it was all real, an incredibly complex, scandalous saga spanning fifty years of secrecy and deception.

So, what now? She couldn't approach her editor, at least not right away. The only way to handle it would be to surreptitiously work on the story while she did her other assignments. Eventually, perhaps she would actually be able to find credible, on-the-record sources and tangible evidence. The documents and tapes would have to be authenticated by experts, the sort of verification that might withstand the scrutiny of her editor.

"Robert, can you tell me what sort of contact you've had with our source, and do you have any idea who he is?"

"Haven't the foggiest," he said. "He rang me at home on several occasions. Started calling about two weeks ago, I think. Seemed to know all about me and my book in progress. I imagine he got wind of it after I began badgering industry chaps, both current and retired. I mean, certain people in the aerospace community are well aware of my project because I've been poking about for a while. And I think you will agree after reading my manuscript that I have amassed one hell of a lot of circumstantial evidence. Problem is, no one directly involved would talk to me. Oh, I riled a few old boys. Went right up and knocked on their doors. Eye-balled the SOBs. A few of them looked downright scared, maybe terrified. I knew they were among the chosen few who really ran things thirty-forty years ago. No way they would help me. Then again, maybe our mystery man is one of the guys I tried to corner. Hell, I wouldn't recognize his voice."

Marsden stopped talking and gazed toward the ceiling, looking like a man trying desperately to focus his thoughts.

"Anyway, this phone chap suddenly starts calling. He says you are working a big story. He says you've got something I need, and he's not gonna duplicate efforts, and so on. We have got to talk this guy into speaking on the record, and we have got to convince him that others must do the same, or we will never be truly successful in our attempts. And that's not gonna be easy. I mean, what's in it for him? Why does he care? Whatever it is, I can tell it's eating him pretty badly. Maybe all we need to do is press him hard enough."

"Never mind what's in it for him. You keep saying 'we,' but what's in it for moi?"

"The big one," he said simply. "The big one."

"I have the broad strokes right here," he said, patting the manuscript box. "The most plausible chain of events, the political players, those men who most likely shaped the policy of absolute secrecy back when it all started. What you have is the smoking gun. But without the broad strokes, the smoking gun is hardly useful. You need context. We need each other."

Marsden took on a mischievous expression and asked Jane, "So, what other goodies can you show me besides this fascinating video?"

She got up stiffly from the floor in front of the TV set and walked over to the parcel, picked up the box and carried it over to Marsden, where she gingerly placed the heavy package near his chair.

"This is the extent if it."

Then she kneeled down next to the box and began to carefully pick through the items, setting them out on the floorboards.

"Haven't even had a chance to review a lot of these things. Stuff related to R&D, or something. I really don't know."

The two of them emptied the contents of the box onto Jane's bed, and, at Marsden's insistence, they began arranging the materials into separate piles.

"You see, what we've got to do is catalog this stuff because …"

"Oh, I almost forgot," Jane said, retrieving the envelope she had found on her desk the day it all began. "One day, this just showed up at the office, hand-delivered."

She turned the open envelope upside down and emptied it onto the bed. Marsden placed the VHS tapes, various paper documents and film reels in discrete piles. Then he stood back and scrutinized the materials as though pondering a work of art.

"What have we here?" he asked Jane rhetorically.

"Actually, our mutual friend made it easy for us," she told Marsden. "He wrote a vague little summary that includes, well, a sort of shipping manifest."

Jane rooted through the stack of documents, found the single-page letter and handed the memo to Marsden, who read it eagerly and began poring over the photocopied laboratory documents. The papers contained neatly drawn tables and various narratives seemingly describing experimental setups and findings, punctuated with an occasional mathematical equation and sketches of hardware. Marsden appeared to be straining to comprehend what he was reading.

"I'm a little rusty on physics and non-linear algebra," he said sarcastically, "but I think I know some chaps who could review these papers for us."

They stayed up most of the night, looking over the documents, watching all of the VHS tapes and mapping out a strategy to find experts who might be able to make sense of it all. The laboratory records were dated from the mid-1950s to late '60s. Some portions had been blacked out, apparently to hide certain identities. After some wrangling Jane agreed to let Marsden borrow a few documents but declined to share the film reels until she could have them analyzed.

She pulled a sleeping bag out of the closet and unfurled it on the floor. Marsden seemed exhausted and numb. He looked blankly at the sleeping bag.

"Thanks," he mumbled as he removed his shoes and crawled into the down bag.

Jane turned off the lights and undressed, sliding between the covers of her small bed. She fell asleep almost immediately, her mind saturated with unresolved issues. Not surprisingly, she dreamed of flying saucers. Like most dreams, nothing made any sense. A bunch of guys in lab smocks were standing near the craft. One of the guys was her editor. All of a sudden he lifted off the ground, literally hovering around the object, taking notes with a pad the whole time and looking very analytical. A voice came over a loudspeaker: "Assume your posts, assume your posts. Takeoff imminent. Takeoff imminent," came the voice, followed by a klaxon-like horn.

Jane awoke abruptly to the grating sound of her buzzing alarm clock. Six o'clock. She immediately reached over and switched off the buzzer, the strange dream still fresh in her mind. What did it mean, a flying boss?

She sat up in bed, her eyes falling on the space where she'd last seen Marsden curled up in the sleeping bag.

The bag was folded neatly, and Marsden was not there.

CHAPTER 9

Marsden had vacated the premises early. As Jane slept, he moved in careful, silent increments, transferring one of the sixteen-millimeter film reels and a VHS tape to his valise. Then, just as silently, he crept off into the night.

She grinned upon discovering this thievery in grudging admiration of Marsden's stealthy opportunism, even if it had come at her expense. The box containing his manuscript lay on her desk, and she toyed with the idea of playing hooky. She phoned Marsden's hotel, but there was no answer. Tracking him down would be a waste of time and energy, so her next call went to the newsroom to inform the boss's secretary that she was feeling a little under the weather and wouldn't be in today.

Jane settled down with a cup of coffee and Marsden's manuscript, "The Quest for Antigravity: America's Biggest Top Secret Since the Atomic Bomb Project."

"Jeez, the title's a bit much," she thought.

The first chapter was busy with hypothetical events at the close of World War II. The U.S. Army had just raided clandestine Nazi laboratories tucked away in the hinterlands of Poland's Sudeten Mountains. American military teams, hastily scooping up the spoils of war as the Russians advanced, were uncovering sophisticated hardware related to rockets and nuclear technology, but they were left scratching their heads over several bell-shaped machines and seemingly related high-voltage equipment.

Jane, ambivalent at first, read on with interest. Then, suspending her disbelief, she surrendered herself to Marsden's manuscript.

ଓଓଓଓ

Private first class Herman Schneider, descended from German immigrants and fluent in his ancestral tongue, recognized some of the wording in the notes, papers and other technical paraphernalia littering the workbenches.

"I think it says electro-gravity, or electro-gravitics, whatever that means, sarge," he told his commanding officer.

The Americans spirited away the mysterious gear and assorted research documents. Later, after analyzing the tons of technical booty, U.S. scientists were astonished by what they had uncovered: The Nazis were close to perfecting a breakthrough technology called electric field propulsion. Essentially, it promised to make possible an entirely new kind of flying vehicle that defied gravity, traveled silently and had no conventional airframe or wings.

She liked Marsden's fictional style and his facility for storytelling, but she wondered about his speculative approach. Marsden described how the Americans would learn more about this unprecedented technological achievement in the months and years immediately after the war. How a select group of military brass, scientists, engineers and policy experts at the Pentagon would come to fully appreciate not only the horrors of the Nazi war machine but also its technological prowess.

He skillfully wove real historical elements into the strange cloth of his own conjecture. Jane continued reading:

> *The Pentagon people, their fingers trembling, breath redolent of tobacco, skin clammy from days on Army-issue amphetamines, would examine in great detail the crates of German documents. These materials would tell a story of how, just as the Nazis had surged ahead of everyone else in mastering missiles, jet engines, buzz bombs and various machinations of war, the Überengineers of the Third Reich had aggressively pursued and achieved another -- albeit unheralded -- wonder: antigravity.*

The Pentagon, Marsden explained, quite naturally would have assumed the Russians had acquired comparable intelligence and hardware from the Germans. That they, too, might be working feverishly to understand the science behind the technology:

> *So the Americans, all jacked up on white-cross pills and an occasional nip of Jim Beam, labored around the clock. They would discover that this feat of propulsion had its origins in the United States way back in the 1920s, when physicist Thomas Townsend Brown proposed the underlying principle that would*

make it all possible. But a technologically myopic U.S. government paid little attention to Brown's work.

All these things the Pentagon people would learn as they cloistered in their offices like some tripping college kids pondering the symbolism of Waiting for Godot. The pill-popping, chain-smoking Pentagon guys eagerly carpooled daily in spacious Packard sedans. For they constituted a special class of people who knew things nobody else did, just as the geopolitical climate began to congeal into a frightening bipolar reality that would be known as the Cold War.

They would learn the truth, aroused by the comingling odors of musty paper and black ink, of perspiration and fear and pages stuck together by dried, mathematical secretions. Records that described how Germany's keen military brain trust had rarely misunderstood the potential war-making utility of unconventional concepts. Marshalling vast sums of money and intellectual might, the Nazis had nurtured an array of high-risk research-and-development ventures that branched off into numerous tributaries, each more esoteric than the next.

The Pentagon dweebs learned that one of those R&D estuaries probed Brown's basic concept: that is, that a properly designed capacitor -- oversize versions of those used in countless radios and electrical devices -- when subjected to the precisely correct high-voltage current would be propelled through space.

The astonished Pentagon men, heady with feelings of speed-induced omnipotence, would discover how the Nazi scientists used this idea as a starting point to create a plate-like "gravitator." Applying a positive charge to one side of the plate and a negative charge to the other side caused it to move in the direction of the positive pole. This gravitator could be driven straight up or in any direction.

Of course, it wasn't quite so simple, the Pentagon people would discover. The innovative Germans added a few dashes of genius here, a few risky modifications there -- brutally killing countless slave laborers along the way. This was the atrocious provenance of field propulsion.

In short order the Americans would track down the Bavarian brainiaks responsible for the advance. These engineers and physicists would live their remaining years in anonymity, housed in U.S. military facilities. They sometimes came out, to be admired like polished gemstones, cavorting at stag parties and inhabiting church pews. They were treated reasonably well.

When suitably liquored, the Germans would boast of how the Nazi war machine had gone so far as to test fly prototypes; various strange contraptions cooked up in labs tunneled into the mountains of Poland and Czechoslovakia. One of the unlikely machines would be referred to simply as "the bell." Others were little radio-controlled spheres operated remotely to shadow U.S. bombers toward the final days of war. And then there were the original flying saucers capable of phenomenal performance, climbing to thirty thousand feet and reaching speeds of more than a thousand miles per hour. The Nazis had broken the sound barrier in 1943.

All of these bewildering contrivances were revealed to the Pentagon's antigravity cognoscente in the months and years after the war. And from this knowledge a handful of powerful men would formulate the nation's secret destiny.

ଔଔଔଔ

Marsden's manuscript included a compelling firsthand account from a retired Air Force pilot who accidentally stumbled upon the flying saucer story. How he actually saw one of the discs and spoke with personnel involved. Marsden laid out the story using various hypothetical historic scenarios, an approach Jane found unorthodox but entertaining.

The manuscript moved deftly from anecdotal accounts to scientific theory and the chronological underpinnings of antigravity. It was actually quite good. She had expected something largely unreadable, rife with non sequiturs, spelling and grammar issues and various unfinished threads. But the writing was concise and journalistic and the concepts well organized.

Somewhere around page forty Jane had an epiphany, a profound clarity of mind: The conspiracy just might be real.

Marsden's manuscript was on cruise control at this point. Jane was no longer a reader but a passenger. She could no sooner put it down than jump from a speeding locomotive. Marsden retold in tantalizing detail how he visited Lockheed Martin's Skunk Works in the desert scrubland of Palmdale, California, and how a tour of the plant turned up something fishy. The Skunk Works was the center of the universe of America's black projects; birthplace of the U-2 spy plane and the SR-71. The bustling facility pulsed with the traffic of four thousand workers, but the company had few official projects -- certainly nothing to justify this hyperactivity. What were all of these people doing in their windowless laboratories?

He had come to a stark realization: The Skunk Works might have absolutely nothing to do with antigravity, a technology that would shake the foundations of the aerospace industry, which depended on the science of aerodynamics -- wind tunnels, advanced computational modeling, precision design to reduce drag and friction. Sure, the enterprise was very busy, but not with flying saucer contracts. Rather, they were almost certainly working on far more traditional black projects: perhaps some advanced scramjet- or rocket-powered creatures.

Marsden's adventure had taken a turn, adding a new element that served to keep the reader's attention. Who was leading the saucer project? Was the work based initially at the White Sands Proving Ground in New Mexico? If so, that might explain the famous Roswell crash in 1947. It was almost a sure bet the Air Force was involved. But what about other branches? Given the intensely competitive and fiercely territorial struggles within the U.S. military during and after World War II, Marsden doubted the Air Force had a monopoly on field propulsion.

And what of corporate America's involvement? If not Lockheed Martin, then what about Boeing or the handful of other top defense contractors?

Adding some historical perspective, the story moved next to the American southwest in 1945. Hundreds of railroad freight cars loaded with German rocketry hardware had been seen trundling across the desert to White Sands. Newspapers reported that the cars stretched two hundred miles, occupying every railroad siding from El Paso, Texas, to Belen, New Mexico. A cadre of captured Nazi scientists, led by rocket scientist Wernher von Braun, followed the caravan.

Marsden asked the reader: Wouldn't it have made sense for postwar America to locate all of its German-derived propulsion projects -- rocketry as well as antigravity -- in the same location?

He told of how earlier that year top German officials thwarted Hitler from destroying the antigravity labs and hardware housed in underground research bunkers as the U.S. First Army swept over the fatherland. SS General Hans Kammler devised a successful scheme to meet with the Americans and trade his freedom for a mother lode of top-shelf technology.

Marsden reasoned that Kammler's best bargaining chip would have been the antigravity hardware, along with associated blueprints and experimental documentation. And why not? The Americans already had their fill of rockets and jet aircraft technology, seized in abandoned factories where numerous V-2 missiles and aircraft lay in various stages of completion. But they were completely unaware of the saucers and the existence of subterranean antigravity research-and-development facilities. U.S. officials would certainly be willing to pay any price for such engineering treasures. A maze of facilities tunneled into the mountains south of Poland harbored a variety of prototypes and testbeds, notably "the bell," an acorn-shape machine the size of a Volkswagen Beetle that glowed with a blue aura when activated. The contraption was spirited away shortly before the Russians would overrun the facilities.

Then there was the research led by Viktor Schauberger, a scientist who applied his unorthodox views to harness energy using a spinning vortex of air in a levitating saucer. He had conceived of the device in 1939, filed papers with the Reich Patent Office in 1940, and by war's end his team had succeeded in building the first working saucers.

But Germany's defeat radically altered the trajectory of antigravity research. Just as der Führer was ordering the underground facilities burned and scientists shot, Kammler and Minister of Armaments Albert Speer defied Hitler's edict. They told terrified plant managers that the facilities would be needed to rebuild Germany's economy after the war. At the same time, they quickly arranged to evacuate personnel critical to various programs, handing them over to the Americans before the Nazis could have them all executed.

Soon the German propulsion scientists watched the alien and arid landscape of New Mexico passing by as they traveled by railway in absolute anonymity. Richard Miethe, Rudolph Schriever, Klaus Habermehl, Georg Klein. Hardly household names in the nation's lexicon, yet arguably the biggest haul of brainpower to come under American control.

While von Braun and his staff baked under the klieg lights of public scrutiny, these field-propulsion gurus enjoyed their obscurity and laid the groundwork for what would become America's shadow space program. Marsden described how the U.S. military perfected antigravity during the 1950s, instituting an unprecedented degree of secrecy.

All records pertaining to the project were strictly off-limits to the public, shielded under the National Security Act of 1947. The Germans worked under the most oppressive conditions of secrecy, perhaps even more draconian than their experience in the homeland. All correspondence was meticulously monitored and censored, and they couldn't speak of their work to anyone other than the tight circle of people in their respective labs. Violating this code meant life in a military prison or sometimes death, carried out execution style with no court hearing. End of discussion. People just disappeared.

Then came the 1960s. With America and the Soviet Union poised on the brink of mutual annihilation, the saucers were tapped for a role never anticipated: an antimissile system capable of matching a projectile's supersonic trajectory and blasting it out of the sky with artillery.

The story segued to various entertaining scenarios. One section discussed the accounts of two retired aerospace executives, people afforded extraordinary access to information during the seminal period of saucer development. Jane found the hypothetical storyline to be perfectly plausible, the sources compelling. There was no actual proof, but enough good circumstantial evidence for an Oliver Stone movie. On second thought, perhaps too much good circumstantial evidence for an Oliver Stone movie.

A particularly entertaining passage recounted how Marsden trekked to the Nevada desert's legendary Area 51 military range to sleuth out evidence of antigravity technology in white-world aircraft, specifically the B-2 stealth bomber. Several aerospace experts told Marsden they thought the B-2 might be using some sort of "antigravity assist" to reduce the airplane's weight by five percent. Such a significant weight reduction could be what enables the bomber to fly unprecedented distances before needing to refuel, they suggested.

Jane read on to learn that according to Marsden's sources the airplane might be equipped with a gravitator-like leading edge charged to millions of volts, the product of a growing black budget that had likely spawned at least two new types of advanced vehicles since the stealth fighter and bomber were unveiled.

Marsden assiduously laid out a sequence of key hypothetical events. He eloquently described how the Pentagon readily understood field propulsion for what it was: Uncle Sam's personal mojo in a world full of vile communists, tyrants, dictators and villains of every stripe.

Jane brewed another pot of coffee and sunk further into Marsden's manuscript:

> *The world was getting crazier and its problems more complex and pernicious, while man's inherent virulence was being honed through the wondrous tools of science. Logic, therefore, would dictate that only the acute instruments of science would let America throw elbows in a barroom full of mean characters artfully conniving her demise. The nation needed an edge, a technological juggernaut.*
>
> *Sure, there was the bomb, but the Russians also had it, and soon the other major powers would as well. On the other hand, nobody had Uncle Sam's own personal mojo. But it was a mojo that required nurturing and*

a constant care and feeding. A mojo that could only be maintained so long as the United States enjoyed a monopoly on field propulsion. Excluding antigravity from the rest of the world, however, could prove to be a tricky and sordid business. It would require brutish behavior and drastic measures and penalties up to and including death for anyone seeking to betray the code of secrecy surrounding the project. Large men dressed in cheap suits might be called upon to enforce this code, to preserve Uncle Sam's personal mojo. It would necessitate ample sums of money and various ongoing secret authorizations from the executive branch. President Truman must be informed. He must be made aware of the incredible stakes. The nation's very survival might hang in the balance of his decision!

Only with the president's endorsement could the Pentagon operate a covert program to perfect antigravity and create a new type of interceptor that would be far superior to any jet fighter.

At least, that was how they would sell it.

Although, the Pentagon men mused privately, the saucers couldn't be used for interceptors because that would require technology commercialization, extensive collaboration with the aviation industry and other military contractors, patent filings and the like. Before long, flying saucers would go mainstream and become available to any nation.

This was unthinkable.

The Pentagon men murmured to one another in darkened hallways, in small gatherings. For they were a very small group, an exclusive club made up of only twelve key members and a handful of handpicked, carpooling aides, adjutants and experts. People with MIT and Harvard degrees riding high on the social and political capital they'd earned during the war. People who'd been accepted into the privileged penumbra, the charmed circle, of antigravity. People who luxuriated in the savoir fair of their special position, who eagerly drank in the intoxicating nectar it provided. An analytical lot, like master chess players constantly casting prognostic glances toward the future.

How, and when, might antigravity be unveiled?

Perhaps never in their lifetimes, they confidently professed to one another. Far in the future, after the world's turbulent political dynamic has calmed. Some presumptive future when a greater harmony might prevail. A problem for their successors to resolve, no doubt.

Of course, if the shit really hit the fan, Uncle Sam always had his own personal mojo.

If, say, World War III broke out, aliens invaded or the antichrist emerged, the avuncular bearded one would promptly establish order, brazenly unfurling his secret weapon, the proverbial big stick. Then, there was always the possibility that the Soviet Union had been running its own antigravity program all along and would soon take to the skies in flying saucers.

However, the Pentagon men asked themselves, what if none of the above happened? They were all in agreement about one fundamental precept: There would be no public disclosure, no rollouts on the tarmac with dignitaries and flash bulbs.

Why?

Because, as the Pentagon men were blissfully coming to understand, dominating the wild blue yonder was not the real prize. It was something much larger than that. It was controlling the next frontier: outer space. The Pentagon men, delirious from delusions of power and various other intoxicants, stayed up late writing memos and documents stamped Top Secret. They alone understood that this dream of cosmic dominance might only be realized if antigravity's secrecy could be maintained long enough for American engineers to perfect new space vehicles.

Those early designers didn't really understand the physics. They were, after all, experimentalists primarily, not theoreticians or polymaths. Through trial and error and serendipity the inventors had learned that a powerful thrusting force could be produced by placing ring-shaped capacitors over metal coils through which thousands of volts were passed. They didn't know that Uncle Sam's personal mojo was a de facto demonstration of post-Einsteinian physics; that there existed additional forces beyond those known to science, and these forces were responsible for antigravity propulsion; that the vehicles were tapping into extra dimensions to produce pairs of "gravitophotons," particles that allowed for the conversion of electromagnetic energy into gravitational energy.

The years became a decade, and the tireless Pentagon plotters continued to guide the antigravity project. It evolved into an independent space program that began to emerge even in the earliest days of NASA, a parallel R&D gambit that shadowed the civilian space program. Somewhere among the "what-if" scenarios they considered, the guys in the flying saucer think tank acknowledged the high stakes, the unprecedented nature of the gamble. Imagine the public outrage, the lack of confidence in authority that might result if the program were to be exposed?

Another problem for their successors, they clinically concluded.

The first full-scale prototypes were completed even before test pilot Scott Crossfield cheated death in 1953, when he flew twice the speed of sound in a rocket-propelled airplane called the Douglas D-558-2 Skyrocket. It and other projects that focused on jet engines and rocket technologies served as the perfect smokescreen to keep the Soviet Union from suspecting America's deep dark aviation secret.

The Russians might eventually invent field propulsion on their own, but by then the U.S. would be driving a Ferrari and the Soviets would have but a Model T. This the brilliant Pentagon strategists laid out in one of their what-if scenarios.

The president was skeptical, but in the end he would grudgingly agree with this premise.

Later, as the two superpowers locked horns in the Cold War, hundreds of millions of tax dollars would be funneled into antigravity research and development, drinking from a nearly limitless resource: the Pentagon's burgeoning black budget.

Then, sometime in the early 80s came a startling breakthrough. The antigravity team had been tinkering with a theory called the Casimir effect, predicted in 1948 by Dutch physicist Hendrik Casimir. The theory proposed that a circular arrangement of closely spaced, parallel plates positioned in a particular way would create an envelope of "negative energy," a "warp bubble" around the craft, allowing it to skip through time and space faster than light.

This innovation, when combined with the existing field-propulsion technology, made possible a hybrid, two-speed drive. The standard gravitator, capable of accelerating well beyond the speed of sound, was married to the new Casimir motor, which was nothing short of warp drive.

Now the Pentagon really had a tiger by the tail: starship tech.

And Uncle Sam had his own personal mojo.

ଓଓଓଓ

Marsden's manuscript moved along at a brisk pace, now probing the plausible and pivotal details surrounding the early flying saucer program:

The pilots and engineers flying prototypes in the late 1940s were vexed by a host of risky research-and-development unknowns. The technology was so new that a raft of problems had to be overcome before the saucers could be deployed. No one, not even the Germans, really understood why saucers flew at all. Their testing was purely Edisonian, a trial-and-error approach with no real grasp of the fundamental physics of antigravity. The result was often disastrous.

Sometimes the propulsion system would abruptly "decouple" from the Earth's gravitational field. The wingless ship suddenly went wobbly and fell like a stone while the engineers frantically adjusted dials and flipped toggle switches in hopes of regaining control.

Sometimes the heavy gauge, triple-redundant circuits overheated or blew up because of the kilowatts of power needed for the system. Overloaded vacuum tubes, analog switches, transformers and capacitors sprayed bewildered crew members with red-hot shrapnel within the saucer's cramped interior. There was a fine balance between achieving the "critical capacitance" needed to generate antigravity and blowing up the whole wireworks.

The handful of test pilots assigned to the project refused to call what they did "flying." Rather, they likened it to driving a very finicky, very dangerous sports car. But instead of crashing into a guardrail at a hundred miles per hour you plummeted twenty thousand feet to your death at supersonic speeds.

Relatives received cryptic next-of-kin letters expressing terse condolences.

The unpredictable nature of saucer technology was manifested publicly one July day in 1947 over rural New Mexico. The saucer took off from its hangar at White Sands Proving Ground, skimming desolate gypsum dunes in the Tularosa Basin and skirting the barren peaks of the San Andres and Oscura mountains before making a loop around an Army airfield some one hundred fifty miles away. It was a familiar rout for the saucer's crew. They'd flown it dozens of times, usually in the cover of darkness. But something went wrong this time. Maybe it was the thunderstorm that caused the electrical controls to go whizz bang. Townspeople had reported heavy lightning.

The little saucer crashed on a cattle ranch, breaking in half and killing everyone onboard. Initially, the crash was reported to Army airfield officials by the rancher, and the base's public affairs guy issued a news release about the event. But the feds came fast and furious, quickly squelching the story. The rancher was threatened with life imprisonment, as were the few military personnel who responded to the scene.

The lid was slammed shut on the story, for the time being. But it would emerge decades later, much to the delight of disinformation specialists. They adroitly took advantage of the crashed-saucer yarn's new widespread popularity, introducing a viral sort of propaganda: bogus "witnesses" who reported wholly fictional accounts of extraterrestrial bodies, an "alien autopsy" film and other specious elements.

Roswell would forever be associated with crackpot conspiracy freaks. Nobody, it seemed, would see it for what it really was: a clue to something truly important.

଻଻଻଻

Jane phoned Marsden's hotel room again, with the same results as before. She returned to his manuscript, which concentrated now on the postwar years:

Harry Truman sat behind his large walnut desk in the Oval Office pondering one of the most profound problems of his presidential tenure. Since occupying the White House he'd proven his mettle. He'd dropped nukes on civilians in Japan, and, more recently, kicked off a brand new war on the Korean peninsula while initiating development of the hydrogen bomb. These and other hawkish deeds he offered up like patriotic salves to the American public.

But now he was faced with something entirely different: whether to approve a large black-budget funding outlay to support a shadowy Pentagon program based on antigravity. The money would enable the military to build a fleet of vehicles operating independently of other defense programs.

The president wore an old-fashioned green eyeshade, looking like a miserly bookkeeper as he scrutinized a bound proposal lying open on the top of his neat, meticulously organized desk. He removed his thick, round glasses and rubbed his tired eyes.

"Why, we could practically finance another Air Force for this kind of money," he grumbled, eyes fixed on the bottom line of the briefing document.

New Deal politics aside, Truman had the fiscal instincts of a small-business owner. Until the Korean adventure had spurred dramatic hikes in defense spending, he'd slashed the military budget and was determined to keep it from ballooning out of control regardless of the USSR's expanding might.

A picture frame on his desk displayed a motto by Mark Twain: "Always do right! This will gratify some people and astonish the rest."

Doing the right thing seemed especially critical in those early days of the Cold War, not long after the Russians had unwrapped their own nuclear menace. Joe McCarthy was giving everybody the heebie-jeebies about communism and spies and double agents. The Soviets were rapidly developing atomic weapons, guided missiles, biological warfare agents, a more capable air force and a new class of submarines to patrol the high seas. Who's to say they weren't also developing antigravity? It would be naïve, and even dangerous, to assume otherwise.

With an arsenal of antigravity warships at Stalin's command, there would be no limit to his ambitions. Flying saucers would make the perfect delivery vehicle for all those Soviet nukes rolling off of the assembly line.

These and other concerns had four years earlier catalyzed creation of a special Pentagon panel of eminent scientists, a handful of top military and government officials. It was not unlike FDR's highly secret Interim Committee on S-1. But S-1, code for the Manhattan Project to build the first atomic weapon, was FDR's venture, his legacy, his responsibility.

Antigravity had become Truman's project, whether he liked it or not. So he approached it with the same methodical diligence that marked his political career, forming the foundation of perhaps the most remarkable clandestine military project in history.

Yes, this was Truman's project, and it was called Majestic.

ઌઌઌઌ

It was just past noon, so Jane brewed another pot of coffee and resumed her reading. The story took a dramatic turn:

Issues vital to Majestic soon came to a head. Fiscal commitments had to be made, provisions written, policy formulated. The Pentagon panel, known as Majestic Twelve, urged the president that he had no choice but to funnel as much money as prudently possible into the program. Truman, however, had some nagging doubts about the whole thing. He knew the technology worked in the laboratory, but would it actually function as advertized in a real-life battle situation? Then again, naysayers had asked the same question about the atomic bomb.

"I'll tell you one thing that's absolutely mandatory," the president told a coterie of military brass. "I want a demonstration. Something that tells me why these things are so superior. I want them to fly right over the Capitol, right over the damned White House."

Truman enjoyed brilliant displays of fire and thunder as much as the next guy, and he had a penchant for the dramatic. He'd made a similar demand three years earlier, when he ordered proponents of Northrop's "flying wing" to showcase their new aviation marvel by buzzing the U.S. capital in 1949. The aircraft did just that, flying from California to Andrews Air Force Base near Washington and then passing directly over the president's abode on the return flight. Unfortunately, the trip home was marred by catastrophic engine failure, and the plane had to make an emergency landing in Arizona.

The flying wing program was scrapped shortly thereafter.

Such trials had a way of stifling dreamers, even those occupying the rarified atmosphere of aviation genius, and Truman privately expected a similarly underwhelming outcome for antigravity's acid test.

"Let's see how well your flying saucers perform when they're being chased by the U.S. Air Force," Truman demanded, purposely pronouncing "flying saucers" in a mocking tone.

So, on the night of July 19, 1952, the saucer prototypes flew two thousand feet over Washington.

Air traffic controllers were perplexed and concerned when nearly a dozen blips suddenly appeared on radar screens at National Airport and nearby Andrews and Bolling Air Force bases. Spotters on the ground saw the objects as lights meandering in loose formation. The saucers easily evaded two jet fighters scrambling from New Castle Air Force Base in Delaware. Air traffic controllers watched the bizarre things flit across their screens until dawn, cruising with free rein over the capital.

The test was so impressive that Truman ordered an encore a week later. He wanted to see what would happen if there were more direct interaction between jet interceptors and the saucers. The result: a classic close encounter as one of the jets neared the cluster of saucers.

The pilot radioed controllers.

"I can see those bogies now," he reported. "I'm at maximum speed. They are bluish-white lights. I'm going in for a closer look."

Airport tower officials looked out of the windows and were stunned by what they saw: The objects had no distinguishing characteristics such as wings, nose or tail sections. Much to their astonishment, the craft were clearly round or saucer-shaped.

A few seconds later the pilot sounded much more anxious.

"The objects are surrounding me! What should I do?"

The controllers were at a loss for advice, but before they could answer the pilot's plea the situation quickly resolved itself. The UFOs pulled away from the jet and abruptly disappeared.

A media blowout ensued over the next few days, with front-page articles in the Washington Post and various major daily newspapers across the country. The papers featured alarming headlines like: "UFOS OUTRUN FIGHTER PLANES" and "SAUCERS SWARM OVER CAPITAL."

The Post quoted anonymous government officials, who said they were uncertain what the objects were and acknowledged that they "could be flying saucers." Then again, they might be "weather-related phenomena."

President Truman pretended to be as baffled as everyone else by the strange events, while the Air

Force issued a statement promising to keep jet fighters poised to chase the saucers, should they return. Far from reassuring the public, this only caused more angst. Some scientific observers even warned the president not to attack the UFOs, reasoning that it could incur the wrath of a superior power.

And the media clamored for answers.

Lacking any credible information, newspapers were reduced to gossip mongering and rampant speculation. Persistent rumors circulated that the saucers were actually the product of a secret Boeing project based at a remote military site. In part to squelch such dangerous chatter, which was not far from the truth, Truman ordered the Air Force to stage a press conference. Any talk of top secret U.S. flying saucer technology must be swiftly put to rest by decorated men in uniform.

A minion of print and broadcast journalists sat attentively on hard folding chairs during the largest Pentagon press conference since World War II. And like the entranced devotees of some semi-secular, bureaucratic cult, they eagerly accepted the sermon offered up by military authorities.

Journalists were told that UFOs had been witnessed since "biblical times," suggesting an element of superstition or mythology to discredit the sightings. And the radar blips might have resulted from a temperature inversion in the atmosphere. In other words, a layer of warm air at high altitude produced false echoes. The news conference concluded, sending reporters rushing back to their offices in deadline frenzy. In the end, the temperature-inversion theory emerged as the most likely explanation, newspapers authoritatively proffered.

This conclusion provided a perfect tongue-in-cheek segue for journalists: The familiar hot air of Washington politics ultimately was responsible.

Case closed. The press stopped asking questions.

And somewhere deep inside the Pentagon certain people watched with a rapt and intense curiosity. This had been a crushing victory for them, especially on the disinformation front. More importantly, they had a key new advocate: President Truman had become the political patriarch of antigravity.

ଓଓଓଓ

Marsden's manuscript probed further into Truman's putative place in the history of flying saucers and his crucial role in funding the above-top-secret field-propulsion program. The author framed the alleged events of this chronology in the context of the Cold War, a powerful R&D catalyst.

Jane sipped her coffee and read on:

The outstanding performance of the prototypical saucers only ratcheted up pressure on Truman to make a major financial commitment. If they could fly rings around U.S. jet fighters, they could thoroughly dominate any air force anywhere in the world. This technological fantasy was only bolstered by a desperate political backdrop: red scares, tales of espionage and military assessments suggesting the Soviets were planning to overrun Europe.

The United States simply must perfect the platform first, Truman decided, or the Russians just might sweep over the free world like a plague of locusts.

Funding for the project would be neatly disguised among the multifarious, vague and jargony budget lines that roughly defined military spending. The same sort of extraordinary demand was made once in 1943, when FDR requested a whopping 1.6 billion dollars in additional funding for the Manhattan Project. The request was not only met, but it was provided without a trace of evidence to show how it was spent -- 1.6 billon dollars -- in 1943.

By comparison, Majestic would require far less capital. The project had been crawling along with only a few million dollars annually. Now Truman was being asked to infuse the program with half a billion dollars. Still a sizeable chunk of change, but easily procured if requested under cover of national security. The president would answer this call for funding by neglecting research and development for long-range ballistic missiles. Truman's successor, Dwight Eisenhower, would inherit this legacy, and he would later pay a political price for failing to keep pace with the Soviet's missile program.

Perhaps at no time in American history were the patriotic French horns blaring louder than they were in the 1950s, accompanied by jingoistic shibboleths and platitudes galore, integrated skillfully into movie scripts, mouthed so enthusiastically by Hollywood stars.

And Ike was president - the White House having shed the more civilian vestiges of FDR's regime – Truman having exited gracefully.

Simultaneously, the early years of antigravity brought tantalizing hints, dropped here and there by military bigwigs and aviation-industry honchos. When asked about UFO sightings, General Nathan Twining said in a secret 1947 memo that "it was within U.S. knowledge" for American engineers to build a flying saucer. He was even specific enough to claim the saucers might have a range of seven thousand miles at subsonic speeds. As head of Air Materiel Command, he would have been an exceptionally well-informed source on such matters.

The general speculated in his memo that the craft were possibly "of domestic origin – the product of some high-security project not known to … this Command," or that, perhaps, "some foreign nation has a form of propulsion, possibly nuclear, which is outside of our domestic knowledge." Twining had urged in his memo that an extensive investigation be conducted.

But the investigation didn't happen: They made him a member of Majestic Twelve instead, and never again would General Nathan Twining pen memos about flying saucers.

There were other intriguing clues about the secret project, including lofty suggestions that a new class of "gravity engines" could change the face of civilization, offering everything from levitating cars and trains to interplanetary spacecraft.

"The jet engine will soon be obsolete," one aviation doyen proclaimed in an article in 1955, jubilantly adding, "We are on the verge of fielding an entirely new type of transportation technology that will usher in the space age."

Various industry big shots concurred. They said the nation was close to perfecting antigravity propulsion, and their comments were published in aviation magazines. Sensational remarks attributed to CEOs from several prominent military contractors; the corporate cognoscente who had provided the bulk of U.S. air power for World War II and were now in the forefront of advances in jet turbines and rocketry. Heavy hitters in the fast-emerging military-industrial complex.

One of the articles was a sensational cover story illustrated with a drawing that depicted a sleek wingless craft floating a few feet off the ground, its hatch swung open and stairs extended invitingly. A headline, in sixty-point Bodoni bold, screamed "The Gravity Engines are Coming!" A subhead followed, "A New Class of Vehicles Will Travel Faster Than Light." The article quoted a reputable aviation-industry executive.

"Because the propulsion mechanism is based on gravity, its occupants will feel no G forces, much like people on Earth do not feel the tremendous speed of the planet as it whizzes through space," he explained. "Whereas pilots in conventional jet aircraft pass out if they try to pull more than a few G's, these super

anti-gravity planes will be able to cruise far faster than is humanly possible in today's aircraft."

Someone stuck the article in Vannevar Bush's mailbox, and he nearly choked on his smoldering briar pipe when he read it. As head of Majestic Twelve, it was his job to keep such rumors under wraps. The MIT-trained electrical engineer had administered the most covert research programs in American history. Under his guidance, the United States developed and deployed instruments that turned the tide of World War II. Radar and the proximity fuse chief among these new weapons. He had ably skippered the Manhattan Project and relentlessly fought to protect America's atomic secrets, even as Roosevelt sought to share nuclear know-how with the British.

Now, alarmed by the public outing of antigravity, Bush formulated a policy of secrecy and disinformation to squelch any official indiscretions and neutralize high-level gossip. The hammer came down, and it came down hard. Key industry leaders were summoned to a series of tense high-level meetings with Bush and company. The gatherings were preceded by a sharply worded memo hand-delivered to every person invited. Under National Security Council letterhead, it was signed by a four-star general and contained the following message:

"On authority of the National Security Council and the National Security Act of 1947 all information regarding MAJESTIC must remain in the confidence of proper federal personnel and must not be discussed openly. Divulging any information pertaining

to MAJESTIC will carry the most severe penalty mandated by military law. The special circumstances mandated under this project require that all documents and hardware be housed in prescribed federal facilities."

It may have been couched in bureaucratic mumbo jumbo, but the salient point was this: If you ever, ever talk about this the best possible outcome will be that you will live the rest of your life in prison.

New guidelines also forced the transfer of all related research, data and documents from the commercial sector into the covert military project, to be kept under lock and key and constantly monitored. America was in the process of constructing what would become the most elaborate conspiracy in history. Not a peep would ever be heard again from those executives who had so confidently confided to the media about the coming of antigravity. Nobody dared defy the new rule of law.

A methodically controlled sterile laboratory. A vacuum, where even the slightest spark would quickly suffocate and the most audacious missteps would be completely quashed. And there were some huge missteps along the way.

Not long after Eisenhower took office the flying saucer people lost one of their toys, then another, and another.

Researchers were testing one of their bell contraptions, a juiced-up version of the original German design. Technicians had bolted it to the reinforced-concrete floor of a cramped rocket-engine test cell in a remote section of the White Sands Missile Range.

Laboratory workers were putting the bell through its paces when all of a sudden the whole test cell broke loose from the parched earth and shot skyward. Dumbfounded onlookers watched in awe as the multi-ton structure, a fortified mass of concrete and steel that had no business being airborne, hurtled upward toward the heavens. The soaring structure produced a mystifying and frightening sound, a whooshing-whistling ruckus that seemed to echo from other dimensions.

And then, it was just gone. Dead silence. A chill sort of calm swept over the site like a noiseless wind from the desolate deserts of Antarctica. A calm rooted partly in fear, the knowledge that what goes up must come down.

The scientists watched the sky for signs of their misplaced building.

It was hell for the three unfortunate men trapped inside the test cell. They'd been running the experiment from behind a blast-proof wall. Now they were holding on for dear life, a white-knuckle death ride as the small building reached nearly thirty thousand feet, came to a stop and plummeted toward the ground at supersonic speed. It made quite a violent crater in the otherwise peaceful New Mexico landscape.

People raced to the scene in jeeps, finding body parts mixed with rubble. Officially, the men died as the result of a "malfunctioning thrust chamber" in a rocket experiment. It would be reported that way in hometown newspapers.

The disaster was one of a series of R&D mishaps that year alone.

Antigravity propulsion units on several flying saucers went completely haywire in flight, launching the craft hundreds of miles into space. The vehicles were not pressurized, so everyone aboard died excruciatingly painful deaths. In effect, the marooned vehicles became the world's first artificial satellites four years before Sputnik.

Beating the Russians to space would have been cause for great celebration and fanfare if it hadn't been for the loss of life and the dome of absolute secrecy surrounding the program.

Afterward there was no way to track the doomed saucers, but experts calculated that they were likely in rapidly decaying orbits. This presented all sorts of potential problems: Where would they come down? Would they disintegrate or miraculously land intact?

The uncertainty prompted a mad scramble to quickly put together a tracking station, an effort led by noted astronomer Clyde Tombaugh, discoverer of the planet Pluto. Sky-sweeping telescopes searched near space day and night for the orbiting objects. The project involved all military branches operating under the aegis of "Army Ordnance Research." Officially, journalists were told, astronomers hunted not for manmade satellites but for natural space rocks. Along these lines, Time magazine in March 1954 published an article headlined "Second Moon?" The survey was to extend one million miles from Earth using ingenious techniques developed by Tombaugh, the article said.

The story, however, did little to quell titillating gossip. Media reports repeated rumors that the military had launched a satellite and that a new system was desperately needed to track orbital assets. News accounts even included details about the satellites, notably that one had been observed traveling sixteen thousand miles an hour and was eight hundred miles up.

These murmurs, however, soon faded from public discourse, lacking valid sources and verifiable data.

And, with a knowing smile, Uncle Sam exulted, confidently patting his own personal mojo like a trusty ray gun holstered at his side.

Jane contemplated the profound implications of Marsden's manuscript. Massaging a stiff neck, she called the hotel again, but still no Marsden. By now it was late afternoon, and she could read no further.

CHAPTER 10

Two days had passed since her fact-finding session with Marsden, and she was conflicted.

A part of her kept saying she was onto the biggest story of her career. Another part, however, reluctantly acknowledged the practical reality: Without some sort of official confirmation no reputable journal would ever publish anything about flying saucers, even if she were able to secure on-the-record sources.

Newsroom culture generally didn't encourage adventurous explorations into such dubious genre as ufology and fringe conspiracy theories. You simply didn't go there. At least, not with a straight face. For the sake of your own reputation, it was just too risky. The prospects of professional suicide and financial ruin were by no means trivial concerns. Jane didn't want to find herself working for some dipshit industry newsletter or subsisting on freelance assignments, anxiously awaiting payments in the mail like a junkie craving the next dime bag.

Yet she ached to tell a fellow journalist about her dilemma, as if the burden of what she knew -- or thought she knew -- was too much to bear alone. Scanning the newsroom, Jane scrutinized her co-workers. Thompson's

Defense Weekly employed 32 reporters and editors, but Jane doubted she could really trust any of them; smug professionals, mostly, who generally lacked humility and the capacity for sympathetic introspection. The unapproachable Doctor William Walsh; the stuffy associate editor Byron Braun; various and sundry assistant editors and staff writers.

One by one she considered, and then eliminated, each of them.

In the end, only a single possibility remained: old Samuel Barr, an ancient columnist who worked part-time to file his commentary, The Barr Code. Considered the dean of aviation writing, he was a holdover from an era when magazines and newspapers printed with "hot type" lead characters and the memory of World War II yet burned fervently in the minds of Americans.

Now pushing eighty-five, Barr was said to have met the magazine's namesake, Randall Scott Thompson, who founded Thompson's Publishing Company back in 1909, just six years after the Wright Brothers' first flight. Everyone sort of adopted Barr as their surrogate grandfather. He arrived at the office, tousled and weary in a threadbare sport coat, frayed trousers and faded necktie. The old man composed his columns on an equally antiquated relic, pecking away at his manual Underwood typewriter, and then a secretary retyped it into the computer.

Much of his past was mysterious, and rumor had it that Barr had been a spy in the OSS, precursor of the CIA, during the war. He was still quite sharp, with a quick wit and penchant for sarcasm. But his powers of concentration waned soon after the lunch hour, when his Parkinson's palsy seemed to get the best of him and he longed for the solace of his recliner.

No. She couldn't confide in the old man. He likely wouldn't, or couldn't, understand.

ଓଓଓଓ

Jane wasn't exactly sure how she was going to broach the subject of flying saucers with her hard-ass editors, most notably Bill Walsh. But she had to do something. It was gnawing at her like angry insects. She couldn't think of anything but the damned story, Marsden and his fucking manuscript.

A woman sitting near her on the subway was reading a weekly tabloid. The front-page headline screamed: "Air Force Fights Off UFOs!" Artwork under the headline showed three flying saucers pursued by fighter jets.

That just magnified her obsession.

When she got to the office, Walsh was busy editing some writer's copy, gnashing his teeth and muttering disparaging comments, his nose buried in the computer monitor. This was definitely not the time to bring up the subject.

Calls to Marsden's hotel room went unanswered.

Jane was determined to resolve two issues: the veracity of the films and the identity of her anonymous phone caller. She consulted her overstuffed Rolodex for the phone number of a contact, flipping through the rotating file until she recognized the business card she'd stapled to one of the tabs: Gregory Ginsberg Productions, Inc.

Jane had been to his house for some sort of holiday party years ago; the friend of a friend of her ex-hubby. Ginsberg ran a production company from the furnished basement of his suburban New Jersey home. The card displayed a plain black-ink drawing of a video camera mounted on a tripod. She dialed the phone number. He picked up on the second ring.

After a brief reintroduction, she described her quest for an expert on corporate celluloid of the vintage kind.

"What I'm really trying to do is authenticate a couple of old films."

Jane could hear dogs barking in the background and remembered that Ginsberg had some sort of little pedigrees, poofy things all dressed up with hair ribbons for the holidays.

"Well, I've worked with enough sixteen, thirty-five and eight millimeter films to know the lay of the land," Ginsberg said. "Had a few contracts to convert 'em to video for archives and that sort of thing. What kind of shape are these reels in?"

Jane explained that she knew absolutely nothing about film technology and was hoping he could take a look at the footage in question. He told her to come by his studio with the reels.

She'd already dumped a feature story into the news editor's queue for the next issue and had a few minor pieces to crank out by Wednesday's deadline, so Jane decided to visit Ginsberg that day. She took the subway home and hopped in her beat-up Toyota Corolla, which seldom saw active duty and was almost permanently parked in a garage near her apartment building. Jane navigated the perilous passage down Route 17 amid a haze of auto exhaust, dodging at least one fallen muffler and yielding to predatory, tailgating truckers.

Ginsberg's house was a nondescript Cape Cod. It was in a tidy neighborhood like so many others in a colorless suburb dominated by shopping malls, office buildings, chain restaurants. She rang the doorbell and immediately heard the frantic yelping of small dogs. Several minutes went by without any answer, and she was about to ring again when she heard footfalls. A man's spectacled face appeared through small panes in the door, followed by the sound of the lock opening.

"You must be Jane Hale," Ginsberg said.

She thought she detected the faint smell of marijuana wafting through the open storm door as he extended his hand toward her. Jane surveyed his bloodshot countenance while three Yorkshire terriers barked and peered curiously up at her.

"Don't worry about them," he assured her, leading the way toward his basement video-production enclave.

However, she felt less threatened by the diminutive canines than by the scruffy forty-something Ginsberg, who had at least a day's worth of stubble, wore a faded Rolling Stones T-shirt and a pair of ancient patched blue jeans. Was it safe, she wondered, as he escorted her downstairs amid the vocalizing terriers?

The walls of his video-editing suite were adorned with old movie posters, large photographic prints of nature scenes, miscellaneous New York Yankees memorabilia, and various professional credentials. She noticed a framed diploma on the wall: Bachelor of Fine Arts in Photography and Imaging Technology, Rochester Institute of Technology.

"My ex is a Red Sox fan. Hates the Yankees," she commented.

"Yeah, it's rough being a Yankee fan," he kidded. "I admit it's a character flaw. Kind of like being a child molester or a Reagan Democrat. You know it's morally wrong, but you can't control yourself. I mean, you are what you are."

Jane chuckled at his self-deprecating pseudo existentialism, opened her briefcase and pulled out an aged metal film can.

"Well, here it is," she said. "Seems kind of heavy."

Ginsberg sized up the gray metal canister, labeled "Moore Aircraft Company" and dated April 1955.

"It's in good shape," he said. "No dents or corrosion."

Ginsberg sat down at a small workbench and turned on a bright table lamp. He lifted the canister, and, tilting it slightly away from him as if expecting something toxic to spill out, he tugged on the cover. It easily separated from the bottom half of the can, revealing a film reel. He slipped on a pair of white cotton gloves before handling the film.

"It's already on a projection reel. That makes it easier to look at."

He carefully took the reel out of the can and carried it over to another table so that he could view the film using an apparatus consisting of two hand-cranked "rewinds." The antique-looking mechanisms were bolted a few feet apart on a piece of plywood.

Ginsberg mounted the reel onto one of the rewinds and gently unspooled the film, threading it onto an empty take-up reel on the opposite rewind. He squinted through a magnifying glass to examine the film, illuminated with a light box positioned between the two rewinds. Cranking the take-up reel slowly, he stopped now and then to view specific frames.

As he wound the film slowly from the feed to the take-up reels, he trailed his fingers along its edges to detect any defects. Ginsberg moved the magnifying glass away temporarily so that he could take a whiff of the film, like a wine connoisseur sampling the bouquet of a fine burgundy. He was trying to pick up the smell of vinegar, a tell-tale sign of decay.

"Hmm. No shrinkage. It's sixteen millimeter. Looks like standard black-and-white Kodak stock, probably polyester. It's in good shape. I don't see any real deterioration or mold. It's been well cared for."

Ginsberg continued winding the film forward.

The dogs had settled down, and now the room was entirely silent except for a soft, incessant hissing noise coming from one of those ionic wind air filters. Jane surmised he must be using the gadget to mask his pot smoking, but it wasn't doing the trick. The smell was stronger in the basement than it had been upstairs. Still, this didn't bother her in the least, as she had always found the odor rather pleasant.

She wondered how Ginsberg was going to react to the images of flying saucers and laboratory scenes of strange hovering experiments. But the guy remained surprisingly clinical, studying the film as though it were someone's old vacation reel.

"Let's see what the edge codes say. Usually, you can get a pretty good idea about the age of a film by markings along the edges. Yep, there they are. Here, have a look."

Ginsberg motioned for Jane to view the film through the magnifying loupe.

"Now, see those funny-looking symbols along the side of the film?"

She gazed through the lens. After a few seconds, she nodded affirmatively.

"Yes, I think I see them."

He opened a drawer and rooted around for something, pulling out a sheet containing a table entitled Eastman Kodak Date Code Chart. Then he squinted into the magnifying loupe again, straining to pick out the edge codes. He looked back at the table of codes and ran his index finger down the list until he found the matching symbols.

"These codes indicate this movie was produced in either 1935, 1955 or 1975. So the date on the can looks right. Yep, ya see, this is what we've got," he said, showing her the symbols on the chart: a plus sign and a solid black square.

"Here, have a look."

Jane peeped into the magnifying loupe, spying the codes as Ginsberg slowly advanced the film a few frames at a time.

"Before 1951, film stock manufactured in different countries, like the U.S., Canada, France and whatnot, used different codes, but after 1951 they all used the same codes," Ginsberg said. "Different sequences in specific years of manufacture, and these sequences repeat every so many years."

"I see, so that makes it pretty unambiguous, in terms of when the film stock was made, but how soon afterward would this footage have been shot?" she asked.

"Oh, probably within months. I'd say the year of manufacture is a pretty sure way to date these reels, give or take a year. Excuse me," he said, laying a hand on Jane's shoulder to motion her away from the magnifying loupe.

Ginsberg continued winding and rewinding the film and viewing certain frames with great interest. After a few minutes, he looked up at her and asked, "What the hell are we dealing with here?"

Jane considered his question.

"I'm not one hundred percent sure, but I was sort of hoping you could tell me whether you thought this film was authentic. Is there any way this could be a fake?"

"From what I've seen so far, it certainly looks authentic. If you're asking whether it could be fake, I guess anything is possible, with enough money and effort. I would recommend a scientific analysis of this film by people who have access to the best equipment, either a company specializing in film restoration, or a university with a top-notch film program. This is gonna take more resources than I have at my disposal."

Jane looked dissatisfied and perplexed. She wasn't very keen on letting the reel out of her sight, even temporarily.

"Well, maybe that would be premature," she hedged. "At this point, I'm only just exploring the possibility of looking into this further."

Ginsberg excitedly resumed his examination of the film as Jane continued to downplay her interest in it. He eventually rewound the reel and placed it back in its metal case.

"Well, thanks for your help. What do I owe you?"

But Ginsberg, with a wave of his hand, casually dismissed any notion of monetary compensation for his services.

"That's okay," he said amicably. "I can recommend some people, if you need a detailed analysis. Give me your email address and I'll send you some information."

She handed Ginsberg her business card.

On her drive back to the city Jane had the nagging sensation of being followed. She checked her rearview mirror periodically, seeing only the usual highway traffic: frenetic motorists changing lanes, high-priced Beemers and rust-ridden beaters, taxicabs and commercial vehicles. All flowing inexorably toward the great metropolis.

The urban landscape grew closer and closer until she merged with it, crossing the George Washington Bridge and then onto the Harlem River Drive south into Manhattan. She arrived at her office shortly after 4 o'clock to find a few items in her mailbox. A hard copy of her feature story with Walsh's comments scribbled in the border; some assignment leads bearing Post-It notes from the news editor: "Jane, fyi."

But nothing from Marsden.

This irritated her greatly. She was more than ready to confront him about the missing film reel. Actually, it could all work to her advantage, she told herself. The film and other newly acquired evidence could strengthen Marsden's manuscript, or at least add to its entertainment value, especially if he managed to find sources to comment on the film's authenticity. At the same time, she expected to piggyback on his efforts and perhaps even tap the same sources for her own purposes.

As much as Marsden was using her, she intended to return the favor. Between the two of them, maybe they could learn the identity of their mysterious telephone caller and interview him on the record.

That was the most important thing.

CHAPTER 11

It was a gloomy Saturday morning. A steady rain pelted her apartment window, and still no word from Marsden. Jane resolved to plow through the second half of his manuscript.

The story ventured next into the origins of the military-industrial complex and its control over the embryonic flying saucer program. Marsden revisited General Twining's stunning memo from 1947, a vital piece of anecdotal evidence. The reader was reminded of its most startling implication: The United States already had the knowledge to build flying saucers "... capable of an approximate range of 7,000 miles at subsonic speeds."

This was awfully specific information, Jane thought. How could he have possibly estimated the range of these mysterious vehicles unless he had received intelligence from knowledgeable sources?

Because the memo's authenticity was never in dispute, it amounted to an amazing confirmation from an unimpeachable source in a communication that was obviously not meant for public consumption. The language of the classified memo lacked the usual subterfuge of UFO-related announcements cooked up for the masses: It made no attempt to assign mundane explanations such as astronomical or meteorological phenomena, conventional military aircraft, weather balloons, swamp gas, the Northern Lights, ball lightning.

Was this memo actually just a portion of an ongoing conversation -- a leaked snippet -- one small piece of a dialog between military officials? If so, it sure would be nice to know the rest of that conversation.

Jane had read more than half of Marsden's book by now, and the story continued to hold her interest. The author was just catching his stride, merging real history with his own hypothetical yet conceivable chronology:

> *Vannevar Bush spoke amid a miasma of acrid tobacco smoke, a white plume puffing constantly out of his pipe, a simmering nicotine-delivery system that infected everyone with its toxic belching. His voice never rose above the normal decibel range of casual conversation, but the tone was intimidating, sometimes menacing. It was a raspy, grating voice.*
>
> *"Well, Mr. Cutler, I think we have a consensus that the project must be given the highest priority and maintained in the utmost secrecy. I have given much thought to this issue, and it is clear that following your approach would be contrary to the extraordinary measures we must take to ensure national defense. This is a conclusion one can only reach by a careful, in-depth study of the matter, which we have undertaken."*
>
> *Robert Cutler, President Eisenhower's national security advisor, listened to Bush's gravelly voice drone on about the awesome "responsibilities" foisted on the*

committee, the burden of leadership, and bla, bla, bla. The committee - Majestic Twelve - was the bane of Eisenhower's presidency. As Truman's successor, Eisenhower had inherited oversight, but he was loath to condone the group's bureaucratic control of the antigravity propulsion program. Unfortunately, challenging MJ-12 and its imperious leader was a lonely lesson in futility.

A bilious Bush continued his condescending, one-sided conversation with Cutler.

"The project is very vulnerable and subject to potential compromise, considering the fact that some of my best men came from the commercial sector. Although this is a very select, handpicked and closely monitored team, the potential for leaks is an issue. We also remain fairly certain that the Soviet Union is ahead of us. As far as the technology itself, field propulsion is by no means ready for service. We have fundamental design challenges that we simply must overcome if we are to prepare ourselves for future conflict with the Soviets."

He disagreed with most of Eisenhower's ideas, especially the president's "new look" strategy, which concentrated on deterring Soviet attacks by threatening a massive nuclear bombardment. In theory, this tack would enable the United States to trim military spending by reducing the nation's defense presence around the world. Logically, the Soviets would be unlikely to provoke a nuclear strike, allowing the United States to cut back on military personnel abroad.

But something didn't wash, as far as Bush was concerned, and he wasn't alone in his criticism of Eisenhower's overall national security concept. Other scientists had demonstrated the need for defensive measures. Presumably, they groused, the Soviets would be working on their own ways to thwart a U.S. nuclear strike, eventually negating the threat and exposing America to surprise Russian attack. Instead of relying exclusively on the deterrent value of nukes, the nation must develop a multifarious defensive system to repel potential Soviet salvos.

The linchpin of this sophisticated shield should be "an air defense system far tighter than that of Russia," Bush had argued, a force of interceptors capable of catching up to and shooting down any long-range Russian bombers. A saucer squadron tasked only with nuclear defense; an overwhelmingly superior presence to safeguard the country.

Eisenhower, on the other hand, thought Bush's line of reasoning was pure hogwash. Stalin was finally dead, and it was peacetime, after all, notwithstanding the horrifying specter of the Soviet Union, described by Eisenhower's own advisors in 1954 as "an implacable enemy whose avowed objective is world domination."

The memory of Pearl Harbor had been seared into the nation's psyche, and Americans were generally freaked out by fears of nuclear ambush. Even so, the president was extremely wary of demands by Congress, the Pentagon and top generals to expand the U.S. military, ramp up missile research, build new Polaris attack submarines, nuclear-powered aircraft carriers and long-range bombers, all bristling with the latest weapon of choice: hundreds of hydrogen bombs.

The Defense Department engulfed half of the federal budget, spending more annually than the twelve largest U.S. corporations combined.

An exasperated Eisenhower marveled at the alarmist zeal sweeping over the country, and he fought hard to contain defense spending, rhetorically asking, "How many times do we have to destroy Russia?"

MJ-12 and other high-level groups were beginning to wield too much influence, Eisenhower feared. The committee was a tall gathering of alpha males. Guys like Admiral Sidney W. Souers and General Hoyt S. Vandenberg, both central intelligence gurus during and after World War II; Rear Admiral Roscoe Hillenkoetter, the first CIA director; and General Twining, who headed Air Materiel Command at Wright-Patterson Air Force Base.

Anchoring this dream team of military specialists were two key players in the Truman power structure: Secretary of Defense James Forrestal and Bush, president of the Carnegie Institute and head of the Office of Scientific Research and Development during the war.

He was regarded as perhaps the most politically connected inventor and scientific advisor since Benjamin Franklin; lionized by the national media as a superlative gadgeteer, a genius who had nearly single-handedly saved the world from the Nazis; a technical czar who stood up to the likes of Churchill and shunned left-leaning liberal scientists, even Albert Einstein.

Some would say he was a bully whose brilliance and ambition were surpassed only by his hunger for domination and control.

Even before Sputnik's overflight energized the Cold War, the men in charge of the antigravity program sweated out many a sleepless night. Bush was dictatorial, a fierce patriot and a military technocrat obsessed with advancing the national defense. MJ-12 was really his idea. Just as he had forcefully urged its creation, Bush would remain its most ardent supporter in the years that followed, the backstage wizard who so skillfully manipulated the knobs and levers of the flying saucer project.

It was a stealthy stewardship: Keeping secrets was second nature to Bush, hardwired into his keenly suspicious intellect.

Majestic was a symptom of the anti-communist, nuclear-age hysteria gripping the nation, an ethos that would dictate the course of antigravity. The nation's second-biggest black research program after the Manhattan Project, it was concealed from members of Congress and nearly all top military brass. Hardly anyone had a "need to know," and most of the scientists, engineers and technicians on the project were compartmentalized, working in isolated divisions. Few people really understood the total package; only the pilots, MJ-12, and a handful of researchers and officials from the defense community.

And, of course, the president.

As allied commander during the war, Eisenhower had been informed about the raids on Nazi labs, knowing only that the Americans had removed gear related to "advanced propulsion systems." He'd heard rumors of UFO encounters, but chalked them up to adrenaline and faulty perception in the fog of war.

As president, however, he soon learned the truth.

One day in February 1955 the president was spirited away from a watchful national media under the pretense of suffering a head cold. But instead of a trip to the infirmary, Eisenhower conducted a sort of white-glove presidential tour of a flying saucer at Holloman Air Force Base.

The president's plane taxied to a stop, sunlight glinting off its shiny aluminum fuselage in the severe morning glare of the New Mexico desert. The big four-engine Lockheed Constellation sat at the end of the base's most distant runway. Stairs were rolled in place and the airplane's cabin door opened just as a saucer glided overhead, put down its landing gear and settled gently on the runway. Eisenhower deplaned and stood by himself at the foot of the stairway, blue eyes agleam under blue skies, square-shouldered and composed.

There was no red carpet or brass band.

The base commander and officials heading the saucer project drove out to the plane in a jeep, greeted the president and escorted him to the landed saucer, where they briefed Eisenhower.

The craft was twenty feet in diameter and had a lustrous titanium skin. A hatch opened on the bottom and doubled as a narrow ramp to gain entry to the small interior. After discussing the saucer's design and basic performance characteristics with the president, one of the military officials walked up the ramp and Eisenhower followed him inside, stooping slightly to squeeze through the slender portal.

Another saucer approached the area and hovered nearby for the duration of the presidential tour, which lasted less than an hour.

The experience was extraordinary, but as the months and years passed, Ike's wonder turned to cynicism. The president was particularly concerned about MJ-12's cozy relationships with the anointed few industry moguls and academics privileged enough to be in on the secret. He was especially suspicious of big defense programs that sidestepped official government scrutiny.

Was it prudent to allow an exclusive club of powerful men to deprive common culture of such a technological wonder as antigravity? Think of the potential commercial benefit, the president mused. Antigravity could fuel a new world economy, facilitated by a sophisticated global transportation network for business and commerce. Suddenly, space exploration would be an affordable endeavor and the rich resources of the solar system accessible to the world.

At the very least, Eisenhower believed, the saucers should be moved into the U.S. arsenal as soon as possible, perhaps superseding nascent jet technology, which was evidently inferior. But no matter which course to pursue, the decision ought to be made by a broad range of Congressional and military leaders. Cloaking the program prevented Congress from shaping policy on antigravity.

Bush, on the other hand, thought it extremely unwise to trust Congress, and the public at large, to make the right decisions about crucial science and technology programs. Politicians were scientifically illiterate, and the unwashed citizenry even more incapable of comprehending the increasingly specialized technologies of war, he reasoned.

The only sure way to keep America safe was to let the experts run the show. Install an elite corps of civilian technocrats, a patriarchal ruling authority immune to the dysfunctional infighting that permeated postwar American society. The less meddling by the public and top government officials, the greater the possibility of success. So much was at stake, Bush believed: perhaps the difference between survival and ruin.

Bush knew that an increasingly fearful public -- fixating on Russian intercontinental missiles and the prospects of nuclear annihilation -- might be perfectly happy to sacrifice certain democratic safeguards, ceding control of sensitive military projects to the experts.

Fortunately for Bush, he didn't really need the president's approval to design and build working prototypes. Ever since 1941, when Roosevelt created the Office of Scientific Research and Development, Bush had been empowered to produce small batches of weapons and equipment developed in his labs. This autonomy gave him extra leverage, which he applied often in debates with political and military leaders if they balked at moving forward with a new weapon.

He would simply produce a prototype, successfully demonstrate the technology, and then dare his opponents to ignore it.

In certain respects, Bush felt, representative democracy was an impediment to homeland defense. Congress, the public and press were deliberately kept in the dark about the atomic bomb and a collection of deadly weapons of the last world war. There was no national dialogue about these critical technologies. And if the lessons of the last global conflict had taught him anything, it was that allied complacency had invited Nazi aggression.

There was only one way to prevent history from repeating itself: Create a new relationship between the military, industry and scientific elite. This "military-industrial-academic" complex would guarantee America's technological dominance by spearheading and maintaining research programs, some in secret and some openly. Winning, or preventing, a modern war simply depended on a linkage between these elements.

He had proved that research to perfect new technologies could be fast-tracked, supercharged with military funding and yet shrouded from the public.

And all for the better of humanity.

In Eisenhower's view, this was how America incubated her biggest sin of the postwar period: the unjustified influence given to a tight inner circle of experts, military and industry insiders operating in a vacuum. Their recommendations were practically rubber stamped by only a small group of Pentagon brass.

But this sea change swept across American culture like multiple tsunamis set in motion by the rumblings of the Cold War. An animal response to fear fed by nightmarish recollections of Hiroshima.

No single president dare stand in its way.

Indeed, Eisenhower was already dogged by accusations that his penny-pinching in military spending had led to a "missile gap" that gave the Soviets an edge in delivering intercontinental nukes. He was in no position to shine a spotlight on the saucer program, which he reluctantly supported. And by the time he suffered a stroke in 1958, the president's misgivings were irrelevant. Antigravity was taken over that year by the newly formed Defense Advanced Research Projects Agency.

NASA's more muscular twin, DARPA sprang up in response to the Soviets' launch of Sputnik and would initially handle many of the most sensitive defense-related space ventures, just as MJ-12 was being dissolved. Vannevar Bush, taken out of the flying saucer picture, was free to raise turkeys on his New Hampshire farm and reflect on a lifetime of thwarting evildoers. Free to ruminate solemnly about decisive moments that had determined the destiny of thousands.

By then the lid of secrecy had been securely tightened over the aviation industry. Aerospace VIPs were no longer promising the advent of antigravity. DARPA automatically adopted Vannevar Bush's "doctrine of independent genesis," which held that the U.S. field propulsion project must remain secret at least until the technology's invention by other researchers in the commercial sector or by a foreign power. In other words, so long as America held a monopoly, the saucers would remain hidden from public view. And, concurrently, the latest intelligence was revealing that the Soviets didn't have antigravity.

A few years later, John F. Kennedy's defense secretary, Robert McNamara, would increase funding for space research and begin a program to test the saucers as potential antimissile gunships. He was ostensibly opposed to an "anti-ballistic missile system" because, he said, it would be too expensive and ultimately ineffective. But that wasn't the real reason; it was because America already had a potentially superior antimissile system in flying saucers.

Antigravity was now seen as critical to the national defense. Anyone privy to information about the program would be subjected to an ongoing and intensive scrutiny and their immediate family members examined under a microscope. Because circumstances surrounding the flying saucer program were unprecedented and the implications of failure so potentially grave, the penalties were suitably draconian.

Military personnel caught publicly divulging information about their research would be court-martialed, imprisoned, dishonorably discharged. Likewise, military pilots who had chance encounters with flying saucers were forbidden under similar threat from speaking about their experiences. Private sector whistle blowers would be blackballed from the feeding trough of military contracts. They could be tried for treason and go to prison for a long, long time. Or worse, pay the ultimate price for their transgressions. Simply cease to exist. Becoming mere crime statistics under that mundane but thriving category: missing person, no evidence of foul play.

Such things could be arranged in the name of national security and for the express purpose of maintaining the conspiracy. It was a system that worked on the principle that people are motivated primarily out of fear. The kind of fear that kept strong men quiet until they lay quivering on their deathbeds, senile and mumbling incoherently about flying saucers. Not that punitive extremes were often needed. The warning alone was sufficiently intimidating. Besides, people endeavoring to design, build and test weapons of mass destruction for the U.S. government occupied a fairly staunch segment of society. They tended easily toward unflinching loyalty.

The secret of antigravity would remain safe, perhaps forever.

ଓଓଓଓ

Only three chapters remained of Marsden's manuscript, as the story transitioned to the 1960s:

Uncle Sam's own personal mojo was in a major state of flux, what with competing ideas and designs and various technical challenges. Getting the tiger by the tail proved a risky maneuver that often turned dangerous. Like the time in 1964 when test pilots took off from a secret military base in the southwestern desert. They were flying a prototype that combined a liquid-fuel rocket for vertical lift with a gravitator for overall propulsion. Something went horribly wrong, though; the egg-shaped thing skewed wildly off course, like a shanked golf ball, ending up well outside of the test range and into civilian airspace.

That's when police officer Benjie Alvarez got involved. He was in the middle of a high-speed chase, trailing a stolen Chevy Impala that had just been heisted by a couple of juvenile delinquents.

There was no quit in this cop. The thrill of pursuit always touched off something primal in him; sweaty palms and cottonmouth and an exhilarating sense of one's manliness.

Alvarez was speeding westbound, and the bright sun hung like a burning disk over the dry basalt-capped buttes of the high Mojave Desert. Even though he was wearing dark sunglasses, the cop squinted to keep his focus on the speeding car. Suddenly a dramatic column of flames and smoke erupted eighty feet into the air to his left. His mind raced, thinking in fragments. Could be a plane crash. Obviously a major accident. Definitely an explosion. Could be dynamite.

It certainly wouldn't be the first time an old mining shack went ka-boom in his largely rural Arizona jurisdiction.

He immediately abandoned his car chase and drove in the direction of the plume, proceeding slowly along a gravel road in the rugged desert terrain. The squad car shambled noisily on the narrow, bumpy road, rising and dipping alongside a small arroyo. Alvarez tried to keep an eye on the remnants of the now-dissipating plume, just beyond a nearby ridge, without careening into the ditch.

He came to a summit overlooking a gully, seeing what appeared to be an overturned car roughly a hundred yards away. Two people dressed in white coveralls were doing something around the vehicle. One of them seemed startled at the sight of Alvarez, who cut an imposing figure standing next to his squad car, arms akimbo, revolver holstered on his hip. The officer reached for the radio handset inside the car, advising dispatch that he was going in for a closer look.

"I got a possible ten forty-four, and I'll be ten-six out of the car, checking the vehicle down in the arroyo -- looks to be overturned," he said in a monotone voice that belied the peculiar nature of the situation.

Maybe some joy-riding four-wheelers drove their jeep into the gully. Perhaps others were pinned under the vehicle. The cop proceeded on foot, losing sight of the object as he hiked the dipping terrain before coming to the top of a small hillside directly adjacent to the accident scene.

At this point things really got strange.

The two people were gone, and Alvarez realized that the "vehicle" was actually an ovoid object sitting on silvery legs. It was either white or some sort of shiny metal that glimmered in the desert sun. There didn't seem to be any windows or doors, and there was a red insignia on the side.

He heard several thumping sounds that resembled metal hitting metal, followed by a deafening roar and a blue-colored flame shooting from the bottom of the egg, then a whirring sound as the craft rose out of the arroyo, legs retracting. The object hung motionless, and the flame disappeared as it became completely silent.

The astonished officer ran back to his car and tried to call headquarters, but the radio was on the blink. The egg moved parallel to the desert landscape, accelerated and sped away. Just then the radio started working again, and Alvarez called dispatch to request help from the Arizona State Police.

Word traveled quickly, and within twenty-four hours the government sent its official UFO investigator, who never was able to solve the mystery. After all, Alvarez was a decorated war veteran, a police officer who served with distinction, a church-going family man and a pillar of his community.

The officer stuck to his story no matter how many times he was grilled, and physical evidence seemed to support his claim: charred vegetation, deep indentations from the vehicle's legs and an array of footprints.

Nevertheless, tales of Alvarez's adventure drew so much ridicule that he soon quit the police department and took a job at an auto-parts store.

"I dunno what the heck it was," he told a local newspaper reporter many years later amid the fan belts and radiator hoses. "All I know is what I seen. I'm not saying I think it's from outer space. If it's some kinda new type of plane, man, it sure is strange."

ଔଔଔଔ

Marsden's manuscript consistently reinforced a recurring theme: the government's masterful record of covering up mistakes involving the antigravity program. Sometimes the mistakes got way out of hand, like one night in the Pennsylvania countryside:

> *Only a year after the Alvarez encounter the military lost control of another toy. This time it was a drone-like experimental platform loosely based on the Nazi bell design.*
>
> *The radio-directed prototype was supposed to land at Wright-Patterson Air Force Base but overshot its mark by quite a margin. It was on a cold, cloudy December afternoon in rural Pennsylvania when the fiery object streaked horizontally overhead, crashing in wooded property on the outskirts of a little town.*
>
> *Fourteen-year-old Bobbie Filmore and his friends were sneaking a smoke on the loading dock of an abandoned warehouse when they witnessed the strange thing; a flaming ball that traveled parallel to the ground. At times it seemed to actually start climbing higher in the sky.*
>
> *"It wasn't falling down like no meteor," he told a radio newsman. "It was flying more like an airplane."*
>
> *Volunteer firefighters rushed to the scene but were perplexed by what they found smoldering in the thick underbrush.*
>
> *"It kinda looked like a big acorn-shaped thing," said fire chief Joel Smithson, according to the local newspaper. "There was no wings. There was no engine.*

There was no propeller. We didn't know what the heck to do with it."

Soon they were confronted by a stout military official and a cordon of soldiers marching briskly toward them down the sloping terrain.

"You men have to get out of here, right now," the officer told them.

"Now see here," Smithson protested. "We're responding to an accident, and we're going to do our job."

One of the soldiers immediately seized him from behind, roughly holding his arms behind his back, as several other military personnel trained M1 rifles on the firefighters.

"You are either going to leave the area or you're going to spend some time in jail, one or the other," the officer shouted at them.

The firefighters were hustled away from the crash scene under guard.

Within minutes the hilly, forested site was swarming with soldiers. An hour later a flatbed truck arrived, and a short time after that the vehicle was seen speeding away from the scene, hauling a tarpaulin-covered hump about the dimensions of a Volkswagen Beetle.

Local print and broadcast media buzzed for days. Some journalists bird-dogged the story for years, but they never were able to learn what the mysterious cargo was. And, although an official report was filed and later obtained through Freedom of Information Act requests, the document made absolutely no mention of the strange acorn-shaped thing that was forcibly extracted from the rustic hillside that evening.

ઌઌઌઌ

Mid-morning had turned to mid-afternoon, and Jane started skimming chapters to skip redundant content. She settled finally on a chapter focusing on the domain of disinformation, a Machiavellian realm dominated by dispassionate actors working toward a single purpose: to deceive the American public into believing flying saucers are not of this world. Marsden capped this portion with a disclaimer informing the reader that the central character was a fictionalized composite constructed with information from sources. With that caveat, he dove into the heart of the matter:

Donald W. Johnson, Ph.D. in communication theory, was a tall, imposing, chain-smoking man with a resonant, erudite-sounding voice. He would have thrived in academia, but he opted instead for a life of anonymous service to the U.S. government. Oh, he was paid very handsomely, in both monetary and figurative terms: a true patriot. Yet his brilliant application of communication concepts never would be published in the scientific literature or described in textbooks. His pivotal contributions would remain hidden between the lines of history.

Johnson was a specialist, a master of mendacity who led efforts to engineer the UFO disinformation machinery. It all started way back in the 1950s, when he was a young post-doctoral fellow at a federally funded think tank. Ever since that nasty rumor circulated that the saucers over Washington might have been manufactured by Boeing as part of some mysterious U.S. defense project, Majestic Twelve recognized that a professional "perception management" campaign would be needed to mislead the public.

Still fresh from the hallowed halls of Harvard University, the feds tapped Johnson to lead a group of propagandists tasked with forging an indelible link between aliens and flying saucers through popular media. Moviemakers had already started this association all by themselves in the 1956 science fiction film Earth Vs. The Flying Saucers. It was one of the first times Johnson could remember seeing aliens depicted as macrocephalic extraterrestrials, an image that would later morph into the iconic "greys" of UFO lore and mythology.

He had studied the greatest philosophers and communication theorists: Socrates and Plato, McLuhan and Chomsky. Now he distilled their pearls of wisdom into an intoxicating brew of disinformation, feeding it like nectar to an eager populace.

Dr. Johnson harnessed the expertise of his skilled staff to manipulate the public mind. His team gained access to the impressionable underbelly of the American psyche by engaging its universal angst and insecurities and employing McLuhan's maxim: The medium is the message. They used vivid images in film and TV programs to engrave the association between aliens and flying saucers on the mass mind. For the various print media, they appealed to more intellectual sensitivities:

the human obsessions with fantasy, paranoia and conspiracy thinking.

The disinformation program represented a natural evolution in a long history of authority-sponsored propaganda. Messages designed to foster a pseudoreality bolstered by simple stereotypes and emotional impressions to channel the communal subconscious, corral the bewildered herd. Operating under the mundane-sounding Division of Information Services, it was an effort the likes of which hadn't been seen since Woodrow Wilson's Committee on Public Information, an assemblage of the leading persuasion and propaganda experts charged with selling World War I to a wary electorate.

The most effective messages in any such effort were usually rooted in something inherently unsettling: eternal damnation; an alien threat; imminent demise.

The universal driver was fear.

A fear powerful and pernicious, a fear Dr. Johnson thought was nearly palpable. He could almost feel it pulsating among the masses while riding the subway to and from work. Always there. Omnipresent yet unseen. An energy source waiting to be tapped. He sensed it while observing others reading their newspapers and magazines, their trite tabloids. That's why Dr. Johnson, a man of considerable means owing in large part to family wealth, insisted on taking the subway to work nearly every day. Mentally recording the facial expressions, the body language, the nervous conversations. They were like laboratory mice to him.

Or possibly even less significant: paramecia.

He likened his manipulations to a rudimentary biology experiment often performed by undergraduates. The task was to introduce a viscous medium onto a microscope slide full of the tiny aquatic critters. You see, paramecia swim too fast for students to observe their ciliated locomotion, but you could slow them down by adding the syrupy liquid to their environment. The disinformation was not unlike that sticky medium: impede cognition so that people never really make the connection between the military and flying saucers.

The entire affair would have all been so comical if it weren't such serious business, he often thought with sadistic delight: to watch the people squirm.

Johnson and his staff had no idea whether flying saucers existed. They didn't care. Their job was only to make people associate them with strange and frightening creatures from other worlds. To this end they grooved their imagery into the fabric of existing mainstream culture, then sat back and watched with a detached scientific curiosity at what unfolded.

One simple message reverberated from a constant background drumbeat of the concepts they cultivated: Aliens ride in flying saucers.

This overarching theme was muddled because the public initially gave some credence to the idea that human engineers, not aliens, were behind the saucers, a sentiment that had existed ever since one crashed in the New Mexico desert in 1947. General Hap Arnold, the putative father of the U.S. Air Force, let slip that the discs could be "a development of United States scientists" that had not yet been perfected.

Any such associations between saucers and the military, subconscious or otherwise, must be expunged, or, at the very least, overlaid with the alien-saucer paradigm.

Dr. Johnson measured his success by what he read, watched and heard. Always tweaking the messages, the "products" generated by his office. The DIS exploited mainstream culture like a sharp instrument to promote the ET-flying saucer myth. Johnson's crack team of media experts, psychologists, literary scholars, sociologists, linguists, journalists, advertising and communication wonks would do a number on the American psyche.

It was a scientific bastion for the nation's best liars. Most central to their modus operandi was the fundamental truism that propaganda is most powerful when least conspicuous.

Specialists wrote military reports debunking high-profile UFO events. These were masterpieces of deception, filled with mounds of technical jargon and falsified data sculpted into plausible, workaday explanations for the most potentially dangerous sightings, encounters that might lead people to finally start putting two and two together.

Handwriting experts at DIS forged the signatures of everyone from Albert Einstein to Ronald Reagan, their names appearing impressively in reports, memos and dispatches. Documents, photos, reports, illustrations. They did it all, a one-stop shop for disinformation; planting their seeds of subterfuge, then watching them sprout and take root. They provided nourishment over the years with granules of half-truths precisely packaged and distributed for maximum effect.

The greatest concoctions were the well-crafted reports and books and the fabricated witnesses linking flying saucers to alien visitors, and, by extension, to the lunatic fringe. This was a substantial body of work, a brilliant compendium of stealth marketing.

DIS planted writers on the production teams of popular television programs and motion picture houses. A major coup was a TV series of the mid-1960s, originally pitched to producers by writers working for Dr. Johnson. "The Intruders" brought flying saucers into American homes every week for two years. Each episode opened with a flying saucer ominously approaching Earth, piloted by two aliens impassively observing the planet growing progressively larger in their view screen. Aliens from another solar system bent on making the Earth "their world."

Sometimes the DIS served as impromptu censor, like the time Dr. Johnson was tipped off to details deemed "sensitive" in a Hollywood script for a seemingly harmless fantasy about invaders from Mars. He swiftly informed the film's director that the movie could not be released in the United States without changes mandated by the Pentagon. The DIS then proceeded to cut a sizeable chunk of footage from the film, snipping out dialogue and a sequence of illustrations and models resembling top-secret technology being tested by the military; things that had been reported as UFOs by newspapers, magazines and broadcast media.

Oddly, though, a "British version" of the film released in the UK retained the offending naughty bits, a subtlety missed by moviegoers.

Dr. Johnson's product-placement wizards also were the instigators behind a wildly successful flying saucer toy "for children of all ages." The product description on the box said it was an alien spacecraft based on revelations from an alleged whistleblower who had worked at Area 51, the secret military facility in Nevada. The whistleblower was actually a government plant, and his story a complete scam concocted to perpetuate apocryphal accounts of attempts to "reverse engineer" ET technology.

DIS also spearheaded various alien-abduction reports, which invariably involved flying saucers and telepathic extraterrestrials. They bribed the wives, siblings and descendants of deceased military personnel to tell tales about alien corpses and government misdeeds at purported flying saucer crash sites. They created bogus informers who claimed to have had first-hand knowledge of extraterrestrial contact and secret programs.

At first blush, these sources seemed legitimate. But with a stroke of disinformation genius the purveyors of propaganda artfully wove inconsistencies into their backgrounds so that they appeared just a little too flaky: Maybe they never actually earned that master's degree from MIT as alleged on their resume. Maybe, on closer scrutiny, key elements of their stories were too easily refutable to be taken seriously.

To further taint the legitimacy of flying saucers, the DIS played a role in the emergence of a whole new investigative genre -- ufology -- and with it a bevy of mostly strange and eccentric doyens: ufologists. Some, supported with disinformation moneys, helped to cement the alien-flying saucer myth with specious disclosures about UFO crackups and star-hopping space creatures.

Ersatz ufologists figured prominently in Majestic Twelve lore. In 1981, the DIS leaked a terse 1947 memo from President Truman to Secretary of Defense James Forrestal authorizing a special classified executive order to form "Operation Majestic Twelve." After its disclosure a series of bogus documents were planted in the National Archives and revealed to a select group of UFO investigators.

The original Truman memo was dated the day after Twining's secret memorandum, which had been prompted by a spate of saucer sightings. Both the Twining and Truman memos were authentic. The latter was penned by the president himself with the utmost care to say absolutely nothing of substance while laying the logistical foundation for a critical bureaucracy to guide the project. The memo was so vague that it revealed little more than the committee's title and the fact that Truman wanted ultimate decision-making authority over the group.

Then, the DIS created several fictitious MJ-12 documents as companion pieces to the Truman memo. The collection included an alleged Eisenhower briefing memo supposedly prepared in November 1952 by

Roscoe Hillenkoetter, the first CIA director, concerning crashed alien spacecraft in the southwestern United States and northern Mexico. What actually crashed were U.S. saucer prototypes.

Conspiracy theorists were intrigued to learn that Eisenhower did indeed receive extensive briefings during the same timeframe in 1952, including meetings at the Pentagon with military types who'd been revealed as MJ-12 members.

This was a matter of public record.

Adding to the intrigue, however, was the fact that these briefings would remain classified virtually forever. The material covered during the meetings, hashed out in sometimes heated exchanges between Ike and Majestic, wouldn't be accessible to the general public for several generations, if ever.

Of course, the president did meet with MJ-12, and the men did discuss issues concerning antigravity and flying saucers. But of a very terrestrial nature.

Other fake MJ-12 papers in the DIS collection amounted to a veritable anthology of disinformation: They included documents concerning such matters as proper military procedure during close encounters with aliens, diagrams and records of UFO testing, missives on spurious cover-ups, and items that allegedly contained statements from Truman regarding UFOs.

By the early 1990s, the alien-saucer myth had been permanently tattooed on the mass mind, stamped into the gray matter of the public consciousness. No one, it seemed, even entertained the possibility that people were being had. The DIS was all-but dismantled.

Dr. Johnson, by then an old man, continued reporting to work for a time, like a professor emeritus craving continuity. Scanning the papers and magazines. Watching the numerous UFO documentaries. Even perusing the Internet. So far as he could see, all accounts possessed a singularity. He luxuriated in this singularity, in the proverbial pronouncements, now simply taken for granted: "What I saw was not of this world."

And, occasionally, he indulged himself in a wry chuckle.

After all, he'd earned the right.

ଔଔଔଔ

The manuscript's final chapter rehashed key elements, exploring various clues and suspicions about the antigravity program. By the 1970s flying saucers were nearly passé; the program had matured and now included a variety of platforms of assorted shapes and sizes.

Marsden cited documents from the U.S. Geological Survey, which keeps track of earthquake activity, revealing that a new type of aircraft with a unique acoustic signature was producing "airquakes" while speeding east from the Pacific coastline toward southern Nevada. The seismic data supported eyewitness accounts of a large airplane that had a tendency to leave in its wake a strange contrail punctuated regularly with puffs of exhaust resembling knots on a rope.

Marsden tracked down experts who thought the odd combustion remnants might be evidence of a special type of high-performance engine called a scramjet, which, in theory, could deliver rocket-like thrust. An aircraft equipped with such an engine might achieve "hypersonic" speeds, perhaps Mach eight, they said.

Budget analyses also strongly suggested the feds were developing an array of other exotic aircraft. In other words, scramjets might be just the tip of the iceberg.

During his investigation, a group of engineers floated to the surface of the murky world of black projects to educate Marsden about their covert activities. They had made a conscious decision to break the government-imposed code of silence, believing that the end of the Cold War meant it was high time to begin spinning off certain technologies into the white world of commercial aviation.

Unfortunately, the sources were all unnamed: They insisted that coming out entirely constituted a danger to their families. Their stories, however, were quite persuasive when woven so skillfully into a tapestry of other evidence, pictures and documents, Jane thought.

Marsden's sources also laid the groundwork for another revelation: unlike the stealth fighter, which uses primarily its angular surfaces to keep radar signals from bouncing back to their source, the B-2 stealth bomber apparently was equipped with something different. In addition to the bomber's radar-absorbing skin and its slippery shape, the plane was surrounded by an intense envelope of electromagnetic energy. The speculation was that gravitators onboard the bombers served a dual purpose: provide stealth by interfering with radar waves and also boost the plane's aerodynamic efficiency by reducing drag on the airframe.

The conclusion of Marsden's manuscript offered a cynical, perhaps ominous assessment that spanned the Reagan years and glimpsed the future:

Presidents would come and go; Congressional leadership would change hands; wars would be fought; social mores challenged; the doors of perception unhinged; and people would walk on the moon.

But flying saucers remained Uncle Sam's own personal mojo, Vannevar Bush's doctrine of independent genesis holding sway over the decades, ensuring that antigravity would continue to evolve in the dark; Eisenhower and Truman the only presidents to ever have had a direct, first-hand knowledge of the saucer program. Their immediate successor likely never informed - although JFK might have had suspicions - his murder evidently unrelated to the conspiracy. Then, in the chaos that followed, a 'need to know' was not restored to the Oval Office. And for a whole generation no defense secretary other than Robert McNamara was privy to the intimate facts surrounding field propulsion.

Air Force General Curtis LeMay, a key player in antigravity R&D, informed McNamara that the saucers were by design the perfect foil against Soviet intercontinental ballistic missiles. LeMay, who despised McNamara and his intellectual disposition, strong-armed the defense secretary into boosting resources for the antigravity program.

Tests ordered by LeMay were conclusive: Just flying alongside missiles and unloading a few hundred rounds from a 30-millimeter cannon was all it would take to neutralize nukes. Or, better yet, hover over a missile silo and barrage it with electromagnetic pulses to overwhelm the controls.

The weapons people were testing both options by 1967, inducing terror in the hearts and minds of military personnel on both sides of the Cold War. Missile silo operators at U.S. and Soviet bases reported UFO encounters that temporarily shut them down.

On other occasions, Air Force and Army engineers reviewing films of missile tests were surprised to see flying saucers shadowing their rockets and shooting what appeared to be a ray gun. The "ray gun" was actually a high-intensity strobe lamp flashing rapidly to simulate cannon fire. Sometimes word leaked out to the press, fueling speculation of alien visitation and interstellar intrigue. All films were sent to the Pentagon and studied by project leaders. Analyses confirmed that flying saucers were the only effective defensive weapon against ICBMs.

This sort of testing represented a dramatic development: The big brains in charge of antigravity realized the best way to evaluate their new weapon was in the real world. Cribbing a page from Truman's playbook, they'd fly over cities and near military bases in America and Europe and then watch the fireworks. The idea was to pit antigravity vehicles against first-class air defenses and radar systems.

America was fine-tuning the ultimate weapon, and the program got a big boost during the Reagan years, when the black budget tripled. A mysterious line item labeled "Aurora" went from eighty million dollars in 1986 to more than two billion the next year.

Back-channel scuttlebutt alleged Aurora had experimental scramjet engines, designed to provide the thrusting power of rockets while scooping air from the atmosphere like a jet turbine. The scuttlebutt was a smokescreen. Sure, the Aurora actually did exist, but only as a superficial testbed to divert attention away from field propulsion; a cover story to confuse journalists and the aviation community while most of the money was routed to the antigravity program.

Reagan never knew the particulars, yet under his watch exploring the solar system and traveling to the stars became practical pursuits. Vehicles equipped with the new hyperdrive could skip through space with instantaneous acceleration, leaping from point to point like a kid hops boulders in a creek.

Instead of months to reach Mars, it now took only hours, and excursions to the nearest stars but a few weeks.

Astonishing developments by any measure.

CHAPTER 12

Tommy Swift led the "Belgium Campaign" of 1989-1990, taking orders directly from the admiral in charge of the fleet. The mission was designed to see just how well the antigravity vehicles could dominate a first-class air force. The results were spectacular: Big Black Delta ruled the skies over Belgium for cumulative hours, easily outperforming F-16s scrambled from Beauvechain Air Base.

Captain Swift coordinated the series of simulated "attacks," which climaxed in March 1990 southeast of Brussels. BBD assumed a staging position at an altitude of a few thousand feet, releasing two interceptors. For the next four hours they darted about, terrifying the public and taunting the air force.

The operation netted a profusion of data for the Americans, revealing key tactical details, exposing air-defense weaknesses and showing exactly how successful the raid had been. Every time the F-16s tried to lock their radars onto the intruders, the UFOs pulled maneuvers that would have rendered any jet pilot unconscious, instantaneously flitting from place to place.

The Belgians tracked the interlopers, took photographs, compiled several thousand eyewitness accounts and reams of technical information. Belgian media interviewed top air force officials, who publically admitting they were at a loss to explain the phenomenon. Military and government leaders dismissed any possibility of U.S. involvement, telling reporters they would be more inclined to suspect an extraterrestrial origin. Afterward, the nation's air force released a comprehensive report chronicling the events of the night.

The Americans requested a copy.

ଔଔଔଔ

Later in the same decade Captain Swift skippered BBD during the Arizona campaign. Big Black Delta's primary role would be to carry out the opening phase of a mock military incursion, surveying the hypothetical battlefield for high-priority targets.

A critical mission objective was to evade detection while penetrating military and commercial airspace over a large metropolitan area. Commander Swift brought her in from the north, gliding low over Nevada, then into northern Arizona and south to Phoenix.

The ship's reconnaissance run would be followed by a bomb-training mission two hours later. Four A-10 warthog ground-attack aircraft would fly over the Barry M. Goldwater Range southwest of the city and drop illumination flares. The warthog pilots were entirely unaware of Big Black Delta and her mission that night: They didn't have a need to know, but their flares would provide the perfect diversion, after the fact.

The invasion unfolded quietly around 8 p.m. Tommy Swift's reconnaissance footprint skirted Nellis Air Force

Base north of Vegas and later Luke Air Force Base near Phoenix, cruising at low altitude over major population centers along the way.

Running with no lights in stealth-recon mode, the ship melded into the cloudless night sky of the desert Southwest. Several hundred people did happen to look upward and were startled at the sight. BBD, however, attracted no attention from the military, its crew collecting strategic data that would have proved crucial in neutralizing the enemy's air and ground defenses. This information included the precision coordinates of radar sites, airports and military runways, power plants, vital bridges and thoroughfares and communications towers.

The whole thing took less time than a round of golf. Then, a couple of hours later came the warthogs' routine exercise over the desert bombing range near Phoenix. The bright flares descended in a wide arc, illuminating dummy targets below, a gaudy spectacle observed by thousands of people. Citizens excitedly shot amateur video and pictures of what appeared to be the outline of a giant starship hovering over the city.

Big Black Delta's appearance was timed perfectly to befuddle the public. While a small number of reliable sources, including the state's governor, witnessed the huge ship slinking over the city, the vast majority had instead seen the dramatic display of flares. The scant number of eyewitnesses to BBD's incursion would be overshadowed by the multitude reporting the flares, complicating the interpretation of events.

By any measure the mission was a success. The military tested Big Black Delta's indisputable air superiority, and the public remained thoroughly confused.

ↈↈↈↈ

Arizona was reminiscent of Big Black Delta's earliest foray into the living lab. Back when Tommy Swift was in high school flying Cessnas his predecessors executed BBD's first stealth-recon drill over the Hudson River Valley, 25 miles north of New York City.

The ship's maiden mission in 1983 provided unambiguous proof of just how effective it could be. For the next three years BBD mesmerized roughly five thousand witnesses to her magnificent mastery of the skies over the Hudson Valley and vicinity.

Onlookers marveled at the ship's stealthy silence. Many observers said they wouldn't even have noticed BBD if not for her bright strobes. Witnesses who would have been deemed respectable in any court of law -- doctors, cops, executives -- watched it loitering over the skies of New York, Connecticut, New Jersey and Massachusetts. Traffic came screeching to a halt on Interstate 84 and the Taconic Parkway. Police officers stood in awe.

"I couldn't believe there was no noise whatsoever," one cop told local TV news. "I wasn't scared. There was no time to be scared. It was just there and gone."

And, people said, the thing seemed to hang ever so close to the ground.

"I think I could have hit it with a rock," remarked an electronics engineer who spotted the object while fiddling with his car radio, which had inexplicably gone dead. "I pulled off the road to get a better look. A couple of other drivers did the same. I said to one guy, 'Wow, what the hell is that thing?' But he just gawked at it. He never did answer me. I'll tell you one thing, though: It was not of this world."

CHAPTER 13

Lev Levine double-parked his Ford Crown Victoria outside Samuel Barr's brownstone at 8:15 in the morning. Barr had been waiting patiently in his sitting room for half an hour. Upon seeing his driver pull up, he stood and waved to Levine.

A man of considerable size, the driver hustled out of his car to assist Barr. Levine operated a private taxi service, and he did modestly well by concentrating on only a handful of well-to-do, mostly elderly or otherwise mobility-compromised New Yorkers.

He was a laconic man whose Israeli past was a bit murky. Whatever he did was bad enough that he couldn't return to his homeland. Maybe he worked for the Mossad. Maybe he knew too much, or killed the wrong person, or had too many wives. Maybe he could deftly extinguish a human life using only his thumbs.

At some point he married an American and gained citizenship. Now, the American wife was long gone. Levine was a difficult man to live with.

Barr's failing vision had become a driving hazard, and he was too frail for mass transit, so he began using Levine's service a couple of years ago. It was a bumpy twenty-minute ride in the Crown Vic from his house on the Upper West Side to the midtown office of Thompson's Defense Weekly.

But Levine was more than a driver. When it rained or snowed, he helped his fare walk to and from the car. And if there was some critical need of transport he could usually be counted on at all times of day. Perhaps most importantly, he listened to stories. He commiserated. He offered support, in his oddly cautious way.

He became an acquaintance, sharing stingy but telling snippets of his own life, narrated in a strong Israeli accent. He was twice divorced. He had a grownup daughter in Israel somewhere. He had served in the military and knew martial arts, which he referred to as "just dirty fighting."

He was a staunch capitalist.

He wasn't merely a driver. That was only what he did to pay the bills. He was a man of ideas. Ideas bordering on schemes, most of them having something to do with private security, his true passion.

He was an opportunist, a confidant, a makeshift bodyguard.

It might be true that just under the surface something violent lurked, a spring-loaded menace waiting to be unleashed.

But he was not, ultimately, a bad man.

ᏩᏩᏩᏩ

Barr hadn't left the city in years, and he was not happy about doing so now, but the sense of urgency in Glenn Moore's pleading phone call made the trip unavoidable. He'd known Moore since the war. The well-bred descendant of paternal aviation genius, Moore had been instrumental in developing fighters and bombers that helped defeat the Axis powers. He was an American hero who personally flight-tested nearly every type of aircraft manufactured by his company.

Thompson's Defense Weekly had published many flattering articles about Moore; his proud family tree of engineers and mathematicians, his Scottish lineage, his aeronautical excellence and Stanford University credentials. Ever since, the two men had been on a first-name basis.

Moore led efforts in 1946 to form the Strategic Research and Development Group, later renamed STRAND, with his old war buddy General Curtis LeMay. Barr was on the frontlines of aviation writing back then, and he wrote extensively about STRAND, a think tank that gathered mountains of information about military technology for the feds.

Later, during the '60s, '70s, and '80s, Barr wrote about Moore's involvement in spy planes and stealth. Then came retirement and personal tragedies: a son was killed in an Air Force training exercise. Then, his wife, a recovering alcoholic, committed suicide, and Moore dropped out of sight. Barr hadn't heard anything from Glenn Moore in many years, until the day he called Thompson's ranting something about "the most important issue of our time," and, "a matter of the utmost national significance," and, finally, "the biggest story you will ever have."

And this from a man who was not given to superlatives, but it was all too sensitive to divulge over the phone, he said.

Barr feared senility had overtaken his old friend. Aging sometimes has a tendency to magnify one's ego. Perhaps, having many years in retirement, memories of his life's accomplishments had percolated and then boiled over to the point where he'd lost all perspective.

Nevertheless, Barr owed him a personal visit at the very least, so he booked Lev Levine's services for an entire day: It was a three-hour drive to Albany. Their journey would take them initially along the Taconic State Parkway, the same scenic road where BBD wowed the citizenry a decade earlier during her three-year-long series of living-lab operations.

Barr asked his driver to turn on the classical-music radio station. Then he promptly fell asleep on the backseat, reclining awkwardly, snoring amid the dulcet tones of Bach and Beethoven and the new-car-scented air freshener Levine used to mask the Crown Vic's musty interior.

They sped past the pines and willows of upstate New York, a serene natural theater, and he awoke somewhere outside of Kingston, cued by Levine.

"Mista Baah, Mista Baah, the exit."

Rolling up to the gate of Moore's estate, Levine pushed the intercom button to announce their arrival. No one responded, but a few seconds later the gate's electric mechanism sprang into action.

Driving up the circular driveway, the two men were impressed by the classic colonial-style house and accompanying barn. A slow-moving Moore emerged from the front door, walking with a cane.

"Give me a few hours, will ya Lev?" said Barr, struggling to extract his ancient little body from the Crown Vic's cavernous cabin.

He declined Levine's offer for assistance: Barr hated to look feeble in the eyes of old acquaintances. It was okay around strangers, but not in the company of people who had known him as a far younger, more capable man. He told Levine to cool his heels in town for a while.

Barr had assumed Moore's intention was to provide his final reflections on a brilliant career; the kind of stuff that made for great columns or feature writing, a sort of proactive obituary.

He couldn't have been more mistaken.

Moore stood in the open threshold. He held his cane in one hand and rolled a small cart containing an oxygen cylinder with the other. Plastic tubes extended from the tank, hooked behind his ears and fed oxygen into his nostrils via little prongs.

The two old men sat down at a long table in Moore's library. The large room occupied much of the home's first floor and was lined with built-in bookshelves from floor to ceiling.

"You probably wondered why I called you up here in such haste, and I do apologize, by the way," Moore said, the oxygen cannula issuing a subliminal hiss.

The room was utterly quiet except for the breathing apparatus, and the air had a pleasant aroma of ink and old book bindings.

"I am not well. In fact, I might have a year, the doctors say. As a result, I find myself quite desperate."

"Well, I, now I understand," Barr said awkwardly.

"No, I don't think you do," said Moore. He was distracted for a moment as he checked a gauge on his oxygen tank and adjusted a valve.

"Technology: can't live without it," he joked.

"Ah, where to begin? I guess the only thing that keeps me from going public is my family, but after I'm gone, what can they do?"

"They?" asked Barr.

"You have no idea, do you? I mean, you people in the media."

Barr fumbled to answer his borderline-rude host.

"Please take no offense," Moore said, disarming Barr's pique. "You are no hack, my friend. I suppose I would behave the same way if I were in your shoes. But that is neither here nor there. What we now have before us is a grave injustice."

Moore slid a stack of papers across the table.

"This summarizes the situation. It includes official photographs and schematics. Basically, we have been lying to you for a long, long time."

The pile of papers was topped with a black-and-white, eight-by-ten glossy of a flying saucer parked just outside of an open hangar. A classic F-86 fighter jet could be seen in the background, sporting an unmistakable U.S. Air Force roundel insignia.

Barr's eyes opened wide, and his facial expression betrayed a glimmer of confused skepticism.

"Glenn, what?" he said. "Flying saucers are real?"

"Sammy, what I have to tell you goes so far beyond flying saucers, at this point. It all started right after the war," Moore said with labored breathing. "General LeMay was heading up R&D, and that's when we started STRAND. We were doing what we thought was best for the country. And it was, initially. I was one of the naïve ones. Thought we'd be mass-producing flying saucers by 1960. And I hinted as much to you, if you recall. I still have the article you wrote. What was it, 1956, I think."

"Oh, yes, the so-called gravity engines," Barr said. "I do remember. But then, nothing ever became of it."

"We started STRAND to fast-track field propulsion because we thought the Soviets were doing likewise. But it wasn't true. The Russians never had it. We were pretty sure about that by the '70s. Still, secrecy was more than justified because of the geopolitics of the day. But then game glasnost and perestroika, the wall coming down. It's time."

Moore stopped talking, and the room was as quiet as a tomb, save for the old man's oxygen equipment.

"Time for what?" Barr asked.

"Nearly all military brass, the president of the United States, virtually all members of Congress. They don't have a need to know. The people we entrust with the nation's future, the policy makers, the economic brains, the long-term strategists, are all ignorant of the most profound technological development in human history. More significant than nuclear power and the bomb."

Barr was speechless. He'd thought all those rumors of flying saucers had been dispelled long ago.

"Glenn, are you going to blow the whistle? Is that why you called me here? To blow the whistle on flying saucers?"

"It's not that simple. It's just not that simple, Sammy."

"Well then, what?"

"You work for a big outfit. I mean, it's not the New York Times, but it's got some cachet, some credibility and respect."

"Yes, this is true. But to make a big splash, to really bust this open, you need to hit the bigs: the Times, the Washington Post. You know, the Capital Gang."

"Sammy, don't you think I've been trying. I've approached them all, and no one will listen. Oh, sure, I came close. Some guy at the Times seemed really interested.

Right up until the time his editor told him the Old Gray Lady doesn't publish articles about flying saucers, period. I tried some other places, but I couldn't even get past the front door. I believe you media people call it the palace guard. I started trying the news magazines. Hell, even The New Yorker, if you can believe that. Everyone thinks I'm a kook."

"So, I'm your last resort."

"Sammy, I've got to get this off my chest if it's the last thing I do. And now it looks to be just that. I mean, I've got it all laid out for you, the whole timeline going back to 1946. Like I said, we were doing the right thing. Extraordinary steps were justified at that time. To protect the country, I mean."

For the better part of the next hour Moore lectured Barr nonstop about the history of antigravity. How LeMay, the celebrated World War II hero who'd bombed the Germans and Japanese into submission, recommended that an independent military unit be established just for the saucer project. That the secret of antigravity must be maintained at all cost, requiring steps even greater than those adopted for the Manhattan Project.

He dwelled for a time on LeMay, and how the general received just about everything he sought. It was, after all, only a year after the war, and he'd been perhaps its most ardent champion, a fearless pilot and bombardier, a ruthless gladiator. Now, in the afterglow of his many military triumphs, he was at his flourishing best.

The general had an uncanny knack for simplifying complex problems, a talent that would serve him well during these times. The Air Force was moving into uncharted territory, a complex future of jets, missiles, rockets and satellites. Before the war, it had all been the stuff of Buck Rogers, but not anymore.

Moore told of how he and the general worked out of the Pentagon, initially heading a fledgling think tank of technology and policy wonks, forming a blueprint for how to deal with this quantum leap in military weaponry; the guidelines and recommendations, logistical parameters and restrictions and a research timetable.

Moore continued the narrative, recounting how he and LeMay were powerful and influential forces in their respective professional circles and riding steep career ascendancies. LeMay would later guide efforts to protect Europe from the Soviet menace and lead the Strategic Air Command. Moore would control one of the most successful military contractors in history, building sophisticated spy planes and pioneering stealth technology.

He explained how LeMay was obsessed with the threat of communism. He had no confidence in arms-control efforts, and, as SAC commander was constantly monitoring the Russians, following their every military movement, probing their capabilities near the sensitive European boundaries and using any tools at his disposal. Spy planes and bombers flew regularly into Soviet territories. And by the time LeMay left SAC in 1957, the new field propulsion technology was being pressed into service in reconnaissance missions.

That's when UFO reports started to spike. Flying saucers were no longer entirely experimental. They were becoming operational, albeit only for very specific roles: snooping on Mother Russia and other Cold War adversaries.

Moore schooled Barr about the whole secret history of flying saucers, Barr sipping tea, Moore sipping oxygen in the friendly confines of the wood-paneled library. He described how Defense Secretary Robert McNamara and LeMay became the oddest of bedfellows, the gifted intellectual and the cigar-chomping hawk. McNamara was convinced that the way to enhance American security was to vigorously exploit U.S. technological advantages, but in a manner that would not threaten the stability of deterrence. Translation: There must be no publicly disclosed antiballistic missile system. Either side possessing such a system could dangerously compromise the delicate U.S.-Soviet nuclear deterrence imposed under the doctrine of mutual assured destruction.

Any attempt to install systems to shoot down Russian missiles would result in a self-perpetuating tit-for-tat strategic tug of war between the two superpowers, an endless series of measures and countermeasures, of antiballistic systems, then anti-anti-ballistic missile systems, and so on.

LeMay despised McNamara and his liberal sentiments, and he couldn't care less about diplomacy. However, field propulsion represented common ground for LeMay and McNamara, a secret dual-use platform offering both antiballistic and first-strike capabilities. These new strategic possibilities effectively strengthened previous restrictions laid down by Vannevar Bush: The ban on commercializing antigravity wouldn't be lifted anytime soon.

This was something that didn't sit well with Moore, and he looked forward to the day when flying saucers would burst onto the aviation scene. Then he'd be well-positioned to shepherd commercialization and large-scale manufacturing.

He watched and waited, but that day never came.

Decades had passed, all of the principals were gone and the Soviet Union dissolved, but still no flying saucers. Meanwhile, Moore quietly kept his own private archive on field propulsion locked away in his library. The sixteen-millimeter films, the laboratory notes, photographs and official classified memos.

"I've always fantasized about spilling the beans, but just never had the stones," he now confided. "I guess, the thing is, you always think you have more time than you do."

"Glenn, if this is true, it changes everything. The ramifications are global, huge economic implications. We're talking space mining, colonization, militarization. The whole ball of wax, virtually every economic sector dramatically impacted. Nothing would be the same. Our entire culture would be shocked into a new reality."

"Yes, but I can't get anyone to listen," groused Moore. "No one who is anyone, at least."

"Tell me what you want me to do," Barr said. "Ah, but I have only my column, and an old man scribbling about UFOs will be interpreted as a sign of senility, I fear."

"Well, how about your staff? There's gotta be someone."

Barr made a mental survey of the newsroom. Thompson's had barely twenty writers and a dozen editors. It was, after all, a specialized weekly publication. Not some high-powered daily operation.

He thought about the stable of editors handling Washington, the Middle East and Africa, Europe and Asia. The Columbia Journalism Review crowd, the reporters covering various beats: naval warfare, land forces, defense-contract analysis, satellites and space research. Several had come from daily newspapering and wire services, covering business, market and labor issues, Congress and regulatory agencies. Some had impressive awards and credentials, a Harvard degree here, a top aerospace-journalism award there. Then there were those with military backgrounds: pilots and technical experts who'd made the unorthodox jump to journalism.

It was largely an old-boys' club.

Barr thought out loud: "We need someone who isn't in the club, someone unconventional, I think."

"What's that you say, Sammy? Oh, by the way, there is one thing I should mention. Some Brit's been banging on doors lately. Says he's writing a book about antigravity secrets, but I sure don't trust him."

"Well, who is he?" said Barr.

"Like I said, a Brit who says he's writing a book. I'm not gonna trust just some guy writing a book. I want a journalist, a real journalist, with credentials, and backed by a professional organization."

Moore produced Marsden's business card and showed it to Barr.

"Let me check on Robert Marsden, find out if we've written about him, find out if any of our people have heard of him," Barr said. "Who knows? Maybe we'll be able to use this guy to our advantage."

Moore was heartened by the phrase "our advantage," as if he now had an ally in his lonely crusade to out the U.S. military on field propulsion.

"Give me a few days," Barr said to Moore as the two wound up their meeting.

He ruminated on the whole confounding conundrum. Flying saucers. The military-industrial complex. Moore's rapidly declining health. Barr had been shaken by the revelations from Moore, the most unimpeachable of sources. A poster child for patriotism, capitalism and all of the other isms that defined apple-pie America. Had he gone off his rocker? Not likely.

On the ride back to the city, Barr popped half an OxyContin to dull the pain of rampant arthritis. He dozed sporadically, at times failing to discern the difference between fact and fantasy, dream and reality.

And Lev Levine played the radio with the volume turned way down.

ଓଓଓଓ

The next day Barr visited the magazine's archives, otherwise known as the morgue. The room held endless rows of tomb-like filing cabinets containing numerous, narrow drawers specially designed for news clippings.

The articles, uniformly folded and labeled, dated and stamped to specification, were filed under the source and subject. The archivist, Kendall, was an untidy, bookish man who enjoyed talking about politics, philosophy, the virtues of anarchy, and, above all, his attractive Filipino wife. Her photos graced his workspace. Kimmy gardening. Kimmy behind the wheel of the couple's old Volvo. Kimmy in a bathing suit at Jones Beach.

Women coworkers shied away from the archivist. He had, they said, a propensity to often "adjust" himself. It was probably just a nervous habit, not anything sexual or perverse. Still, it was an odd behavior. The kind of thing people tried to ignore.

Despite his disheveled weirdness, though, he was a very thorough librarian.

"Got anything on a guy named Marsden, Robert Marsden?" said Barr.

The archivist was sitting behind a timeworn battleship-gray metal desk, leaning as far back as his creaky office chair would tolerate, hands behind his head. It was an unflattering pose that both accentuated his flabby midsection and his shirt's yellow-stained underarms, indelibly acquired over many years of bad laundering.

Ordinarily the archivist would encourage people to search for themselves, but he always made special allowances for Mr. Barr.

"Marsden, you say? I don't know, let's have a look."

He found the "Ma" drawer and thumbed through the many articles stored there until settling on a very small clipping for "Marsden, Robert."

"Well, son of a gun, there is something here, and by our very own staff writer Jane Hale."

The archivist handed Barr the news brief Jane had written about Marsden's eerie UFO sighting in the North Sea.

Barr barely knew Jane. Although her desk was just beyond whispering distance, his part-time status as columnist emeritus provided limited opportunities to mingle. Nevertheless, the few interactions he'd had with her were very favorable, particularly the times she patiently provided guidance on the latest office technologies that were anathema to the manual-typewriter set: navigating email, opening attachments or operating that confounding new photocopying machine.

Now he read the short clip with great interest, bordering on glee at his lucky find. Sitting at his workstation, reviewing the news brief about Marsden, his eyes wandered in Jane Hale's direction as she pecked furiously at her keyboard on some deadline assignment. He wondered how receptive she might be.

She looked up once or twice from her keyboard, as though feeling his gaze.

Later that day Barr called Moore to tell of his discovery and suggested that a meeting be arranged.

"Sammy, let me think about this for a day or two. I want to approach it the right way. Systematically, if you know what I mean."

Moore contemplated the situation in the quiet solitude of his library, and a loose plan began to materialize in his mind. It was a cunning plot that would hinge on anonymity, exploiting Jane and Marsden as complementary pawns.

Jane, he reasoned, would be less likely to ignore the flying saucer story if goaded on by Marsden, whose book stood to benefit in a big way by new revelations contained in the evidence she would come to possess.

Barr was taken aback when told of Moore's deceptive modus operandi.

"Jeez, Glenn, why not just go public right now? I don't like all this conniving crap. It's a little too manipulative for my blood."

"This is just how I have to do it, Sammy. First, test the waters. Then, if your Jane Hale is game, and if this Marsden character turns out to be the real deal, I will come out completely. Expose everyone, my friends, name names."

Barr grudgingly complied, but he didn't like it. After all, he knew Thompson's editors weren't ever going to publish an article about antigravity without at least one solid on-the-record source. The elderly columnist privately decided to step in if things got out of hand, if Moore failed to fully identify himself in a timely manner, if his colleague's good name was ever in jeopardy.

So he stood by as Moore set his duplicitous scheme in motion, the mysterious night caller confiding in Jane while simultaneously alerting Marsden about her involvement. Moore would lead Marsden to Jane in a cryptic letter, suggesting that she might be working on a story about field propulsion.

Barr cautioned Moore that it was unclear whether Thompson's would risk its credibility to wade into the morass of government conspiracy. However, it was a chance worth taking, they both agreed. If it worked, an article in Thompson's would lend a modicum of legitimacy to the whole flying saucer story.

So, one day at noon while the newsroom was largely vacant, Barr placed an envelope on Jane Hale's desk.

CHAPTER 14

The police detective thought autoerotic asphyxiation was usually a young man's game, but anything was possible these days, he surmised. Marsden's body was found on the bed in his hotel room, necktie anchored to a bedpost and knotted around the deceased man's throat. He was naked, and pornographic material festooned the bed.

It had all the hallmarks of that sexually deviant art: depriving the brain of oxygen while simultaneously masturbating, thereby intensifying orgasm. Medical science didn't know why it worked, but men the world over had dabbled in the practice. Sometimes they got carried away, applying slightly too many pounds of pressure and collapsing the carotid artery, inducing unconsciousness within seconds.

The official coroner's report would read "accidental fatality." Barbiturates were found in the man's system, but this was explained by the vial of prescription sleeping pills on the bedside table. Investigators ruled out suicide or foul play: case closed.

The coroner's conclusion, however, was wrong.

Earlier that day Marsden had endured a harrowing in-your-face conference with his editor, during which he dropped the bombshell about "unexpectedly obtaining" the flying saucer film footage. Marsden insisted the smoking-gun evidence merited the addition of a whole new chapter, one that dramatically strengthened the entire premise of the book. His editor was mortified by the news. The publisher, however, granted Marsden's request for a deadline extension, but not before some lecturing and metaphorical finger waggling.

He returned to his hotel shortly before five o'clock, beleaguered and weary. Marsden took off his shoes and massaged his feet. He was famished, but going down to the hotel restaurant was out of the question. He picked up the phone on the nightstand and called room service, ordering the special. Forty minutes later, as a hotel attendant rolled the dinner tray out of the elevator, he was approached by two men in suits.

"Hello, son. I'm Carlos and this is Ray," said one of the men, betraying a slight Honduran accent. "We're old personal friends of Mr. Marsden, and we'd just like to play a little practical joke on him. You see, it's been a long time since we've seen each other. And, well, would you mind if we delivered this to him?"

As the attendant began to protest, one of the men stuck a hundred dollar bill in his shirt pocket. These suits weren't taking no for an answer. They handled the kid like a couple of wise guys.

The operatives had been shadowing Marsden since his arrival in the United States. They had bugged most of his conversations with Jane, covertly invading their lives. They wired Jane's apartment and Marsden's hotel room with various audio and video devices and gingerly perused their personal belongings, recording any and all details that might be useful in their mission. They became quite familiar with the intimate nuances, the precise patterns and movements and liaisons of their quarry.

They were professionals.

Carlos had learned his trade during the Contra war, when the CIA came to his native Honduras, hat in hand seeking recruits for Ronald Reagan's anti-communist crusades in Central America. The Hondurans were essential for logistical support and infrastructure in the CIA's covert operations to bolster the Contras, or counter-revolutionaries, assembled to fight Nicaragua's Sandinista government

He trained at the U.S. Army School of the Americas at Fort Benning, Georgia, a specialized academy for Latin Americans doing the Pentagon's dirty work in the region. Carlos was among the most elite of the CIA's "unilaterally controlled Latino assets," expert in sabotage, explosives, and the heartless anatomy of mayhem. He was not averse to the most brutal, lethal and demoralizing tactics: destroying schools, clinics, cooperative farms and child-care centers; tormenting peasants in the pristine Nicaraguan forest, the air smelling of cold mountain springs and gun smoke.

It was all justified, in his mind, so long as the communists were uprooted. Besides, the professional benefits were significant: a whole new career path. Carlos first rubbed elbows with Oliver North while mining Nicaraguan harbors for the CIA. He and Ollie, a National Security Council staff member and ex-marine, became fast friends during their various raids and exploits.

At some point word leaked of the whole CIA-harbor-mining business and other bad behavior. The newspapers learned that money from U.S. arms sales to Iran evidently had been diverted to fund the Contras, engendering additional negative press that led to the cutoff of military funds to the rebel force. By then, however, young Carlos had made powerful friends and was well on his way toward U.S. citizenship: It was hard to find immigrants with his skill set, a virtual Ph.D. in the arts of torture, extortion, asphyxiation and the like.

Ray was equally credentialed.

He'd been a Navy SEAL, and, like Carlos, profited from Ronald Reagan's hyperkinetic anti-communist agenda of the 1980s. The son of a cash register repairman whose pride and joy was a full-dress Harley, he grew up amid the nurturing aura of motor oil and WD-40 and dad's constant abuse. The old man was an imposing guy who wore his obesity with pride and was always cursing over some mechanical task in the garage, threatening harm to his children, wrench in hand, if they happened to get in his way.

This paternal model Ray took to heart, brutalizing his own way through life. First, as a kid who incessantly picked fights, spouted anti-Semitic nonsense and found comfort in the suffering of others. Then, as a star defensive lineman in high school football, where his only true objective was the infliction of pain, regardless of who won or lost.

This also seemed to be his rule with women.

"I'll tell you what, nobody ever hurt that bitch as much as me," he proudly asserted after a particular breakup.

He went straight from high school into the military, where he excelled in close-contact killing, finding his niche with the SEALS.

For others in his line of work, liquidation was a necessary but unpleasant end. But not to Ray. He derived some sort of voyeuristic stimulus from it: a quickening of the pulse, a heightening of the senses, a hard-on. To him, it was pure sport.

He'd been snuffing communists, Marxists and other people deemed dangerous since the early 1980s, thwarting the Soviets at every turn with his buddies from SEAL Team Six. By the end of the Reagan era, Ray had terminated hundreds of people and fine-tuned his craft; a grim catalog of deadly tools and tactics.

So much so that others took notice of his resume.

The CIA would draw young talent from the special forces, like a farm system of pernicious players, and Ray was recruited by the agency for an elite assassination squad. It was the perfect environment within which to channel his infinite wellspring of violence; a serial killer on the government payroll. Now he had truly found himself.

There had been way too much humanity in the SEALS for his blood; too many good eggs. Presently, there was no humanity, and this he enjoyed immensely. Once he even offed an American; some asshole who knew too much and was determined to use it.

Officially, Carlos and Ray were "civilian contractors." The Pentagon budget entry was always tricky, though. Some apparatchik once listed them as "window washers." The name stuck, and now they were routinely referred to by their line item, which usually tallied six figures per assignment. After all, window washing might seem simple enough to the casual observer, but it was not. It required ropes and pulleys and a great deal of expertise and planning. Otherwise, disastrous things could happen. It was a job that was best not left to amateurs.

Sending the room service attendant on his way, the men wheeled the dining cart into their own room, also on the same floor, where they spiked Marsden's iced tea and mashed potatoes with a barbiturate. One of the agents changed into an official-looking hotel uniform and delivered the cart to Marsden's room.

About an hour later Marsden had passed out from the drugged dinner. Carlos and Ray entered the room, one of the men toting a small suitcase, and strangled the sedated Marsden with his own necktie. He never put up a struggle. Indeed, until his last few heartbeats Marsden wasn't even vaguely aware of being strangled. He awoke, gazed up at his assailants with a surprised expression, reaching out with both hands like a blind man flailing, groping.

Afterward, the men carried on light conversation as they stripped Marsden. Chatting about their lives on a most superficial level: what they did over the weekend, girlfriends, the weather, plans for the evening. One of them plopped their little suitcase on the bed, opened it and removed several porno magazines, which he splayed artfully near the corpse. The other man pulled a medication vial out of the suitcase and placed it neatly on the night table. The drug vial was labeled with an expertly forged prescription for sleep medication listing Marsden as the patient and some pharmacy in London.

Finally, the coup de maître. The men used Marsden's own credit card to order a porno movie. The skin flick, complete with raunchy dialogue and bad music, would still be playing on the TV when the dead man was found in this preposterous position.

The honor of discovery would fall to Jane, who had been calling the hotel all afternoon. She'd left a message with the front desk and also voicemails on the room's answering machine.

Jane hated few things more than being wantonly exploited. The very idea burned a little hot spot that persisted annoyingly all day as she tried to go about her business in the newsroom. Like a magnifying glass fixed to a wad of dry kindling. A continuous, caustic itching that intensified as long as Marsden failed to return her calls.

"The coy British fucker's toying with me," she grumbled to herself.

Finally, she decided to pay Marsden a visit before he had a chance to check out of the hotel. Arriving shortly after 6:30, she rang his room from a phone in the lobby. No answer. Jane paced for several minutes, growing more irate with every pass of the plush carpeting. Convinced he had given her the slip, she asked the front-desk clerk.

"We do have Mr. Marsden listed as a guest," the clerk said. "Do you want to leave a message?"

"No, I'll just go up and stick a note on his door," said Jane, outwardly miffed.

She rushed up to the room. A do-not-disturb sign hung on the door handle. This really annoyed Jane. She knocked, but there was no response. Taking a notebook and pen out of her handbag, Jane wrote a terse message to Marsden.

"Robert: Where are you? Call me at home!"

She tore the paper from the notebook and stuck it in the door. Then, just for the heck of it, she tried the door handle, which surprisingly was unlocked. Jane opened the door slightly. She became incensed upon hearing the television set. It now became clear that he was deliberately avoiding her.

She burst into his room, witnessing all at once Marsden's dead naked self sitting on the bed, neck in a makeshift noose, dirty magazines scattered about and a porno movie onscreen.

"Oh, Robert, I'm sorry," she blurted.

But then she saw Marsden's curious state, instinctively covering her mouth to suppress a gasp. At that moment she seemed to remember reading once that asphyxiation causes erections, an anecdotal footnote in the annals of forensic pathology and capital punishment. More than a few men executed by hanging had been found sporting one. This observation has never been supported with peer-reviewed empirical data from research into the biochemistry, neurophysiology and hormonal workings of the human body. No precise cellular or sub-cellular measurements had been made of the tissues involved. No scholarly papers had been published detailing the mechanisms and showing exactly why anoxia inspires male turgidity.

Nevertheless, Jane found she didn't need any scientific proof. The evidence, in all of its prurient splendor, spoke for itself.

His mouth was open, tongue lolling off to the side, one end of the taught necktie tethered to the bedpost and the other end constricting his throat, blue tinged and bruised. And the porno movie playing, the male protagonist encouraging his female costar to perform fellatio.

"Suck it, suck it! Yeah, oooh, suck it baby!"

Incongruous female groans, sounding like they were dubbed in, emanated obscenely from the TV set. The porno dialogue could be heard halfway to the elevator because Jane had left the door wide open. For some inexplicable reason she impulsively reached out and tugged on the necktie, as if trying to free Marsden. His limp head slumped forward, erection bobbing slightly.

Thinking back on it all, Jane couldn't remember exactly why she fled the room, slamming the door behind her. Maybe it was the sheer sensory overload -- both auditory and visual -- Marsden's bizarre post-mortem pose coupled with the embarrassingly crude pornographic voices.

Then, wandering the hallway in a daze, eventually ending up at the front desk and mumbling something to the clerk about a dead guy. She later told the cops only that she had discovered Marsden in his room after he hadn't returned her messages. She didn't say anything specific about their professional relationship. But Jane felt certain there was a connection, and in the days following Marsden's demise she tried to make sense of the death. Notwithstanding the coroner's finding, she strongly suspected homicide.

Something just didn't track.

She became increasingly concerned for her own safety. Often a feeling of being watched. She started scrutinizing the nooks and crannies of her apartment: the hanging pictures, bookshelves, cabinets, closets, furniture.

Two suits on the subway, glancing furtively in her direction. And then, she couldn't be sure, but the same two guys milling around outside the Thompson's Defense Weekly offices.

One day they came calling at her apartment building, the desk clerk mentioned nonchalantly.

"Jane -- Miss Hale," he said. "Two guys were looking for you. They didn't say what it was about. I told them to try this evening."

Her phone also seemed to be tapped, as evidenced, Jane thought, by the clicking sound she kept hearing. Or, had it always made that sound? She picked up the phone and inspected its underside for bugs, as if she had any clue of what to look for.

Then came the knocks on her door at odd hours. She'd peer through the peephole, but no one was ever there.

CHAPTER 15

The uniform patch depicted a flying saucer and a stylized map of the United States, a red star marking the Southwest, home to much of the military's antigravity work. The words "NTO -- A Lifetime of Secrecy" hovered over the top of the images. Underneath was the phrase, "Semper En Obscurus," Latin for Always in the Dark.

Captain Tommy Swift wore the patch proudly on his upper right sleeve, as did every member of his crew, who collectively dreamed up the design. Like the denizens of other super-classified programs, his people coveted some form of artistic expression for their esprit de corps.

It was a curious industry - most of the military's black programs had similar patches, all making veiled reference to their missions. Mysterious, spooky images of demons and space aliens, framed by inscrutable Latin and Greek mottos. Lightning bolts and laser beams were common symbols, along with metaphors for stealth, surveillance, and various instruments of controlled violence.

All for the sake of a zealous, if sophomoric, need to satisfy male-bonding requirements. Bound in a fellowship like none other; interplanetary adventurers fearlessly poised for the next step.

Big Black Delta was parked in orbit around the planet Mars, and Captain Swift barked out an order to ready the ship for "repositioning" to the outer solar system.

Senior Chief Petty Officer Carl Hand configured the hyperdrive to the proper settings. On command, he activated the propulsion system and, just like that, within three hours, the ship was flung at several times the speed of light to the edge of the Oort Cloud.

Then, Swift, exuding an aura of calm confidence, commanded his engineer to begin computing the proper hyperdrive parameters to send the ship to the nearest star system, Alpha Centauri, 4.37 light years -- or roughly twenty-six trillion miles -- from Earth. The third-brightest star in the night sky, a diamond stud in the constellation Centaurus, it was actually three suns orbiting each other.

Astrophysicists thought it possible that this stellar trio might hold earthlike planets in its "habitable zone," that Goldilocks region not too hot or cold for planets to harbor liquid water needed for life to flourish.

Now the U.S. military would learn whether this was true.

It would take twelve and a half days to get there in Big Black Delta, a huge event in the history of human civilization.

America's secret space force had already plumbed the depths of the solar system, begun to establish military outposts and cataloged a number of asteroids thought to harbor valuable mineral deposits. And all while NASA's space shuttle program struggled amid a series of accidents, various controversies and a turbulent political environment. Just as pundits and professors, historians and cynics alike proclaimed the imminent end of the U.S. dominance of space, America was quietly going where no one had gone before.

The NTOs had spied Jupiter's "great red spot" up close, surveyed the erupting volcanoes and ice-covered oceans of Jovian moons. They'd barnstormed arid Martian landscapes, taking detailed film records of eroded channels, the deep Valles Marineris canyons. They'd skimmed the towering Olympus Mons, which dwarfed Mount Everest as the tallest mountain in the solar system.

They'd flown alongside the tiny Martian moons, Phobos and Deimos, shooting high-resolution pictures and taking data in every range of the spectrum. They'd studied the asteroid belt between Mars and Jupiter.

They'd buzzed Saturn's rings and ringlets and used radar to penetrate the hazy atmosphere of its enigmatic moon Titan. They flew past the blue-tinged Neptune and Uranus, with their methane-rich atmospheres, played chicken with asteroids populating the Kuiper belt and studied the still more distant Oort cloud, a miasma of countless comets and other icy objects.

By then they were already one-third the distance to the nearest star.

They would begin reaching farther out, cataloging the stars and planets inhabiting a circular swath of space roughly fifty light years away. First, Alpha Centauri and then a long list of the nearest stars. Others to follow would be Barnard's Star, six light years away in the constellation of Ophiuchus; Wolf 359, less than eight light years away in the constellation Leo; Gliese 581, twenty light years away in Libra; 51 Pegasi, fifty light years distant in Pegasus; and the star Fomalhaut, twenty-five light-years from Earth, in the constellation Piscis Austrinus.

A fleet of three Big Black Deltas had been constructed so far, and they were bona fide starships. Soon they would be taking inventory of a seemingly endless interstellar menagerie of worlds large and small. After harvesting the low-hanging fruit of nearby solar systems, the expeditions would have a virtually unlimited, more distant outland to explore; the galaxy contained two hundred billion stars, each representing a potential solar system, by some estimates about ten percent of which might hold planets capable of supporting life.

But it was all so new, and most NTOs, including flight engineer Hand, hadn't yet warmed up to the experience of hyperdrive. Once the drive was engaged and the ship began its transdimensional journey through the solar system, everything outside went black. No starlight. No Earth. No moon. No planets. The large viewing screen in the control room showed only complete and utter darkness.

All communication technologies went dead, as well. It was like they didn't even exist. A dark zone, inky black and silent, a strange limbo that lasted until the hyperdrive was deactivated.

The computer calculated how long to remain in hyperdrive for any particular destination. Because the ship was traveling outside of the ordinary realm of physical dimensions, Big Black Delta was impervious to virtually any of the usual hazards of deep space travel. Passing right through all species of the corporeal universe - rocky debris, comets, asteroids, noxious star-forming regions of dust-laden clouds, dark energy, supernovae, hot gases and the entire spectrum of dangerous radiation.

Ostensibly, this was a fairly innocuous way to get from point A to point B. Perhaps the only real occupational nuisance was the boredom, which seemed to induce unusual behavior in some cohabitants of Big Black Delta. Or was it something else, something more fundamental than boredom, something more physiological, that made his crew act a little weird?

Swift was vaguely aware that hyperspace did strange things to people even during those three-hour, puddle-jumping jaunts to Mars. He thought he noticed human beings behaving out of character and duly noted these observations in his daily log. Inhibitions melted away. People came out of their shells. Take Senior, for instance. Carl Hand was normally a very reserved fellow, but his hyperspace persona was quite different. He became noticeably more gregarious, almost chatty.

The skipper was no expert, mind you, but he likened the effects to those induced by amphetamines or cocaine: exhilaration, a heightened libido, a tendency toward risk-taking, an enhancement of compulsive or quirky personality traits.

Why? How? Such basic questions would have to be sorted out by the psychologists and neurophysiologists in the decades to come. This was uncharted territory, both literally and also in the psychiatric sense.

Big Black Delta was tracing a really steep learning curve. As far as Swift was concerned, the only way to cope with so many unknowns was to concentrate on one thing:

completing the mission. All other factors were secondary. So what if his people acted a little odd; sanity was a malleable beast.

Pentagon brass, however, couldn't afford to be cavalier when it came to the mental health of these custodians of America's most important military hardware. The few top commanders with knowledge of Big Black Delta were hypersensitive to any possible side effects of hyperspace, be they of mind or body. As a result, Swift and his medical officers were under the strictest orders to record any and all changes of mood and condition.

This meant checkups every few weeks, a rigid regimen of neurocognitive tests and medical monitoring.

NTOs who had completed previous hyperspace missions, the longest lasting several hours while gallivanting to the outer reaches of the solar system, had complained of a sort of "hyperspace hangover." This was not a concrete thing that could be quantified but rather an intangible sensation, a general malaise that translated into a vagueness of thought. You could do your job adequately, but you just didn't feel a hundred percent after returning to regular space.

Program chiefs voiced concern that the effect, if indeed real, might become more substantial, possibly even incapacitating, after lengthier immersions in hyperspace. Privately, however, many officers thought this idea was ridiculous. It was like all those people who feared breaking the sound barrier could be fatal to pilots or detonating the first atomic bomb might ignite the entire global atmosphere and destroy the planet.

Absurd, they said. Nothing's going to happen to the crew.

However, a simple fact remained: No one knew with absolute certainty whether Big Black Delta and her occupants could endure nearly two weeks in the zone. The physicists who'd constructed the hyperspace parameters weren't even sure the ship would emerge at the proper coordinates.

A week into the voyage to Alpha Centauri, Swift's people were a little jittery. The commander himself had personally experienced one minor side effect. He'd been having the most vivid dreams and nightmares of his life. And the lucidity of these episodes, sometimes horrifying, always bizarre, seemed to be intensifying with each day into the journey. Swift had resorted to self-medication, an occasional snort of blended whiskey, which he had secreted to his officer's bunk several missions ago.

If hyperspace was like a drug, then this was a two-week bender.

The long days in black hyperspace and then the long-anticipated countdown to normal space. First the hours. Then the minutes and the seconds. Ten, nine, eight, seven ...

If all went as planned, the starlight would return. Except for one jarring difference: It would appear from a completely new perspective.

The extended period of nothingness made for a lot of downtime for the crew. Plenty of opportunities to play video games, watch movies, exercise in the zero-gravity gym and hang out with their comrades.

And, of course, drill, drill, drill - mantra of an obsessively regimented - if not slightly sadistic, commander. Swift was especially fond of subjecting his people to emergency preparedness exercises, particularly solar-storm drills. The ship was equipped with radiation safe rooms strategically placed on both decks. The safe rooms were small bunkers surrounded by lead-lined walls as a shield against the potentially lethal streams of charged particles emitted by powerful solar flares.

Hyperspace immunized the crew against any danger from the storms. At all other times, however, ships traveling in deep space, far from the magnetic field that envelopes the Earth and protects orbiting spacecraft, were naked to the invisible menace. Sensors were designed to pick up fast-approaching solar storms, sounding an alarm and alerting crew members to move immediately to one of the nearest safe rooms. The radiation-hardened doorway locked automatically from the inside and a red "emergency" light over the threshold indicated that a room was occupied.

Personnel in various departments quickly stashed sensitive electronic hardware in specially shielded containers before retreating to the safe rooms. Officers timed crew members and issued test scores during later briefings.

Truly dangerous solar storms were rare, to be sure. No Big Black Delta had ever encountered one. Nevertheless, ship commanders were ordered to train vigilantly, lest they find themselves crippled far from home.

Swift also kept his crew guessing with other, more prosaic surprises, such as impromptu inspection of quarters, equipment checks and readiness drills that compelled people to regularly brush up on procedure, protocol and the like. Notwithstanding such official business, twelve days in hyperspace still afforded plenty of time for social interaction among the crew.

Swift and Hand had cultivated an easy friendship and often spoke of home, family, mutual likes and dislikes, during these times. The lanky Hand floated over to his skipper, grasping the railings on the wall to guide his slow-motion trajectory.

Swift was strapped in his chair, a loose-leaf binder containing the mission plan on his lap. Its mundane title, "System Survey One," dramatically understated the historic and scientific magnitude of the event. The plan contained astronomical data about their destination and spelled out a general set of instructions, but there could be no detailed itinerary since hardly anything was known about the star system.

Big Black Delta was to follow an organized, methodical approach: first take detailed pictures, video and film footage of the outermost belt of rocky debris, then the outer planets, if any, progressively drawing closer to the center. Spectrographic cameras would be used to learn the composition and temperature of the planets and stars.

Military scientists at the Pentagon would later analyze these images.

The crew was to spend fourteen days on the survey and seek earthlike planets. If any were discovered, Swift was to spend the bulk of the mission collecting data on these bodies. This was strictly an orbital survey. They would not land on any planets, even if alien Earths did appear to harbor a hospitable atmosphere. In the very off chance that intelligent life and a technological culture were found, Swift was to make no contact, under any circumstances, but gather as much data as possible for program chiefs to study.

Everybody understood their instructions and respective roles, alright, but no one had any idea what to expect. They went about their routines, anxiously awaiting the countdown to normal space.

Because the absolute blackness of hyperspace was unnerving, the viewing monitors bolted to the control room walls reverting to a U.S. Department of Defense screen saver - a dissolving slide show of pages from the official Alpha Centauri mission plan interspersed with colorful military images of aircraft, vehicles, high-ranking officials in uniform. An F-15E Strike Eagle flying over the desert. A nuclear aircraft carrier patrolling the Gulf of Sidra. Apache attack helicopters, tanks, amphibious vehicles, generals in full panoply. A fairly jingoistic array.

Swift saw Hand floating in his direction and closed the mission plan binder.

"'How's the ship looking, Carl?"

"All is well, sir. Did a routine systems check at fourteen hundred hours."

Hand stretched out his slender frame, a posture he was wont to assume in zero gravity. He looked like he was performing some sort of half-ass, weightless tai chi. The skinny engineer rotated slowly, like a thin beam as he chatted with Swift, carrying on a conversation in this preposterous arrangement - the skipper belted into his captain's chair and Hand spinning in slow motion overhead, images from the wall monitors reflecting off his eye glasses.

Their dialogs rarely turned to politics, but somehow this time the two began bantering about current events, settling on the latest revelations about Bill Clinton's infidelities.

"Slick Willy - boy oh boy," Hand said. "I sure never voted for him, but it must be embarrassing as hell, what with all the talk about the cum-stained dress and the size of his unit and how he exposed his damn self."

Swift was sitting there, head cocked to one side, as though seriously considering all matters surrounding William Jefferson Clinton. He always appeared to be contemplative, no matter what the discussion. He could have been talking about issues as cerebral as quantum mechanics or as trivial as the World Series. It really didn't matter. He would stroke his chin or right temple, as though applying his significant intellect to the problem. Then he would speak. Very deliberate, very direct.

"Senior, do you even vote? Somehow, you don't strike me as the sort of guy who actively participates in the democratic process."

"Hey, I voted once, I think."

The engineer, turning languidly in the air over Swift, started floating away and had to push himself back toward his skipper using the handholds mounted on the walls.

"Well, I really couldn't care less about Clinton's sordid sex life and perverted exploits," Swift said. "The newspapers sure are making a lot of hay over it, though. Kind of makes you wonder how crazy they'd get if they knew what we were up to."

"Probably have a kanipchen fit or something," Hand said.

Swift thought about the certain media backlash and public outrage that would result from disclosure.

"You know the political ramifications would be pretty profound," he said. "It would be a nightmare for the government and the military. Can you imagine the size and scope of the Congressional investigations? It would be like Watergate on steroids. The condemnation would be wide and deep. And people would just generally go berserk when they found out the policy makers and presidents had been deliberately kept clueless."

Hand listened intently as Swift continued.

"But I'll tell you what: Extreme circumstances call for equally extreme measures. I can't see any reason in the world why the press or the public should have a need to know. Once that cat's out of the bag, antigravity becomes pervasive. That eliminates our biggest military advantage globally. It makes us like a million times more vulnerable. After all, would you want the Ayatollah cruising over your house in a flying saucer?"

"Hey, you're preachin' to the choir," Hand said. "Hell, I don't think Slick Willy's got a need to know."

"In fact," Swift continued, oblivious to Senior's contributions to the conversation and taking on a professorial air true to his Ph.D. education, "it's not historically unprecedented to exclude the ruling elite from military or cultural knowledge. You can go all the way back to the Holy Grail, the Ark of the Covenant. Only high priests were permitted to see it. Not even kings or members of the ruling class were given access. I can see a definite parallel here. Kings are like commanders in chief. And we're like the high priests."

"Hmmm, interesting, sir," Hand said with feigned fascination and a hint of sarcasm.

He had a dubious look on his face as he rotated away from Swift, as if to say, "Ark of the Covenant, high priests -- where does he get this stuff?"

Hand pulled out a harmonica and started playing some haunting melody in triple time, but the captain didn't recognize the tune.

The music emanated from the control room as other crew members frequented the mess hall or recreation room or lay cloistered in their bunks, reading, sleeping or otherwise enjoying a little personal time. There were even a few occasions of hanky-panky.

Given the carnal awkwardness of communal bunking, dalliances played out spontaneously in various places that afforded more privacy. The radiation safe rooms proved more than adequate. Only, during these liaisons the red light over the threshold signified not a hot solar blast engulfing the ship but the torrid sexual passions of crew members. The NTOs established a milestone that would likely remain forever unrecorded in history: the first humans to have sex in space.

Perhaps it was the very angst of hyperspace that brought people together as they sped across the galaxy in search of god knew what.

Meanwhile, deep within the bowels of Big Black Delta engineers watched over the nuclear power plant, which generated hundreds of megawatts of electricity, enough juice to light a small city. The anaerobic power and propulsion systems allowed Big Black Delta to operate in space for months, perhaps even years at a time.

The reactor compartment hummed the inaudible hum of a nuclear chain reaction as neutrons and fission products flew apart at high velocity. The resulting heat was harnessed to produce steam through a tangle of pipes, pumps and valves, ultimately driving turbines to generate electricity.

The ship zipped toward Alpha Centauri, speeding ever closer to the moment of truth, as Big Black Delta's full complement of NTOs watched the progression of time. They keenly observed the monitors in the control room with a mixture of emotions - disbelief, uncertainty, pitched fear - as the countdown to normal space commenced: Ten, nine, eight, seven, six, five, four, three, two, one.

Blackness was instantly replaced by the subtle reflection of starlight emitted by the grainy outer texture of a new solar system, and Senior Hand's jaw dropped wide open.

CHAPTER 16

Big Black Delta's stunned crew remained silent, riveted to the monitors revealing their new venue.

It had been only a few seconds since the countdown hit zero, deactivating the hyperdrive and instantaneously transporting them from the dark zone to the outer fringe of the Alpha Centauri system. An unfamiliar star field suddenly replaced the absolute, trans-dimensional darkness they'd known for nearly two weeks.

Like a conductor prompting a well-trained orchestra, Captain Swift skillfully directed his crew to carry out their specific roles in the system survey. He himself would lead the science team dedicated to operating a bevy of cameras and instruments to measure various characteristics of the system and its planets.

Most immediately, the wide-field camera would be pressed into service to get a big picture of the system and determine whether it had any planets, specifically any rocky worlds like Earth. The top priority would be the search for intelligent life, with more esoteric studies of the system's scientific nuances performed during latter visits.

The survey would, however, include a more than cursory inventory of the system. The outer rocky debris, the asteroid belts, the lurking dangers and pitfalls for future spacefarers. Every bona fide planet would be catalogued over the next two weeks and a spectrum of its atmosphere recorded. Big Black Delta's science team would drill down primarily on the two stars at the center of the system, Alpha Centauri A and B, both similar in many ways to Earth's sun. Separated by a few billion kilometers, the stars were locked in a gravitational tug of war.

Astrophysicists tinkering with their "adaptive optics" and advanced mathematical models had theorized that the smaller of the two, CenB, might harbor planets like Earth in the habitable zone. Swift wouldn't need any exotic tools, though, to confirm such fanciful theory. He was going to park in orbit around each planet, one by one, and use plain old garden variety scientific instruments: cameras, spectrometers, radar, ultraviolet and infrared detectors, various remote- and direct-sensing devices.

The whole mission also would be documented with a video record of the control room. Every action of the crew would later be studied for military and research purposes, observations to improve efficiency in subsequent missions. Even psychologists would be involved in the analysis of this first survey of an alien star system.

Nevertheless, by far the most critical part of Survey One would be an investigation of the planets and their moons. This close-up initial study would yield data revealing everything from a planet's chemical fingerprint to its topography. Because Alpha Centauri is about the same age as Earth's solar system, it was thought rocky worlds might harbor life. Perhaps even intelligent life millions of years more evolved than humans.

Captain Swift was familiar with such speculation. What if, for example, the Alpha Centurions had not experienced anything similar to the mass extinction that wiped out the dinosaurs sixty-five million years ago on Earth? Why, they could have begun evolving millions of years earlier than humans. Imagine how far human science could advance in millions of years. Such a thing was unfathomable. On the other hand, what if the most recent mass extinction happened only a few million years ago? The most intelligent creature might be a mollusk.

Briefly, however, Big Black Delta's control room remained absolutely devoid of such musings as crew members indulged themselves in awestruck appreciation of their achievement.

"Alright, people, I think we've had our wow moment -- let's get the program in motion," Swift said.

His voice cut through their temporary reverie.

Power to the instrument pod, a single platform about the size of a school bus, was switched on. Big Black Delta's huge cargo bay door in the ship's underbelly was scrolled open and the platform lowered into the vacuum of space.

Lieutenant Junior Grade Regina Klein put her graduate-level astrophysics training to good use, beginning an elaborate process needed to ready the instruments. Some of the equipment would take several days to be "outgassed," a procedure in which vapors trapped inside instruments are allowed to naturally evacuate into space. Otherwise, these traces could damage sensitive components and interfere with the observations.

Klein deftly worked a control panel, switching toggles, pushing buttons, calibrating gauges, jotting laboratory notes on a clipboard. This sort of monotonous preparation went on for three days, during which Captain Swift and his crew completed last-minute mission-plan adjustments. The survey was on a strict timetable. Once the instruments were up and running, Commander Swift would spend no more than four days gathering data from the ship's position on the outskirts of the system, calculating their safest approach toward CenB.

The science team would initially identify all of the system's major planetary bodies and plot courses for each flyby. Then they would skip through the system, spending no more time than required at each survey point, until the job was completed. Afterward, everything would be stowed for the long hyperspace journey home.

But first the instruments had to be readied. Swift and Klein worked together with Senior Hand's assistance to unpack and assemble, adjust and align, power up and fine tune the assembly of technical hardware that would make possible a data-gathering bonanza, the icing on the cake of what would truly be an unprecedented scientific feat: the first human expedition to another solar system.

At this very moment back on Earth scientists were gathering for a meeting of the American Astronomical Society. They were getting all hot and bothered about new findings that indicated Alpha Centauri might contain one or more Earth-like planets. The press reacted enthusiastically, with thoughtful articles in the New York Times, the Washington Post and various journals and science magazines. The second-tier media, tabloids and TV, reported the usual "we-might-not-be-alone" stories.

Scientists had used complex simulations to arrive at their conclusion; elegant theory that married observation with computational models, painting a picture of how the Alpha Centauri system likely evolved. But it was all, in the end, merely intelligent speculation until supported by hard, empirical information. As it was in the scientific method, hypothesis preceded experimental study. Cosmological theory and experimental verification rarely occurred simultaneously, simply because the stars are so far away.

The scientists at the AAS meeting couldn't have known, but even as they were presenting their findings before skeptical peers, people whose names they would never know were on the verge of either confirming or disproving their theory. About halfway through the weeklong conference, Commander Swift's team finished final preparations to begin the survey. Klein switched on the wide-field camera first, and the instrument immediately sprang to life.

She checked a computer monitor, and, after a few taps of the mouse informed a watchful control room: "We're taking data."

Colleagues cheered, looking at one another in giddy amazement. The crew spent the next four days initially surveying the system from Big Black Delta's perch on the outer fringe. It was critical to first create a fundamental map of the system before devising the survey route. Swift and Klein primarily used one of the instruments, a powerful light telescope, to create the map, locating all of the major planets, the asteroid belts, other rocky bodies and potential hazards.

From this schematic, Swift laid out the ship's itinerary like a cosmic TripTik.

"Ok, people, this is what the neighborhood looks like," he said, flashing a basic diagram of the system on the control room monitors. "Ms. Klein, would you care to educate us further?"

Klein, strapped into her seat behind a computer monitor, spoke into a microphone.

"Well, we've identified several gas giants," she said, using a mouse to position a pointer in the diagram. "Here we have the presence of an asteroid belt. And, over in this region we have four rocky planets. Two of these planets are likely within the habitable zone of Alpha Centauri B. We haven't been able to take good spectrographic data yet on these planets, but we think they're good candidates for liquid water and conditions suitable for life."

Captain Swift took over from Klein.

"Navigator, departure time is four hundred hours. We're gonna be patching in the coordinates in a few. All total, we've got seven stops, and count on twenty-four to thirty-six hours at each location. First on the tour is this sucker, Alpha Centauri Bb -- that's big B little b, the outermost gas giant. And you'll be interested to know it has rings a lot like Saturn's. Then we're just gonna go right down the alphabet, ending at Alpha Centauri Bh. Ms. Klein, prepare to temporarily stow the instrument pod."

One thing Swift left unsaid was obvious to every crew member in the control room: now that potentially habitable planets had been located, this particular survey wouldn't just be laying the groundwork for future research but also for possible human colonization, the beginnings of a galactic migration.

"Navigator, configure hyperdrive for the first survey point and stand by to engage," Swift commanded.

The control room ambiance was pure adrenaline.

"Captain, sir, hyperdrive set and standing by to engage," said the navigator.

"Engage," Swift responded.

Big Black Delta shot into the zone, and two hours later began the final countdown sequence. The ship emerged from hyperspace in a distant orbit around the first gas giant, a gargantuan body roughly three times the mass of Jupiter with a ring system of pastel bands dwarfing Saturn's.

The crew immediately buzzed with activity.

"Ms. Klein, deploy the instrument pod," Swift said excitedly.

An hour later all of the instruments were up and running, and four hours after that it was time to stow the instrument pod and skip to the next survey point.

The days passed, as Swift and his staff grew increasingly mesmerized by what they were seeing. They had traversed most of the system, finding that the gas giants harbored several moons that were planets in their own right. Preliminary information indicated that no less than five of these moons had atmospheres and possessed oceans of liquid hydrocarbons, according to the spectrograph and radar data.

However, all paled in significance to the final destination: the habitable zone and its pair of rocky worlds clinically called Alpha Centauri Bf and Bg.

Again came the commands to stow the instrument pod, configure and engage the hyperdrive. Again came the final countdown sequence. The ship materialized in orbit around the first planet. Audible gasps were heard from crew members as they looked upon blue oceans, wispy tendrils of high cirrus clouds, continents and craggy topography.

Again, the busy commotion in the control room as Klein deployed the instrument pod and Swift frantically typed the latest entry for the ship's log on his computer.

Soon the instruments would be humming along, recording all of the vital statistics of Alpha Centauri Bf. However, nobody needed to look at spectrographs or radar blips to interpret what they were witnessing: This was obviously an oxygen-rich biosphere, with temperate zones and frozen polar regions, forests, deserts, oceans and lakes.

For the first time, Swift would be paying special attention to one particular instrument -- a radio receiver designed for a singular purpose -- the quest for technologically advanced civilizations.

Klein panned the instrument, and they both donned earphones and listened intently, hearing only silence. Then, while making an especially wide arc with the instrument, came a sound.

"Wait, hold it there," Swift shouted.

Klein panned the instrument back, and the sound returned. A faint broadcast could be heard, but it wasn't coming from Alpha Centauri Bf. It was coming from the direction of its twin, a small azure dot barely visible above the airglow of the planet's upper atmosphere.

And, after all of the data were taken and the instrument pod stowed safely in the ship's underbelly, Big Black Delta laid in a course for Alpha Centauri Bg.

CHAPTER 17

Bill Walsh sat behind his desk, a puzzled look on his face, drumming his notepad with a pencil. The eraser tip rapped a nervous, uneven tap, tap, tap, punctuating the awkward silence in the room.

Jane had called the meeting because of her growing angst. She was beginning to fear for her life, and so it was time to confide in her editor, even though doing so represented a professional gamble.

She told the story from the beginning and included all the sordid details: the mysterious phone source; the sixteen-millimeter films and the laboratory documents; Marsden's book, his death. She brought in all of her material evidence, which she masterfully presented like courtroom exhibits. Jane narrated the story with remarkable efficiency, describing the sequence of events that had unfolded over the past few weeks.

Walsh's expression had morphed from confused to comical, dumbfounded to doubtful. He glanced at his wristwatch more than once. A long silence followed the presentation, which had consumed forty-five minutes of his precious time.

"Well, that's quite a yarn," he said. "Is any of it true?"

"It's all true," Jane retorted indignantly.

"Oh, c'mon. It's a scam. Somebody's just having fun with you."

Jane was caught off-guard by her editor's jaded response.

"But what about the film footage, the lab documents, the evidence? Why in the world would someone go to such lengths?"

"First of all," he said, picking up the film case, "I'm sure there are plenty of people with the requisite skills and misguided character to create these cellulosic counterfeits. Remember the alleged alien autopsy footage, what, three-four years ago? It was supposed to be some old film of military doctors cutting up an alien. Turned out to be an elaborate hoax. And so is this."

"But, but …," Jane interjected, growing more apoplectic by the moment. "What about Marsden's killing, the guys in suits harassing me?"

Walsh chuckled derisively.

"Marsden's killing? Don't you mean Marsden's mistake? He died just as the coroner said he did."

Jane put her head in her hands and said nothing while contemplating a defense, but then the one-sided conversation abruptly turned to what her editor described as "recent performance issues."

"Jane, I wonder if your obsession with this story is affecting the quality of your work. I can't think of any time in the past when you've turned in such sloppy copy."

The lyrical "sloppy copy" would reverberate in her mind for days.

"Your draft on the piece about defense department satellites was rife with typos, and you had three different spellings for the last name of one of the sources. How is that possible?"

Jane could clearly hear the ticking of her internal doomsday clock, and it was five minutes to midnight.

Walsh kept right on scolding her, but Jane couldn't tell what he was saying. She simply watched his lips moving, in a state of shock, deafened to her surroundings. Everything moved in slow motion.

Later, in the newsroom, Jane stared vacantly at her computer screen. She had finished the reporting for an assignment but lacked motivation to write it. She usually needed a fire under her ass to generate readable text. And now, in the afterglow of Bill Walsh's devastating criticisms, she needed nothing short of a stiff drink.

And soon.

She felt utterly alone, surrounded by unsympathetic, even hostile, forces. Walsh was standing outside his office, bullshitting with a couple of assistant editors. He said something, and they all glanced over at Jane, whispering.

"Was she crazy or simply inept?" they pondered.

Jane had to get out of there. She looked around for someone, anyone to talk to.

Suddenly, a voice from behind made her jump.

"Jane, excuse me, but I wondered if you might help me."

It was old Samuel Barr, standing on somewhat wobbly legs and looking disheveled. He wore a short-sleeve shirt that hadn't been ironed, a bolo tie with a turquoise clasp and a pair of frayed plaid polyester pants. A gray stubble graced his weathered face.

Barr often sought help when dealing with his own personal demon: cyberspace. This time, he was trying to correspond with a source. He escorted Jane to his desk, walking with a shuffling gait that was the result of a recent spate of mini-strokes. At long last, he reached his desk and fell into his chair, breathing a great sigh of relief and momentarily forgetting why he required Jane's assistance to begin with.

"Sam?" Jane asked him as he sat vacuously for a moment.

"Oh, yes," he said, snapping out of his brief cognitive lapse. "You see, it has to do with those infernal email attachments. I keep asking people not to send them, but this Dr. Becker insists it simply cannot be helped. So, would you be so good as to help me print this document?"

The old man fixed his thick eyeglasses on the computer monitor, scrolling his email queue feebly up and then down, up and then down, in search of the offending message.

"Let me see now, where is that thing?"

Jane looked over his shoulder, and her eyes scanned his workstation while she waited for him to find the message. The top of his desk was impeccably neat. Only a blotter and a few books held in place by two heavy chunks of polished agate, which his long-deceased wife had purchased at the Grand Canyon gift shop back in '68, a tattered hardcover Webster's New World dictionary, the Elements of Style by Strunk & White, a paperback copy of The Scarlet Letter and a compendium of short stories by Nathaniel Hawthorne.

"Have you any interests in literature?" he asked Jane without looking away from the computer screen as though reading her mind. "I've always fancied Hawthorne. Ah, but all that sex and redemption. Religion is at best a silly distraction and at worst a cruel exploitation of human frailty. Wouldn't you agree?"

"Well, I'm probably the wrong person to ask," she said.

Old Barr continued searching his email queue with growing frustration.

Jane heard muted laughter and looked up to see the cluster of editors stealing glances at her, many heads turning, like some sort of journalistic Hydra. Walsh turned away, muttering something, but all she could make out were the words "flying saucers," which drew snickers from the others.

The taunting excited those parts of her brain housing painful memories of "plain-ee, Jane-ee, that's ma name-ee," an irrational trigger point. She suddenly felt her body temperature rising with anger and humiliation, and her face flushed an unnatural shade of pink.

"Hey, I found it," Barr exulted, seemingly oblivious to Jane's torment.

But she was already stalking across the room toward her editor, internal doomsday clock mere seconds from midnight.

CHAPTER 18

Big Black Delta parked in orbit around Alpha Centauri Bg and dangled the instrument pod from its underbelly.

The planet resembled its twin. A cerulean marble with continents and oceans, and, ostensibly, flourishing ecosystems. But there were no obvious signs of anything that might be construed as synthetic.

Commander Swift turned on the radio receiver. In no time he heard it again. The voice coming from Alpha Centauri Bg was distinctly non-human, perhaps robotic. Maybe it wasn't even a voice at all; an oddly metallic series of tones.

"Are we recording this?" Swift asked Klein.

"Affirmative," she replied.

Captain Swift had the transmission piped over the ship's intercom system. Everyone stopped what they were doing and listened to the hypnotic sound. They never suspected the tonal transmission was a technological Trojan horse engineered by an intelligence far superior to their own. The radio signal was part of a broadband, multimedia assault on the ship and its crew that enabled the Alpha Centaurians to take control of Big Black Delta, merging with its computers, pulsing the lighting system in synch with the oscillating tones; flashing a mix of colors and patterns on the computer monitors. The combined stimuli effectively turned the ship's audiovisual systems into a mind machine that altered and controlled brainwave activity, opening a gateway into the cerebral cortex, hijacking the synaptic junctions of the brain. A stereophonic, syncopated rhythm of tones and frequencies tuned precisely to the natural resonance of the human mind, inducing a reorganization of brain activity.

The aliens had a neurophysiological password, a de facto backdoor that allowed them to hack directly into consciousness, like a systems designer who knows secrets nobody else does about her own code.

The induced brainwave patterns placed the human mind into a trancelike state, just the proper mix of alpha and theta waves, leaving the junctions between neurons entirely receptive to suggestion and learning. The interlopers, it turned out, knew all about the human brain. They'd been visiting Earth for centuries and had become expert in nearly every aspect of Homo sapiens physiology and cognition. Their mind-controlling music and lightshow induced a condition that was both alert yet relaxed, a cycle of learning and lucid experience and "active dreaming" all rolled into one.

At this time, with the mind completely open to post-hypnotic transmissions, the funky alien telemetry streamed vast quantities of data-rich information directly into the cerebral cortex of every crew member. The message included visual images, auditory and olfactory snippets, along with an informational narrative something like spoken language. The Alpha Centaurians schooled the earthlings about matters both practical and whimsical. Issues as important as the galactic social-pecking order and as irrelevant as alien sexuality.

Captain Swift, along with his entire crew, absorbed these teachings, transfixed, facial expressions evolving from vacant, then vaguely puzzled, and, finally, to a subdued ecstasy, slack-mouthed and drooling with a half smile as the story unfolded.

According to the streaming narrative, the race that ruled Alpha Centauri also dominated the entire quadrant of the galaxy. They'd come from a solar system nearly five hundred light years away. These beings revealed a history that was at once humbling and gratifying. The aliens had explored only a small portion of the Milky Way since they first ventured into space eons ago. The galactic quadrant that was home to Earth and Alpha Centauri held some twenty-five million stars, an expanse even these technological titans had yet to traverse.

Cosmic elders in a galaxy teeming with life, they had discovered only three other spacefaring civilizations. Whereas the quadrant held millions of solar systems, intelligent life could be found on fewer than one hundred of these systems, and technologically advanced civilizations were exceedingly rare. In short, the human race was among an elite class for whom the galaxy was virtually a wide-open frontier with an endless treasure of resources. There were, however, rules: Some planets and systems had been colonized and were off-limits. Protocols had been established and catalogued.

"These truths you must share with your superiors on Earth if there is to be peace among us, and we have provided here an instrument for you to do so," the alien narrative conveyed. "We will use this instrument to communicate, as well."

Captain Swift abruptly dropped out of his trance to find a translucent cylindrical object floating in the middle of the control room. Roughly the size of a person, it was surrounded by a greenish-blue halo. Its purpose was a complete mystery. Then the captain remembered something from the alien narrative: "You will find the controls intuitive, as we have studied how your minds work."

Later, a very tight circle of military officials back on Earth would learn from the enigmatic cylinder.

They, too, would grok the telepathic message. And they would be awed by its power.

CHAPTER 19

Two chief concerns vexed Jane the most: Marsden's mysterious ending and the fact that she'd told her boss to fuck off in the middle of the newsroom, putting her livelihood in peril.

At some point during her rant, Walsh sternly pointed a crooked finger in her direction and said she'd better "take a few days off." Afterward, she skulked at her desk for what seemed an eternity, and then began packing up her things. The phone rang.

"This is Jane," she said, but no one replied.

"Who the fuck is this?" she said, exasperated.

"Excuse me. Is this Jane Hale?" asked a befuddled Gregory Ginsberg.

"It is."

"Well, this is Greg. You know, we met about your unusual sixteen-millimeter movie not long ago, and I was ..."

But Jane cut him off in mid-sentence.

"Greg, this is not a good time, and I was just on my way out of the office."

Undeterred, he continued: "I was wondering if you still had the reel because a good friend of mine who teaches might be visiting this weekend and I wanted him to take a look, and ..."

Ginsberg trailed off as Jane interrupted him again.

"I really do appreciate the followup, but I've had a few setbacks in the story so I'm not sure when I'll get back to it."

"I see," said Ginsberg. "I've been thinking about the film, which was very unusual, to say the least. Certainly, from a historical point of view, I mean. And it raises some interesting technical issues. So, I wanted to talk to you about this, possibly, maybe, I don't know, over a beer or something."

ଓଓଓଓ

Jane wasn't sure exactly what drove her southward at altogether alarming speeds, considering her car's vintage and spotty maintenance history. Perhaps it was just out of the need for companionship or solace or the counsel of someone who didn't think she was crazy.

But she wasn't going fast enough to impress the suited goons in their black Chevy Caprice -- a powerful boat of a car prized for its utility as a police cruiser.

Carlos and Ray easily paced Jane's little Toyota and tracked her to Ginsberg's house. They had already assembled a dossier on Ginsberg, conducting surveillance, documenting his communications, his banking and consumer behavior, even his electricity usage. They would drive by at various times of day with infrared testing gear, collecting data to confirm what they had already suspected: Gregory Ginsberg was growing marijuana in his basement.

The pieces lined up so neatly: terminate the hapless pair, then plant cocaine and heroin at the scene. Homicide cops, upon discovering Ginsberg's agricultural endeavors and the harder contraband, would conclude it was a drug-related shooting. All that was left to do now was plan the fine details and wait for the right moment to strike.

Plan, wait, execute. So formulaic, so elegant in its simplicity.

ଓଓଓଓ

Jane was still wound tight from her editor's reprimand when she arrived at Ginsberg's house. She walked up to the front stoop and was about to knock when he swung open the door.

"I was thinking about wearing only a sarong," Ginsberg said wryly, cracking ajar the screen door to let her in.

"That would have been interesting," Jane said, looking down unconsciously to make sure he was, indeed, dressed.

Carlos and Ray drove by just in time to see the door closing behind her.

"Have a seat," he said. "How about a drink? But all I have is vodka and beer."

Ginsberg came back from the kitchen holding two bottles of beer. She set hers down on the coffee table, noticing what appeared to be the lone stub of a spent marijuana cigarette in an ashtray.

By the time Jane was halfway through her second beer, Ginsberg broke out a small wooden pipe and his reefer stash. He crumbled a choice bud and stuffed the bowl with the succulent weed. The two smoked marijuana, saying little and filling the minuscule pipe several times. Ginsberg expertly burned the little bowls of reefer so that not a single morsel remained. Inhaling. Exhaling. Whatever tension had existed dispersed nearly immediately.

Jane sought refuge in Ginsberg's hospitality. They chatted about various insubstantial matters, exchanging niceties and offering trivial, conversational tidbits. NPR news played quietly on a radio somewhere.

Before long he was giving Jane a tour of his house, which concluded with a showing of his small but thriving basement marijuana crop growing in a room next to his editing bay. Three hooded lamps hung from the ceiling, each issuing a thousand watts. A couple dozen plants, stunted by the intense high-pressure sodium lights, pushed stoutly upward against the artificial sunlight, wiggling in the faux wind from two fans that whirred constantly.

Jane made a joke, and Ginsberg put his arm around her shoulders. After that, one thing led to another. They had sex on an old couch in the grow room amid the pleasantly pungent aroma of marijuana and the educated voices of NPR.

Later, Ginsberg cooked dinner and they both drank vodka, mixed with orange juice until it ran out, then straight up. She got very drunk and told him everything about Marsden and the flying saucers. A rambling recital recorded by the authorities for transcription later.

CHAPTER 20

Lev Levine pulled into the parking lot of a dingy strip mall down the street from Gregory Ginsberg's house. He'd been keeping an eye on Jane for the past week at the request of Samuel Barr, who decided to take advantage of Levine's new sideline.

It was just one of those things he'd floated out there, handing Barr a glossy business card for "Levine Security Services." The chauffeur had received his private investigator license well over a year ago, he happily told his elderly fare, and he also held a concealed-weapons permit.

"I used to be instruct-ah," he said, pointing an invisible rifle at pedestrians at a midtown traffic light. "Pow, gotcha!"

Barr peered over his thick-lens glasses from the back seat, eyebrows raised.

"Lev, is this some kinda joke?" he said.

"Whad, you don't think I have other talents?" Levine said at the time with a laugh. "Oh-kay. That hurts me. That really hurts me. Oh-kay."

But this was before Jane's meltdown over the flying saucer story, the details of which had permeated newsroom gossip ever since her tense meeting with Walsh, who suspected that she probably suffered from "a persecution complex and paranoid delusions." As if being a doctor of journalism empowered him to dispense such a complicated medical diagnosis, which he shared freely with editorial colleagues. Barr, however, thought differently. If something terrible happened to his coworker, wouldn't he be responsible? After all, he was the one who'd given her name to Moore, whose envelope stuffed with flying saucer secrets he'd anonymously deposited on her desk that day in the newsroom.

Levine was more than happy to oblige his client. Playing private eye paid a lot more than playing chauffeur, and the old man forked over cold cash. But the clueless rent-a-cop might have reconsidered the assignment had he known about Carlos and Ray, who were, at that very moment, readying themselves for mortal combat.

They were stationed at a nearby Holiday Inn, feeling right at home with the Muzak and the corporate crowd, planning their attack like it was some sort of business blitz; systematically performing their mission checklist, specialists prepping for an operation.

Surgical gloves to prevent fingerprints: check.

A spare set of clothes in case of excessive blood spatter: check.

Nine-millimeter semiautomatic handguns with spare clips: check.

Silencers: check.

Two-way communications gear: check.

Double-edge combat knife -- razor sharp and serrated -- in case of the unlikely event of hand-to-hand conflict: check.

A detailed getaway route typed neatly in bold print on a single page protected in a plastic loose-leaf binder sleeve: check.

Piano wire: check.

Body armor, various blunt instruments of death: check.

Carlos reluctantly read the plan aloud in singsong fashion.

"I ring the bell while you make entry through the back door. We corral targets. We order them to assume a kneeling position and pepper them with questions to make them think we're just looking for information. Then we cap them both, the male first. Yadda, yadda, yadda."

They weren't expecting any resistance. The data sheet on Ginsberg showed he owned no guns and had never served in the military.

"He's a Mary," Ray said. "Piece a cake."

ଓଓଓଓ

Levine parked his Crown Vic, and the cooling engine ticked something like a time bomb. He took his .357 revolver out of the glove compartment and stuck it in a jacket pocket before setting off on foot in the general direction of Ginsberg's house, nestled among like residential buildings along the pleasant, sun-dappled suburban tract. He mentally recording all of the mundane details. A neat little Cape Cod, yellow with wooden shingles. White trim. Crummy aluminum shutters. Black. All seemed quiet enough. Two cars parked in the driveway. One was Jane's.

Levine moseyed down the block, where he found a quaint little park with a few weathered benches and a rusty swing set. Harry Goldberg Park, according to a carved wooden sign. Deserted. There was a vague whoosh of cars from a distant thoroughfare, and downshifting tractor-trailers comingled with birdsong.

He sat on a bench, but that was no good because shrubbery blocked his view of Ginsberg's house. So then he settled on one of the swings. Foliage still partially blocked his line of sight unless he swung forward and backward. A large unshaven guy on a child's swing, heavily armed, cigarette dangling from his mouth.

The house came into view intermittently as he swung forward, backward, forward, backward.

Carlos and Ray had seen Levine, watching him from inside a panel van labeled "Grimes Electric," and dismissed him as just some local. In the cozy privacy of the windowless van they changed into work coveralls with Grimes Electric legends stitched to the back. The men checked their weapons, chambering a bullet and doing a cursory visual inspection. They ran a quick systems check on their two-way radio gear, complete with Secret Service earpieces and throat mikes.

Confident in their own bad selves, they casually carried out their plan, constantly in wireless communication. Ray yawned as he opened the driver's door, so cocksure of himself that he didn't even don his bullet-proof vest. He approached Ginsberg's house from the rear, looking like a utility guy in search of an easement. Then he expertly picked the lock to the back door, all the while humming a Johnny Cash song.

"We're in," he whispered to Carlos over the two-way radio.

Carlos rang the front doorbell and waited for Ginsberg to answer.

Everything was on track for a successful mission, according to their precise, tactical calculus. But a key factor had been left out of the equation, a critical term introducing an element of mathematical uncertainty: It was Lev Levine.

ଓଓଓଓ

Ginsberg was in the bathroom, gripped by a horrible bout of the hangover shits. Hot and toxic. Radioactive. The ventilation fan clawed at the poisonous air, redolent of the body's metabolic wastes from the previous night's abuse.

He sighed with relief, bordering on ecstasy, upon purging his lower tract. At that very moment sweat momentarily cooled his forehead, yet he felt a flush at the same time. Afterward, he remained on the toilet, head bowed, staring straight down at the faded, cracked linoleum floor.

A prayer-like pose; a special Zen moment.

Then the doorbell rang.

He quickly wiped up after himself and pulled up his gym shorts. The bell rang again, and he rushed out of the bathroom.

"Hold your horses."

Ginsberg unlocked the door and turned the knob.

"Door opening," Carlos informed Ray.

The door flung open violently as Carlos pushed with great force.

"Police, on your knees. Hands on your head," he barked, drawing his handgun.

He closed the front door as a terrified Ginsberg complied. Then Ray burst into the room.

"Where's your girlfriend?" Carlos yelled at Ginsberg.

Ginsberg said nothing and promptly received a smack to the side of his head with something as hard as steel. He nearly passed out.

"Bedroom, ah, upstairs."

"Alright, get up. Let's all have a little talk," Carlos said.

The men took turns pushing Ginsberg, compelling him to stumble on the stairs.

Jane woke up as Ginsberg gingerly nudged her on the shoulder and then a little harder. She sat up abruptly upon seeing Carlos and Ray holding Ginsberg at gunpoint.

"Get up!" Ray yelled.

"What for? Who are you?"

"Just get up right now!"

She climbed out of bed, completely naked, covering her breasts with folded arms but leaving everything else fully exposed.

"Both of you, on your knees. Hands on your heads. Now," Carlos said.

Ginsberg began pleading with the two, his lower lip quivering.

"Officers, maybe there's some kind of mistake? We'll do whatever you say"

"No," Jane cried. "They're not the police!"

Carlos shot Ginsberg point blank in the head with his silencer-muffled weapon, and then once again in the chest. He leveled the gun at Jane.

Suddenly, Lev Levine charged into the room, raising his revolver and firing on Carlos. He automatically wheeled and discharged a round into Ray, who stood bewildered and catatonic in the fraction of a second before his demise. Carlos's head was a splintered mess of bone and pulpy flesh, whereas Ray's chest wound looked tidy in comparison. The results were the same. Blood spurted copiously forth.

"Who the fuck are you people?" screamed Jane.

"Oh sheet! Oh sheet!" Levine said, towering over the scene, the gravitas of the situation taking a few moments to sink in.

He trailed bloody footprints on the threadbare carpeting as he fled the carnage, explaining: "Mistah Baah sent me!"

"Samuel Barr?" Jane yelled incredulously.

Jane grabbed her clothes and fled naked, following Levine's bloody footprints out the door. She drove, hysterical, without direction and primarily sans clothing, at one point parking behind a Dunkin Donuts and dressing in her car like a contortionist, trembling from head to toe.

CHAPTER 21

She never faltered in her flight. Maybe it had something to do with all that marijuana, and the fact that the cops were probably on their way. Or maybe it was the fact that appearing in the local newspaper's police blotter would have killed her career and violated one of journalism's most sacred tenets: News reporters must never become newsmakers. Or maybe it was just a reflex. But whatever the reason, leaving the scene of a homicide was most certainly against the law.

This minor detail she blotted from her mind as she alternated between fits of anger, fear and remorse. Heart palpitating, grappling with the traumatic turn of events, she struggled to fixate only on the immediate. She pulled into the parking garage, using sheer will power to control her trembling. Then she sneaked past the front desk and staggered into the elevator.

It was late morning, and an inebriated senior citizen shambled into the elevator ahead of her.

"Honey, I've been drunk every day of my adult life," he said to her, a satisfied look on his face. "And I raised a family, ran a business."

Bracing himself against the upwardly accelerating car, he didn't notice the state she was in: shoeless and hair matted with dried blood, eyes staring blankly, shirt buttons askew.

She ran to the refuge of her small apartment and immediately grabbed a bottle of Irish whiskey she'd been saving for a special occasion.

Then, in the shower, she slowly washed the dried blood from her hair.

ଓଓଓଓ

Barr fumbled with his manual typewriter, poised a matter of inches from keyboard and paper, eyes straining to make out the print. The fluorescent lighting of the newsroom highlighted the spidery surface veins of his aged face.

Jane cleared her throat to get his attention, but he didn't hear her.

"Why me?" she demanded, arms folded across her chest in a confrontational stance.

Barr didn't look away from his typewriter.

"What's that? Oh, yes," he said with the trace of a smile. "I see what you mean."

It was only two or three hours to deadline for next week's magazine, and the newsroom was busy.

"I don't know exactly what's going on here, but you owe me an explanation," she said. "People are trying to kill me."

Jane was shaking a little.

"I'm only a messenger," Barr said. "He asked me for help. You seemed like the best candidate. Enterprising, unconventional, hungry."

"Who? Who asked you for help?"

Jane had earned capital, big time, and she was going to cash in. She was going to pump Samuel Barr for everything he knew. Then she was going to get a face-to-face with Glenn L. Moore. She was going to interview the bastard on the record if it was the last thing she did.

In short, she was going to blow the lid off the entire flying saucer story.

There was just one small problem: Her would-be journalistic coup lacked a sponsor.

☙☙☙☙

Jane could fit everything from her desk in a single cardboard box. Nearly four years at Thompson's, and that was all.

Everything worth keeping, that is. Omitting the useless paraphernalia of work, the old magazines and interview notes, outdated press passes and business cards from potential sources for stories that never panned out.

All that remained stowed nicely, with room to spare.

It was one of those inevitable career moves. Once you -- more or less -- called your boss an asshole in public, it was all downhill from there. And then there were questions of mental fitness, her colleagues snickering behind her back over flying saucer anecdotes and the like. A pair of plastic Spock ears appeared in her mailbox one day, a Star Trek phaser the next. The work environment had become oppressively negative, the chemistry poisonous. A septic leaching; drip, drip, drip. Like an abandoned nuclear-waste site. The half-life of this particular toxin was more than she cared to endure.

So she explored the job market and came up with a handful of possibilities, only one of which yielded results. Some countywide newspaper in north Jersey with bloated ad revenues, impressive circulation and various bureaus and editions, each as bland as the next.

It was, after all, the 1990s, before the Internet and Wall Street conspired to deal a brutal barrage of economic body blows to the newspaper industry. Things were still good, and Jane's resume was flush with newspaper credentials, most notably her ten years in the field, the Thompson's stint being the only exception. She'd always thought of it only as a temporary life raft.

Most newspaper editors, however, frowned mightily upon people who'd strayed from the daily-print fold to work in other, less-frequent media -- such as magazines, and -- gasp -- trade publications.

Getting back in newsprint would take a good deal of groveling and hand wringing and vocal expressions of remorse. And so, with ample mea culpas, the interview had gone well, but she'd have to take a general-assignment beat, said the managing editor. This meant bad hours and dirty jobs; everything from backing up deadline-strapped police reporters, to chasing down corrupt politicians in the dead of night, to writing an occasional feature story for the business or lifestyles sections.

That was fine. Anything to get out of that snake pit of a newsroom at Thompson's.

But the application process required an extensive "writing tryout," three days of deadline reporting, which she would perform while "on vacation" from the magazine. And all for the privilege of working G.A. for the city desk.

The tryout was a requirement she vaguely took exception to. After all, she was a seasoned professional. And pushing forty, at that. Wasn't she above such rudimentary tests of skill designed to prove one's mettle; to demonstrate spontaneous versatility in the face of rapidly changing conditions; to validate one's overall "enthusiasm" for the job?

But if that's what it would take to beat back the competition, so be it. She showed up at nine o'clock in the morning, reporter's notebook in hand, and her lousy tryout ensued. First, she was dispatched to cover an inane feature story about a good Samaritan and then assigned various other, even more trivial, exercises -- tasks Jane secretly loathed but performed with alacrity. She turned in formulaic, passable prose, and her performance was competent but underwhelming, due in large part to the mundane nature of her assignments. Kids' stuff.

The newsroom's interior was very ugly and industrial, with a really high ceiling and ancient striped wallpaper from the 1960s, stained from years of cigarette-smoking journalists. There was something inherently cold and inhospitable about it.

She could feel her opportunity slipping away, minute by minute.

Then, it happened.

Jane could tell something unusual was going on, a new sense of urgency in the newsroom. Reporters flitted about, hovering around the metro editor's desk or frantically making phone calls. A frenetic photographer ran out of the building without his camera, and, finding himself locked out, had to be let back in. An associate editor threw her hands in the air and wailed something primordial.

About halfway through Jane's shift on the first day of her tryout broke the biggest crime story in a decade. The cops, much to the surprise of the paper's inept police reporter, had arrested a serial killer who'd been preying on prostitutes for a couple of years. So, seizing the opportunity, Jane hustled her ass off, combing through court records at the editor's command, gathering addresses, phone numbers and other pertinent information, interviewing prostitutes, the suspect's neighbors, business owners, toiling late into the night and offering to stay longer, etc., etc.

She tirelessly returned for more work, no matter how much they dished her way.

As a result, her byline appeared in the project more than once. It was a huge spread in the Sunday paper.

When it was all over, Jane found herself packing up and unceremoniously moving across the Hudson, excess baggage and all. Now, from her new perspective the Manhattan skyline limned ambiguously against the horizon. She found herself gazing out of the newsroom's fourth-floor windows, mindlessly tracing the city's jagged outline.

The flying saucer story, meanwhile, languished. It would have to wait until she could reestablish herself, both professionally and personally. She'd have to get used to yet another town, another job, another life. But it wouldn't be long, she told herself. After all, she now had the goods on Glenn L. Moore, courtesy of old Samuel Barr. He'd given her everything, an extensive biographical portfolio together with the flying saucer timeline Moore had revealed to him. She possessed Moore's phone number, his address, and a privileged awareness of the secrets he knew.

The weeks and months passed, and Jane tried not to think about flying saucers or Ginsberg's splattered brains or the cops. She worried that sooner or later they'd stumble across her name, possibly through Ginsberg's phone records. Or maybe a busybody neighbor, alarmed by the outburst of gunfire, had spotted Jane's naked flight. Perhaps this neighbor had jotted down her license plate number. Soon the police would be hauling her in for questioning, match her fingerprints to the crime scene.

She wondered what in the world was taking them so long and constantly checked the papers for any update on the Ginsberg killings. Surely, there couldn't be that many triple homicides in suburbia. She cozied up to the crime reporter in the bureau that covered Ginsberg's town, feigning only professional interest in the slayings. But he said the cops "didn't know from nothin."

ଓଓଓଓ

The obituary was one of those well-crafted standalone postmortems in the New York Times afforded only to important people.

"Aviation innovator Glenn L. Moore" had died in an accidental house fire, it said.

The obit elicited in Jane a feeling of profound regret. The sort of regret that comes from missed opportunities. But regret morphed into worry and finally deep concern. What if the house fire hadn't been an accident?

The article was a bare-bones reading of his life's history, tracing how he had founded the Moore Aircraft Company, its pivotal role during World War II, then the coming of jets, stealth and various other innovations. Toward the end it said Moore had grown "increasingly eccentric," no doubt a euphemism for dementia. It mentioned a gathering in 1992, where he told attendees that the United States "now possesses the technology to travel to the stars."

Not long after Moore's obit a padded envelope appeared from the mailroom. Inside was a videotape and a lengthy notarized affidavit from Moore to be dispatched to Jane upon his death. A sort of legalese manifesto, it recited in very antiseptic prose the chronology of the flying saucer program. The videotape showed Moore seated next to a roll-top desk in his study, reading from the affidavit.

He began with the blunt yet surreal pronouncement that "*... if you have received this, then I am deceased ...*"

CHAPTER 22

Big Black Delta anchored itself motionless in the sky some forty thousand feet over the English countryside and issued a single flying saucer. A computer navigation system aboard the saucer had been programmed to carry out a series of lightning-fast maneuvers, deftly traversing the rolling hills and agricultural acreage surrounding Stonehenge.

It was three o'clock in the afternoon, and the ancient attraction buzzed with tourists. Within a fraction of a second, faster than the eye can register, the saucer arrived at its preset coordinates only a few meters off the ground. Its antigravity drive traced a wonderfully intricate pattern of spirals and circles, as electromagnetic forces emanating from the saucer flattened the wheat stalks with preternatural precision. Then the slender craft darted to a safe altitude, blending into the blue sky, and hovered while its crew shot video and photographs of the large crop circle below, as well as the public's response to it.

Traffic on the A303 London-to-Exeter road came to a standstill, and motorists snapped their own pictures of this complex geometric wonder that had appeared instantly and in broad daylight. New Age devotees noted the formation's elegant design. Skeptics speculated that it had probably been created overnight by local pranksters. Journalists poked fun at UFO believers and couched their stories in trivial verbiage about "little green men."

Like so many things in science, the whole crop-circle effect had been discovered quite by accident. It was 1966, and a saucer had been forced to land in an Australian swamp due to a technical problem. Unknown to the pilot, the saucer's field-propulsion system had reshaped a stand of reeds growing from the marsh. Intense heat and electromagnetic waves flattened slightly scorched plant stalks, bent horizontally an inch or so above the muddy soil and swirling flawlessly in a perfectly balanced, interwoven display.

The first crop circle of the modern media age was born.

A farmer working his fields adjacent to the swamp told reporters that he saw a flying saucer taking off from where he later discovered the circle. That was when the flying saucer illuminati stumbled upon antigravity's creative side. The field-propulsion system, they would come to learn, could be configured to form an endless array of geometric patterns.

Aside from their aesthetic appeal, crop circles might be an ideal medium for disinformation. Research findings revealed a historic underpinning, a mythology originating in the early nineteenth century, when the first simple crop circles were reported. Perhaps a natural meteorological or geophysical mechanism was at work, but that wasn't important. All that really mattered was that they were mysterious metaphysical manifestations. In other words, they could easily be used to marginalize the credibility of ufology by association with the lunatic fringe.

A whole generation of crop circle enthusiasts emerged during the 1980s in response to a dramatic and puzzling proliferation of the pictorial ciphers. The designs featured increasingly complex and enigmatic patterns, inspiring pilgrimages of New Agers, a galvanized following who saw hidden messages couched in the intricate language of Euclidean geometry.

Disinformation gurus started using crop circles en masse as a new tool. Mathematicians created the designs using parameters that corresponded to settings in the field-propulsion system, but they didn't know this. They only knew that inputting certain mathematical expressions resulted in specific features. To them, it was just some academic exercise.

The mathematical instructions were then integrated into computer code for the field-propulsion system. The saucer's pilot and technicians didn't understand the code. Their job was simply to push buttons, instructing the craft's antigravity drive to carry out the instructions. It was a seamless division of labor, and the procedure worked like a charm. Soon thousands of formations had been staged in twenty-six countries, ninety percent of them in southern England.

Success of the disinformation strategy depended on linking the crop-circle phenomenon to the region's mystical identity; the hundreds of weird prehistoric monuments found there. Built from sarsens and bluestones by a people with mysterious motivations, they attracted a steady stream of sightseers, conventional tourists mixed with partisans of the occult who saw the formations as communiqués from god or alien intelligences speaking in the universal tongue of mathematics.

Celtic mandalas, fractals, curlicues, swirls and circles of every variety and denomination, architectures resembling the DNA helix, mind-boggling seven-sided patterns and ancient petroglyphs. Circles within circles, clockwise and counterclockwise, sine waves and flowers, pentagrams and double pentagrams, coiled serpents and origami, super-symmetric spider webs and squares encompassing strange and precisely measured grids.

The crop circle campaign was ongoing, targeting largely the rustic climes of southern England, starting in April when the fields were lush with wheat and barley, through to harvest in September.

Choosing the English countryside was a brilliant strategy, if not a no-brainer for the disinformation folks. Other venues simply posed too many challenges: although China offered vast agricultural tracks, its government-controlled media would have squelched coverage; Australia harbored plenty of prairie but sparse human traffic to bear witness; in the U.S. bread basket, farmers were wont to declare crop circles crime scenes, roping them off with yellow tape and thwarting public access, and the Amish immediately destroyed the formations before anyone could take pictures.

Yes, America was a hostile environment for crop circles, a fact not lost on believers. After all, they reasoned, hadn't the U.S. military already shot down flying saucers, analyzed and reverse engineered them with evil intent?

But England, with its sacred Neolithic sites and continuous flow of tourists, provided fertile ground for the formations as well as the imagination. At the same time, the sudden profusion of crop circles near the end of the century seemed to coincide with various mystical mileposts, namely the prophecies of the Mayan calendar, which marked December 2012 as a time of great change; Aztec artifacts suggested the end of a thirteen thousand-year cycle was at hand, heralding epochal change and a turning point for human consciousness; and the Hopi people had described this time as a period of transition for humanity.

The glyphs were interpreted by crop circle aficionados and said to contain volumes of information, graphical representations of mathematical truisms in geometry, quantum physics, biophysics, alchemy, musical composition, the harmonic signature of god. Believers began reporting that the circles produced "healing energies" and heightened states of awareness.

Others saw in the patterns Gaia's disapproval of humanity's mistreatment of Earth: messages warning of global warming, pollution, war and other environmental and moral wrongs. The planet, taken as one giant self-aware organism, was showing its disgust through these elaborate, artistic semaphores, appearing like telltale welts in response to mankind's malevolence. The formations often manifested near sacred sites for a reason: to reawaken human spirituality, a claim regarded in the mainstream with indifference or ridicule.

The spectacle attracted artists and mischievous hoaxers, who started sneaking onto farmlands to create their own patterns. Even Nick Pope, who investigated UFOs for the

British Ministry of Defence, got involved, saying hoaxes couldn't account for many crop circles and that the scientific community was at a loss to explain how they were formed.

But few scientists took the herbaceous apparitions seriously. Those who would venture into the tall grass of fringe culture suggested the patterns resulted from some unknown natural phenomena, possibly whirlwinds or yet-to-be-discovered geomagnetic influences. Scientists were certain of one thing, however: Crop circles were most-decidedly not produced by flying saucers.

The entire subject of UFOs took another credibility hit.

ଓଓଓଓ

If crop circles represented a cash cow in the profitable enterprise of disinformation, then the whole close-encounter, alien-abduction business was a crowded pasture, an enormous, productive herd.

The ET saga started in the early 1950s, before the inception of DIS, and through the years it adhered to a narrative that featured various strange characters and bizarre claims. It was a storyline that grew from the need to mythologize flying saucers, to counteract the public's growing suspicion that UFOs were a product of U.S. or Soviet military shenanigans, a perception perhaps bolstered by Truman's unorthodox air show over the nation's capital.

Recurring tales evolved into a complex lore, but the plot remained basically the same: Aliens are visiting the Earth in flying saucers, and they sometimes deliberately make contact with people who are privileged to snap pictures and shoot film footage. Sometimes the "contactees" communicate via clairvoyance or hand signals and enjoy amicable interaction, taking jaunts to the moon and back. At other times, however, the communion is unfriendly: alien abduction at the hands of dispassionate creatures of immense intelligence, clinically evaluating human physiology using mysterious medical instruments in examination-room settings.

Occasionally the accounts contained a kernel of truth. Perhaps the contactees did have some sort of a UFO experience, but the stories were embellished and supplemented with government-supplied "evidence." Operatives approached people who claimed to have had close encounters. They were ordered to incorporate various hyperbole into their stories; personal encounters, good and bad; fictional details about the origins of certain cosmic travelers and the purpose of their visitations; an assortment of strange spiritual experiences. Officially, the contactees were informed, it was all part of a Washington program to gauge public reaction to news of extraterrestrials; that they were, in effect, vital components in a social experiment.

The public happily consumed these sensational and often amusing tidbits, recounted by auto mechanics, traveling salesman, housewives, nurses, fishermen and farmers. One guy said a flying saucer took him roundtrip from New Mexico to New York in a half hour. The ship, he said, was piloted by aliens resembling lemurs whose eyes were attached to stalk-like appendages. Others told of mystical experiences and UFOs equipped with "tachyon drives" and secret underground bases in Switzerland and Russia; taking a flying saucer back in time to meet Jesus; aliens from a vegan planet free of conflict; sinister plans to create a hybrid race by breeding with humans.

It was all scripted according to the prevailing social and political sentiments. The 1950s brought Leave It To Beaver, American Bandstand and altruistic aliens who looked just like people, here to provide earthlings with prophetic warnings aimed at saving the human race from its own technological misdeeds. The 1960s brought Psycho, LSD and more predatory space aliens, with supersize heads and the ability to perform telepathy and levitation.

Astronomers regarded these accounts as scientifically absurd. Most of their brethren in other research fields fell in line behind them. The descriptions of flying saucer propulsion made no sense from an engineering point of view. And hadn't Einstein mathematically demonstrated the fallacy of faster-than-light travel?

The narrative, however, couldn't be completely dismissed because of the photographic evidence and film footage, some of which was difficult to debunk. The pictures and movies showed flying saucers cruising high over scenic hills and dales, or hovering briefly. Audio tapes recorded the humming sounds of UFOs. Contactees offered this documentation to the media, to be scrutinized by two generations of journalists and ufologists, skeptics and believers.

Meanwhile, disinformation media specialists were producing a diverse body of documents, vetting books, newsletters and speeches for alien contactees and abduction experiencers; hundreds of pages of "notes," pictures, slides and films allegedly all recorded during close encounters.

The stories became more and more fantastic and frightening. Aliens walked among urbanites and caused the 1965 power failure that blacked out New York City. The

U.S. military was powerless to protect the citizenry from abduction and exploitation by godless critters, descending on the planet like intelligent insects.

Unscrupulous and unlicensed mental health counselors exploited the ET phenomenon, spinning off a sort of cottage industry dedicated to the treatment and study of "post-abduction syndrome." These parsons of hypnotic regression worked to uncover "suppressed memories" of alien abduction. Many abductees might be deluded or simply pretending. In either case, though, their hypnotic regressions could be interpreted as genuine.

Sure, a small number of cases might have been genuine, and occasionally a respected psychiatrist would come forward to support the veracity of abduction experiences. But any semblance of credibility couldn't change one bare fact: The entire subject of UFOs was now fully tainted.

CHAPTER 23

Big Black Delta returned from her extrasolar expedition and delivered the Alpha Centaurians' robotic messenger to the proper authorities.

The machine repeated the same mind-blowing telepathic communiqué that had been force-fed to Captain Swift and his crew, but this time it was for the edification of top brass in charge of the Integrated Space Command. The alien communicator also inexplicably uploaded reams of information in various multimedia formats to a secure military supercomputer; a data-rich compilation that included a catalogue of non-human civilizations inhabiting Earth's galactic quadrant and a listing of solar systems containing planets hospitable to life. Only a small number of systems were labeled off-limits to earthlings, leaving literally thousands of planets open to human exploration. The extraordinary extraterrestrial filings from the Alpha Centaurians would become a working handbook defining protocol for everything from colonization to space mining, militarization to interstellar tourism.

Then the alien gizmo went ominously dormant, its power source and methods of telemetry and telepathy complete mysteries. Officials promptly stowed the machine within the catacombs of some vast military compound in the Midwest, where it would be kept under constant vigil.

Tommy Swift and crew, meanwhile, enjoyed a well-deserved shore leave and then embarked on missions closer to home.

Among their first tasks would be escort duty for a new class of enormous space-station platforms; hulking tube-like architectures a mile long that would be positioned beyond the Moon. It was BBD's job to make sure the platforms were delivered to their proper coordinates.

From these installations military operations could be launched, together with space-mining missions to asteroids possessing valuable assets. Chief among these treasures were "rare-earth" elements needed for weapons technologies like night-vision goggles and laser-guided bombs. The new space-mining ventures could represent a way of skirting China's virtual monopoly on the metals, particularly yttrium, coveted for use in lasers.

Then there were those space rocks rich in platinum and gold and diamonds of every color. Harvesting these commodities promised to bring in untold billions of dollars, which could be funneled into the military's black budget. The nation's secret space force might soon be self-sustaining.

However, building and launching the space stations presented a series of sticky challenges: The whole effort depended on successfully assembling structures as long as the Brooklyn Bridge and then lofting them into space without the public knowing. Both feats were potential showstoppers. First, no hangars or underground facilities large enough existed to house their construction. The only practical place to build them was underwater: specifically, valleys on the ocean bottom that were sufficiently deep to conceal the procedure from the prying eyes of satellites, but not too deep for Navy welders to safely perform their duties.

A perfect spot was discovered in the Atlantic Ocean near the Channel Islands. So the assembly operations commenced. Each of the structures consisted of a dozen or so subsections, including a central nuclear power and propulsion module, built individually at military installations and lowered separately to the seafloor, where they were knitted together by welders. They thought they were assembling offshore missile platforms. That was the false rumor, anyway.

Structural segments were painted neon yellow to improve visibility for the underwater construction workers, who labored in specialized diving suits that allowed them to function at two thousand feet for hours. For their part, the Navy welders never really saw the entire structure, like the parable about six blind men, each inspecting a different part of an elephant and none of them realizing what animal was before them.

The mysterious thing seemed to stretch on forever along the murky seafloor, and the welders came to refer to it as "Big Yellow."

After the assembly was completed another nagging obstacle remained: The structures had to be equipped with gravitators spaced evenly along their entire length to properly hoist the behemoths into the heavens. Because the string of high-voltage gravitators generated brightly glowing plasma, launching the structures at night was out of the question. They would have been impossible to miss, these flying monuments ascending into space lit up like mini suns.

The only sensible alternative, therefore, was a daytime launch. However, this presented potential pitfalls, as well. The dazzling yellow paintjob, while essential for the dusky conditions on the ocean bottom, would make the objects quite noticeable in the daytime skies. The trick was to schedule the launch during a window of time when no commercial aircraft were in the vicinity. Then, the monstrosities were to be ushered into deep space by BBD, which waited at a rendezvous point beyond low-Earth orbit.

The Integrated Space Command completed two of the space stations and would launch the twin structures together. Having scanned the skies for weeks leading up to the launch, a forty-seven-minute window free of commercial air traffic to and from the Channel Islands had been identified. Each of the structures was staffed by a captain and full crew and the machines readied for flight during an extensive three-day countdown.

Nothing could go wrong; the planning was that meticulous. However, something did.

A couple of puddle-jumping charters escaped detection just as the structures were transiting to space. They provided quite a show for the pilots and passengers, these shimmering golden platforms hovering over the English Channel.

British tabloids and broadcast media covered the sightings.

"I never really thought these were from another planet," one of the pilots told a radio host. "I always sort of assumed I was looking at some military thing."

British Ministry of Defence officials said the government wasn't investigating the sightings because there was no threat to national security. Indeed, the yellow apparitions represented not a threat but a new military asset: Just beyond Earth's moon a network of deep-space outposts was taking shape.

Soon George W. Bush would be president, and he would create a sweeping new national space policy, one that would stress the critical need for nuclear-power systems to "enable or significantly enhance space exploration or operational capabilities." It was a framework for the military's secret space program, stipulating that the use of nuclear power systems be "consistent with U.S. national and homeland security, and foreign policy interests," and declaring that "freedom of action in space is as important to the United States as air power and sea power."

Before long the fleet would be visiting military installations near and far.

CHAPTER 24

Detectives investigating the triple homicide had an abundance of bewildering evidence.

First of all, there was that Grimes Electric van parked out front. The police hauled it away and gave it a thorough dissection. They were surprised to find it full of high-tech gear and other paraphernalia reminiscent of professional law-enforcement or military procedure. They also could discover no record of a company by that name in the entire state. And, when police ran identification checks on Carlos and Ray, their efforts led to an endless loop of aliases and ambiguous results, but nothing definitive.

Then there were Lev Levine's bloody footprints, which trailed all the way out to the sidewalk in front of the house. The town had recently installed new concrete walkways, and the ruddy prints contrasted nicely against the chalky cement.

It was, indeed, a very peculiar crime scene.

And, finally, there was the question of a mystery woman allegedly observed fleeing Ginsberg's house. Though, the witness was elderly and myopic and couldn't furnish any physical description of the woman or any information whatsoever pertaining to the vehicle or tag number.

For the time being, she remained anonymous.

ଓଓଓଓ

It was mid-morning, and Jane was muddling through a tedious sidebar for a double-truck layout on the county budget, trying to focus on banal municipal data, lining up figures in a financial table and marking relevant entries with a highlighter.

Her phone rang.

"Hello, is this Jane Hale?"

The very question made her jumpy. It was likely only a matter of time before she received the dreaded phone call from homicide. Maybe this was that call. Maybe the other shoe was finally dropping. A witness had emerged, or the cops had uncovered some new evidence.

But the caller didn't sound much like a cop. His voice had a very proper, academic timbre. It was the kind of affected speech that came only through deliberate effort. Words rolled out of his mouth like cultured pearls of studied perfection.

"I am Ezra Stern, a senior editor at Hopkins House Publishing," he said. "I believe you are an acquaintance of Robert Marsden's?"

He pronounced "Hopkins House" with a pompous inflection, like she was supposed to be impressed just hearing the name. Marsden, he explained, had spoken of Jane to the publisher, specifically referencing the new evidence of a flying saucer cover-up. Of course, the publisher couldn't have known about recent events exposing the source as

Glenn L. Moore, while also introducing a new secondary source in Samuel Barr.

The editor in charge of the project decided a new chapter based on these developments was not only merited but represented a huge shot in the arm to the project. Revelations from Mr. Moore, and his posthumous manifesto, would be integrated. Virtually all of the fixes and additions would be completed within a year, maybe sooner. Jane would be called a "senior book editor."

The content was pretty dubious, and she knew it. Hardly any on-the-record sources and scant hard evidence. In other words, exactly the kind of specious storytelling and slipshod journalism craved by legions of conspiracy freaks the world over. The publisher saw dollar signs. The pay wasn't bad, so Jane labored part-time on the project while working a three-to-midnight general-assignment beat at the newspaper.

She contacted the Moore Aircraft Company with the sole purpose of getting an official denial regarding its namesake's outrageous claims. The PR guy called her a week later: "We're not going to be able to help you on that request," he said. "We just have no idea what to make of it."

The company sent a formal response letter, which would be included in the new chapter of Marsden's book:

"Dear Hopkins House Publishing:

"We have no information related to your inquiry pertaining to 'the secret history of antigravity and flying saucers.'

The Moore Aircraft Company has produced many aircraft types and models since 1937. However, we can find no mention of flying saucers in our inventory, both current and/or discontinued."

Sincerely,
Ryan Small, Director of Marketing

The wording was just condescending enough.

Yes, the project was coming together nicely, but the same couldn't be said of her return to newspapering. It had been just eight months since leaving Thompson's, and already she tired of the daily grind. Her general-assignment shift was a dumping ground. She filled in regularly on the hectic police beat, and when the city hall reporter went on vacation, she covered council meetings. A couple of feature writers were lost to maternity leave, and Jane got an assortment of crummy assignments for the "Lifestyles" section.

"This ain't the New York Times, kiddo," the night city editor had a habit of telling her whenever she indicated the slightest irritation.

Nevertheless, no matter how unpleasant her assignments, being a reporter was preferable to anything else she was qualified to do. She'd rather be a daily hack than PR scum any day.

Her editor seemed moderately intelligent, but she viewed him primarily as an impediment, a lascivious cad with a questionable moral compass who had a penchant for making her job far more complicated than it had to be.

"Try to remember to ask people, 'How did you feel?' What was going through their mind, you know, up here?"

he'd say officiously, tapping his right temple with a tobacco-stained forefinger. "The reader wants to know, and it's what sells newspapers!"

This was an admonition he offered liberally, sometimes as she rushed out the door to cover some breaking news of the day. It was delivered with varying degrees of emotional emphasis, to the point of becoming a nuisance, a caricature. It played in her mind like a stupid, catchy jingle.

"How did he feeeeeel? How did she feeeeeel? Make sure you ask! Did you ask?"

But Jane rarely, if ever, complied with his dictate simply because how people felt was usually irrelevant to most stories. His obsession with brown-nosing the public psyche was all part of a faulty philosophy that permeated management and overall decision making; that somehow engaging the common man would serve to boost circulation. A flawed, unproven speculation that was responsible for the paper's rinky-dink man-on-the-street feature, called *Viewpoints*, which appeared Saturdays in the Metro/State section. Eight people at random were rounded up and polled about some current-events item. Nabbed outside shopping centers and in public venues, bus stops and train stations, their photographs were taken and their opinions scribbled in a notepad. Then, their comments were sliced and diced and bastardized beyond recognition, hopelessly altered and condensed so that they could fit in the meager space allotted under each of the eight mug shots.

Chasing down these public "viewpoints" often fell to the night general-assignment reporter, and it was a big pain in the ass.

How pointless, even maudlin, Jane thought.

"It's what people do that's important, not what they feel," she'd grumble to herself.

The role of a daily journalist was to accurately report on the actions of man, which varied greatly across a broad spectrum of often perplexing, unpredictable and dangerous behavior; but trying to succinctly characterize the hearts and minds of the general public within the limited column inches of newsprint was pure folly. Management would be wise to put more resources into digging up real news instead of wasting time and talent on such misguided exercises.

Real news. Now, THAT's what sold newspapers, she'd like to tell her editor.

This was, however, a sentiment he'd likely call heresy. Then again, what could you expect from a person whose predominant motivation at midlife was the prospect of getting laid as often as possible. He had a wife, once, and a couple of kids, but his young family had disintegrated in 1982, pulled apart by the invisible dark matter of his own deviant cravings.

Since then he'd become a sybarite, assembling an impressively diverse pool of women. And the younger the better. Once he bagged three in a single twenty-four-hour period, and then duly recorded this accomplishment in his weekly calendar, complete with the approximate time of each intimate liaison. "Sex with Marie: 1 a.m.; Sex with Amy: noon; Sex with Suzie: 11:30 p.m.!!!!!!"

He'd even stooped to transgressions against college interns at the paper, and, on more than one occasion, slipped a tape recorder under the bed.

Sordid anecdotes circulated in the newsroom and beyond. Jane really wasn't offended by any of that, though.

As long as he just kept his mitts to himself and let her do her job, she might actually be able to climb out of the general-assignment beat in a year, or, at most, two, she thought.

To that end, she dare not voice too loudly her dislike of *Viewpoints*, bad assignments and bad actors. Having no seniority meant you did whatever came your way.

Her latest assignment was a true gem: a feature story about the surging popularity of skydiving in rural New Jersey, including a first-person reader to describe what it's like to jump out of a plane while hitched to an instructor in tandem. Her editor placed the assignment on her desk one evening.

"Skydiving?" she said. "You want me to go skydiving?"

He explained that the business section had already committed to the project, having assigned a reporter to write the nuts-and-bolts main bar fleshing out the economic and social factors behind the trend.

Jane's task, her editor clarified, was to provide some "color," a narrative from the point of view of a first-time skydiver.

"Did you know that nearly everyone flies in their dreams?" he said excitedly, reading from a printed story assignment. "People are striving to realize a universal fantasy!"

He continued to expound on the merits of the story, perusing the assignment description.

"And more than three hundred thousand people took the plunge last year in the United States alone. Most of them ordinary people, public school teachers, janitors, accountants. Why, nineteen and a half percent of skydivers are professionals, and forty percent have completed college, compared with only sixteen percent of the U.S. population. This is a huge chunk of our readership!"

"That's all very interesting, but ..." Jane said.

"And, you might find this interesting," he interrupted, "more than twenty percent are female, and this percentage is going up!"

"This sounds fascinating, but it seems more appropriate for a sports reporter. I mean, I'm not athletic. I was never athletic."

"Ah, but that's even better. Statistics show most new jumpers aren't big jocks. They are plain old people. Plus, they have this new thing called tandem jumping, where you don't even need training. You just kind of latch onto the skydiving guy and go along for the ride. It's a new craze. A lot of people are doing it!"

"Yeah, but isn't it dangerous?" Jane countered. "I'm no daredevil."

"Why, Jane, I'm glad you asked," her editor said, returning his gaze to the fact sheet. "Statistics show that only about thirty-three people are fatally injured while parachuting in the United States each year. This compares to about a hundred who perish scuba diving, eight-hundred bicycling, seven thousand who drown -- including more than three-hundred in bathtubs -- more than a thousand from bee stings, likewise for boating, sixty while snowmobiling and fifty thousand in highway wrecks."

He handed the assignment to Jane.

"You do the math. It's safer than riding a bike."

"Reassuring," Jane said sarcastically.

ଓଓଓଓ

The articles -- a main story about the business of skydiving and a sidebar on the personal experience of jumping -- were scheduled to front a section in a future Sunday edition of the paper. A photographer had been assigned to the package. It turned out that one of the paper's lensmen was a real adventurer, one of those lean fearless types who crave the exhilaration of high places and pure speed: He'd climbed mountains, scaled buildings and smokestacks, and, yes, jumped from airplanes in the pursuit of the perfect picture. So he lobbied for the assignment and would accompany Jane all the way down.

She conducted plenty of research before the jump and had even started writing the draft. Jane was considering a pullout quote from Ernest Hemingway, just to piss off the chamber-of-commerce crowd: "It is one thing to be in the proximity of death, to know more or less what she is, and it is quite another thing to seek her."

The skydiving place was a model of expediency, she would learn. Because Jane would fall from a plane hitched to an expert skydiver, she needed to complete only a brief training the day of the jump. Her instructor, or "tandem master," turned out to be a very annoying man who went by the name of Mack. Bravado oozed from his pores and lingered like cheap cologne. He'd been an Army Ranger and competitive kick boxer and never stopped gloating about it all.

Jane interviewed him by phone several days before the event, and then she attended the day-of pre-jump instruction. He wore a leather bomber jacket decorated with skydiving badges, showy medallions that testified to his qualifications: the silver-winged U.S. Army Parachute Rigger Badge, an

Army Ranger tab, Military Free Fall Parachutist Badge and other emblems. They were like handsome scars, eye candy for groupies drawn to thrill-seeking bad boys.

Mack described how tandem jumps allowed you to "experience all the thrills" of freefalling from an airplane, but without any of those pesky stresses that come with going it alone. He elucidated how the plane would take them to twelve thousand feet; how he would hook himself to Jane's harness at four points; how they, along with several other jumpers, would fling themselves from the open door; how the tandem master rides on the back and wears an industrial-strength parachute capable of suspending five hundred pounds.

He further clarified how he would apply his considerable skills to ensure that Jane, the "passenger," would enjoy the most exhilarating freefall possible. He explained how they would race ecstatically together toward the drop zone at one hundred twenty miles per hour; how no steps had been spared to ensure safety, and the instructors' helmets were equipped with two-way radios; how the freefall would last only about fifty seconds, until the jumpers reached an altitude of roughly five thousand feet; then, how he would pull the ripcord, followed by deceleration and then a pleasantly panoramic, four-minute parachute ride to the ground.

Mack spelled it all out in textbook chronology, so logically sequenced and precisely timed. But the choreography would break down. Someone would throw a bit of sand into the fine-meshing machinery that permitted people to cheat death while plummeting from the cloud tops.

ଓଓଓଓ

He'd been trying to work up the courage for months.

Mack had wronged him, and wronged him badly. They'd been best buddies, both having served in the military, and they shared so many "core values," moral certitudes to be trotted out during backyard barbecues and fraternal gatherings. Then there was the exaggerated masculinity, the auto racing and motorcycles and the macho, monosyllabic first names that just went with the territory: Butch.

Butch and Mack: best buddies.

Initially their universal passion was skydiving, but soon it became something else. Mack committed the worst sin possible against a good friend. He'd stolen his woman, and not just any woman. His wife. Then the wife moved out and was pregnant with Mack's child.

Butch pretended to accept his fate as the cuckolded, discarded husband; the romantically challenged, deficient spouse. He ostensibly got on with his life, so stoic and venerable, hewing to the maxim that all's fair in love and war.

But it was all an act.

And now guess who was getting even, and at any cost? In his mind, this wasn't going to be the perfect crime: He would gladly face the appropriate punishment. This was purely vengeance, one of those core values he and Mack had often blustered about over a case of beer. But they didn't call it vengeance. They called it justice.

At least, that's how he justified his homicidal scheming to himself. That's what he told himself this was: justice. The Old Testament kind, the kind of justice that was sorely lacking in modern penal systems; the kind of justice that meted out pain and misery and plenty of it.

He wanted Mack to squirm. He wanted Mack to suffer. He wanted Mack to have just enough time to reflect on what an asshole he'd been as he plunged to his death.

Butch contrived his sabotage so as to be virtually undetectable during the final "gear check," when instructors inspect each other's chutes before boarding the plane. This shouldn't be a difficult problem, though. He knew the gear check was never designed to detect foul play for the simple reason that most fatal skydiving events involved human error.

Yes, Butch knew that deliberate tampering was unheard of in his favorite recreational pastime, although the mechanics of disabling a parachute system were actually quite elementary. Pulling the ripcord was supposed to eject a small parachute, or drogue, which, in turn, deployed the larger main canopy. So, cutting the line between the drogue chute and the main canopy should prevent the main chute from opening. To complete the job, straps connecting the reserve chute should be severed, also a simple task.

Butch couldn't care less that investigators would readily discover the crime after the fact. In his own bizarre sense of right versus wrong, he'd willingly pay for his transgression. So, with that concession, the most challenging obstacle was gaining access to the parachutes. However, this, too, proved elementary for a guy like Butch, a trusted and frequent visitor to the skydiving school.

The plan's ultimate success hinged on a weak link in security: the teenagers making up the parachute-packing department. It was their job to prepare the parachutes for each jump, a task they carried out while listening to loud music on an old boom box and salivating over the skydiving groupies -- whuffos in drop-zone slang -- who wandered through the hangar.

They could pack a standard chute in seven minutes and a tandem in twelve, deftly folding the canopies to ensure their proper deployment. At ten bucks a pop, maybe fifty parachutes on a busy day, this was good money for a seventeen-year-old kid.

On the morning of Jane's assignment, the packing crew worked quickly to process the many parachutes that would be needed that weekend.

Butch hauled the sabotaged tandem gear to the packing hangar, and at just the right moment he switched the faulty parachute for the one hanging on the wall under Mack's name. Then he absconded with Mack's pack and threw it in the bed of his pickup truck.

Afterward, he joined the crowd that was gathering at the drop zone and waited for the show to begin.

ଓଓଓଓ

Jane arrived mid-morning with a photographer. The skydiving school also hired its own photographer for the occasion, so there should be no shortage of good art for the piece. The airborne photojournalists donned head-mounted cameras operated with a remote control cable.

It would be Mack's first jump of the day. He grabbed his parachute from the hook, and, as he'd done countless times before, checked the "packing data card" held in a pocket on the parachute covering. The document indicated his equipment had recently been inspected and serviced by an FAA-certified technician.

Everything seemed in perfect order, but Jane got a little nervous when told to sign a waiver, a legally binding document declaring that she accepted "an element of risk" in jumping from an airplane.

She and her photographer went to a locker room and slid into jumpsuits. They emerged to find Mack standing patiently as another instructor gave his pack a going over, systematically eyeballing the parachute's various pins, straps and harnesses. The photographer started shooting pictures of the inspection process. Failure to properly execute the gear check had killed many people in the annals of skydiving pathology, including a freefall photographer who once jumped with no gear at all, details Jane planned to include in her article.

The instructor signaled approval, giving a firm tap to Mack's pack, and then Mack reciprocated, inspecting his colleague's gear.

"Hey, Mack, somebody said they saw Butch a while ago," he said as Mack performed the gear check.

Mack flinched at the suggestion, and then his colleague realized he probably shouldn't have said anything. After all, everyone knew about the bad blood between those two, and it had been months since Butch had shown his face around there.

Mack was still thinking about the alleged Butch sighting as they all climbed aboard the airplane, Jane's photographer clicking away. They were accompanied by four other skydivers jumping solo, super-competitive athletes practicing for an upcoming freefall tournament in the afternoon. A videographer tagged along.

After some time, the pilot started the engine and taxied to the end of the runway. He locked the wheels and raced the engine, causing the plane to vibrate all over as the spinning prop strained against the brakes. The perfume of engine exhaust permeated the immediate environment as the pilot scanned the many instruments on his dashboard and revved the engine again. Then he surveyed the sky for other planes before shoving the throttle home.

"Folks, lean forward," the pilot said loudly over the engine noise.

The aircraft was a twin-engine job with bench seats on either side. Jane perched nervously on the seat in the chilly airplane cabin, trying to suppress a persistent urge to urinate, her mind racing through a series of incongruent thoughts. Hemingway's haunting quote came to mind, which didn't help matters.

"Concentrate on the assignment. Concentrate on the assignment," she kept telling herself. "Concentrate on the assignment. It is one thing to be in the proximity of death … but quite another thing to seek her. Concentrate on the assignment. To be in the proximity of death, of death, of death."

When the plane reached twelve thousand feet, her tandem master announced it was time to "suit up." He attached his harness to Jane's and cinched up all the straps holding them together. Then he directed the pilot to fly over the drop zone. One of the other skydivers reached over and unlatched the plane's swing-up door. He stood in the open doorway and yelled "cut," signaling the pilot to reduce the engine's power. The pilot throttled back, quieting the engine noise as the plane slowed noticeably.

Jane felt queasy as she thought, "My God, am I actually doing this?"

The first soloist to jump stepped carefully out of the doorway and grabbed the wing's supporting strut, bracing himself against the wind and prop blast. Then, left foot first, he perched atop the plane's wheel briefly before letting go. The other solo jumpers did likewise in quick sequence.

Next it was time for Jane and her tandem master. He walked them collectively toward the open doorway and held onto the threshold with his right hand. With the grace of a gymnast, he sat down in the doorway so that Jane was dangling outside the aircraft.

Terrified as she hung from the plane, her tandem master rocked back and forth.

"One, two, three," he said, and with a final pelvic thrust he shoved them both out of the plane.

Jane had trouble catching her breath immediately after deplaning, and the sense of acceleration was mixed with a strange buffeting sensation, like being cushioned by an endless, upwardly flowing and powerful wind stream. They fell for what seemed an eternity. Mack checked the altimeter that he wore on his wrist. Seconds later he checked it again. Finally, at about five thousand feet he pulled the cord. The drogue chute came out, but it failed to deploy the larger parachute and sailed into the clear blue sky.

Mack yanked immediately on the reserve cord, and the result was similar: The chute merely fell away from its cut cords as spectators watched in horror at the unfolding drama. The pair barreled right past the four soloists, their combined weight providing twice the mass and greater acceleration. Instead of a top speed, or "terminal velocity," of one hundred twenty miles per hour, they could hit one sixty without intervention.

The other jumpers immediately knew something was terribly wrong: an obvious canopy failure. The standard "pull time" for tandem jumpers was four thousand five hundred feet, but they had already descended well below that benchmark.

Mack checked his altimeter. They were fast approaching a thousand feet, generally thought of as the point of no return.

Having been schooled in all sorts of hypothetical catastrophic scenarios, including the various types of possible parachute-deployment mishaps, the four solo jumpers had no doubt that they were now witnessing an extraordinary event: a "total malfunction" of the canopy system. On the other hand, the ongoing drama presented an equally extraordinary potential for heroism and glory; a spectacular feat of daring and valor, something of historic significance. In theory it should be easier to pull off a rescue for a total malfunction than for a partial failure, where a chute is deployed incompletely and left twisted and twirling overhead, blocking approach. Still, the plan offered no margin for error: Falling at terminal velocity meant a thousand feet every five seconds. And how the hell was a single parachute going to handle the load of three skydivers? It was a tantalizing opportunity for any red-blooded risk taker.

One of the soloists immediately assumed a diving maneuver he'd practiced many times as a freefall competitor.

Butch, meanwhile, was enjoying the show, watching with a pair of high-power binoculars. He imagined Mack's terror, seeing him wave his arms frantically. He'd been such a conceited asshole, gloating in the absolute factual certainty that he was physically superior to most every man. And this, of course, extended to his carnal experiences, which he often recounted unsolicited.

But he wasn't such a big man now, was he? Not while screaming toward the hard earth at more than a hundred miles per hour. You couldn't kick-box your way out of this one! Imminent death had a way of humbling the overstuffed human ego, of shrinking one's "self-concept" like a splash of high-test gasoline on the scrotum.

Jane observed the patchwork of earth growing closer and closer, defining tall trees and large buildings within the broad lattice of rural roads. Then telephone poles and bungalow houses. Instead of inspiring sheer panic, however, just the opposite transpired: a strange euphoria. Time stood eerily still, and she felt a great, comforting warmth and a sense of peaceful awareness. All of her cares vanished, and she welcomed death like an old, long-lost friend.

Her fearless tandem master was going to pieces, fidgeting like crazy with his gear and the failed parachute ripcord, trying to deploy the damned thing. She couldn't understand what all the commotion was about. Connected, as they were, she on bottom, he on top, resembling rare coital birds in awkward flight.

"I'm going to hit the ground first and cushion the blow," she thought with glee. "Why, he probably won't feel a thing. Hah, funny. He won't feel a thing!"

Then started the end-of-life slideshow. Wow, she thought, it really does happen that way! Her entire history flickered by at blinding speed, yet paradoxically each image was perfectly clear and lucid: the early years, the details of her weird family and messed-up childhood, college, the anxious struggles, being married, being divorced, work.

The slideshow continued, climaxing with the final days, Robert Marsden and all that flying saucer business. Now, only moments before impact, her exhausted tandem instructor had gone limp, silent. It wouldn't be long before the end, she thought, not so much with dread as anticipation. She was already in the process of dying.

But wait a minute!

From out of nowhere another skydiver smacked into them with a terrific thud. He immediately hooked one arm around Mack's waist, deployed his chute and executed a bear hug with all of his strength. The rescuer's harness, an arrangement of nylon straps designed to absorb the force of a rapidly decelerating diver, strained under the weight of three.

Jane cursed her savior, yelling, "no, no," euphoria turning to horror and a whole gamut of things in between. But he'd performed his heroism -- the stupid macho bastard -- and that was that.

The photographers valiantly risked their own lives to capture the event, shooting a series of rapid-fire pictures to chronicle the miraculous rescue before deploying their own chutes.

The drop zone became a dizzying collage of colors and images in the frantic seconds that remained. Jane clenched her teeth in consternation as they slammed into the hard earth. Instead of crashing at one hundred thirty miles per hour and dying instantly, they landed at thirty-seven, breaking every bone in their bodies.

Sirens rang out and ambulances rushed to the scene. A local TV news crew, already filming for a weekend feature package, caught everything. The story aired nationally and was picked up by the wire services, appearing in newspapers coast-to-coast and abroad.

And somewhere among the corridors of power, a curious spook made an entry in Jane Hale's file.

଒଒଒଒

Her recuperation would be slow and agonizing.

Clinical assessments, police reports and insurance claims all agreed that the three had suffered "multiple blunt force injuries" including facial and rib fractures, broken legs and copious contusions and abrasions.

She'd be walking again within several months, albeit with a permanent limp and long-term psychiatric issues, popping prescription painkillers like candy and suffering through physical therapy sessions three times a week. She'd be reliving her skydiving nightmare, played out in dreams and recalled involuntarily during a percentage of every single wakeful moment.

And she'd be writing about it in excruciating detail. The series of articles and photos won major awards from the New Jersey Press Club, and rumor had it that a Pulitzer was in the offing. She'd made brief appearances on *Oprah* and various TV morning shows. Even *60 Minutes* was working on a piece about her harrowing near-death experience.

Of course, police listed Butch among the most likely suspects, and he confessed under questioning. This kicked off a whole new round of media interest. Headlines splashed "Skydiving Probe Reveals Love Triangle," and "Police Charge Estranged Hubby in Skydiving Sabotage."

Marsden's book, meanwhile, had been published with little fanfare and shelved in the paranormal and occult sections of bookstores. Jane found *The Quest for Antigravity* nestled among works on alien abduction, astral projection, witchcraft, ghosts, and the Bermuda triangle. It had posted only modest sales.

The publisher, though, was advertising pretty aggressively in niche magazines and promoting it at UFO conferences and other fringe venues. Marketing gurus also tried an unorthodox promotional tactic: making public the vintage flying saucer film footage from Glenn L. Moore, screening the movies at conferences and offering video to the media.

But the cold truth was that Marsden's masterpiece had bombed. The reading public showed only meager interest in the book and shunned its basic premise as an absurd fantasy; the idea that such a quantum leap in technology could have remained cloaked for so long. Critiques were either scathing or comical, and all made reference to the author's discreditable death by autoerotic asphyxiation. The skeptics "debunked" the film footage as a laughable hoax and labeled Moore a nutcase. Some book critics scorned the late Marsden's speculative interpretation of historic events, others wrote reviews simply as an excuse to ridicule the whole genre of ufology, and the majority paid no attention whatsoever.

It all boiled down to one thing: UFO conspiracies had become passé at best. And, with September eleventh just around the corner, the nation would soon be consumed with a raft of new conspiracy theories reflecting a broad existential angst and a bottomless obsession with homeland security.

Jane, too, had lost any professional interest in UFOs. She was surviving quite well on worker's compensation and devising plans for a new project to investigate her skydiving catastrophe. It was an idea she pitched to book publishers as one of those true-crime readers that expose in minute granularity every aspect of a story, including various subplots, in-depth analyses of the key players and culminating in a sensational court trial. There seemed to be a market for that sort of long-form crime reporting these days, with best sellers on all sorts of grisly and sordid atrocities. And the first-person narrative promised to supercharge the storytelling, she claimed in her pitch. It could be the ideal thing to occupy her time while non-ambulatory and on extended leave from the paper.

Otherwise, Jane Hale enjoyed the unaccustomed luxury of paid leisure, perusing unread books and watching a lot of old movies. In her sabbatical, however, she vowed to avoid anything remotely relevant to UFOs.

Still, on occasion she would think of Marsden, flying saucers and the like. She'd look into the night sky with suspicion and cynical awe.

In the cold darkness above a Big Black Delta floated ever so slowly and then came to a complete stop. The ship's commander configured the hyperdrive and started the countdown for the jump to low-Earth orbit.

Ten, nine, eight, seven, six …

The End

Acknowledgments

I want to thank Jennifer Streisand
for her support.

About the Author

Emil Venere is a science writer who has worked for many years at research universities and at daily newspapers. He lives in the Midwest.

Printed in the United States
by Baker & Taylor Publisher Services